# DANCE OF DECEPTION

An Allingham Regency Classic

Merryn Allingham

# DANCE OF DECEPTION

This novel is entirely a work of fiction. The names, characters and incidents portrayed in it are the work of the author's imagination. Any resemblance to actual persons, living or dead, events or localities is entirely coincidental.

First published in Great Britain 2017 by The Verrall Press

Cover art: Berni Stevens Book Cover Design

ISBN: 978-1-9997824-2-9

Copyright © Merryn Allingham

Merryn Allingham asserts the moral right to be identified as the author of this work.

All rights reserved. No part of the publication may be reproduced, stored in a retrieval system, or transmitted, in any form or by any electronic, mechanical, photocopying, recording or otherwise, without the prior permission of the publishers.

## Chapter One

*London, 1817*

'You will do this for me, for the family.' It was a command rather than a question.

The young woman held her head high, but despite her resolution there was a stricken look in the soft brown eyes.

'Papa, I cannot. Ask anything else of me, but I cannot marry that man.'

Her father, pacing back and forth across the worn library carpet, stopped suddenly in front of her. His expression was angry. 'Sir Rufus Glyde is a respected nobleman. He will give you an elegant home and a secure future. And he will save this family from disaster.'

She looked past her father to the open window, but hardly saw the mass of roses filling the garden with a riot of colour in the late afternoon sun.

'Surely, Papa,' she pleaded, 'the situation cannot be that desperate.'

Lord Milverton was silent. His face, though still handsome, appeared haggard and drawn. He took time to brush the snuff from a velvet sleeve and when he spoke his voice was quiet but insistent.

'The family is virtually ruined. Over the past few months I have had to sell my entire stable of horses and rent out Nethercott Place to a wealthy *cit*. Generations of Milvertons dishonoured by the taint of city money. And now Robert's addiction to gambling is likely to lose us our last piece of security – this very house.'

'In that case,' she responded sharply, 'why doesn't Robert find a way of repaying what he owes.' Her brother's decadent lifestyle was something she could not forgive. 'Why doesn't *he* marry for money?'

'Amelie, you know that it isn't possible. What does he have to offer except debt and unsteadiness? Certainly nothing the matchmaking mamas at Almack's want. You on the other hand have youth, beauty and a steadfast character. Rufus Glyde admires you and wants to make you his wife.'

'But he is nearly twice my age.'

'He is no more than fourteen years older than you. That is no great age. It is well for a husband to be more experienced than his wife. Then he may teach her how to go on in society.'

An image of Rufus Glyde's dissolute eyes and thin, sneering lips swam into her mind and made her shudder. She would not wish to be taught anything by such a man. In her revulsion she twisted the cambric handkerchief she held into a vicious knot.

'I can never care for him,' she declared hotly.

'But do you care for anyone else? You have had an entire

Season to find someone to your taste, a Season I could ill afford. And look what has happened. You have been distant and unapproachable to the young men you have met. Only one was willing to brave your coldness and actually offer for you, and you dismissed his proposal out of hand. So what do you want?'

She smoothed the skirt of her simple sprig muslin with a hand that shook slightly, but when she spoke her voice was firm. 'I want to remain single, Papa. I am grateful for my introduction to *ton* society, but the men I have met have been either shallow or profligate. I shall never marry unless I find a man I truly love and respect. And that seems unlikely.'

'You will be lucky to find any man in the future. There will be no more Seasons. And no home either, if Sir Rufus forecloses on our mortgage,' her father added bitterly.

She caught her breath. 'What do you mean?'

'I had not meant to tell you, but you should know the truth. Your brother has lost this house to Rufus Glyde. In a fit of madness he used it as a stake for his gambling. Either you marry Sir Rufus or we are homeless.'

'How can you allow him to threaten us like this?'

'Come, come, child, the man is willing to make a generous settlement on you, apart from returning the mortgage. He will, I am sure, always treat you with respect and you will have ample money and time to pursue your own interests. Such marriages of convenience are common among our class. You know that.' Lord Milverton paused, thinking no doubt of his own marriage, a love match whose first intoxicating passion had barely survived a year. 'They are often more successful than if one were to marry for love.'

Amelie turned away, unwilling to show the disgust she felt.

'I have no choice,' her father said heavily. 'This is a debt of honour and must be paid, one way or another.'

'And I am to pay the debt,' she cried. 'I am to be the family sacrifice.' It was her turn to stride furiously between the dusty book filled shelves, chestnut curls tumbling free and framing her lovely face.

With an exasperated mutter, Lord Milverton walked towards her and grasped her hands. 'Enough. You forget yourself. You are beautiful and clever, my dear, but you are far too independent. It puts men off and those it does not, you will not have. Think yourself lucky that Sir Rufus values high spirits as well as being a connoisseur of beauty. He has very properly asked me for permission to pay his addresses to you, and I have agreed.'

'No, no, I cannot do it.' She uttered a strangled cry. 'Anything but that! I'll earn my own bread rather.'

'Earn your own bread? What is this? Your taste for the dramatic is regrettable and too reminiscent of your French relations.'

He spoke with disdain, then walked away from her towards the tall windows. When he turned, his face wore an implacable expression and his voice brooked no further disagreement.

'You have been made a highly advantageous offer, Amelie, which will secure this family's future and your own. You will go to your room immediately and stay there. In the morning you will make yourself presentable. Sir

Rufus will be with us at noon and you will accept his offer. Do I make myself clear?'

The interview was at an end. Lord Milverton sank down at his desk and began to leaf listlessly through the scattered papers. His daughter, overcome with angry tears, turned on her heel and banged the oak panelled door behind her.

⁓

Once in her room, she cast herself down onto the damask bedspread and wept. Her grief was intense and though her tears soon subsided, her fury remained. To be forced into a repugnant marriage because of her brother's stupidity. And by her own father! She knew him to be autocratic but never so unfeeling that he would contemplate selling her to the highest bidder. He might try to wrap it up in clean linen, but that is what it came down to. As a child he had been an indulgent parent, reading with her, schooling her on her first pony, bringing surprises each birthday. Yet, if crossed, he could be unrelenting. Until now she had been spared this side of his character, but she knew the suffering it had caused his wife. Her heart ached for her dead mother. Louise St Clair's life had not been a happy one: an *émigrée* from France, an unhappy marriage to an English aristocrat and then an early death.

Lord Miles Milverton must have seemed a white knight when Louise first met him, just months after her dangerous journey from the outskirts of Paris to exile in England. The Bastille would not be stormed for another year, but revolution was already in the air. Signs of dissent and rebellion were everywhere and when the St Clair family home was ransacked without any attempt by the servants to prevent it, Brielle St Clair decided it was no longer safe. She and her eighteen-year-old daughter, disguised as servants themselves, were forced to steal away under cover of darkness and embark on a slow and tortuous journey to the Channel coast. They had travelled by night, resting beneath hedges in the daytime, and ever fearful of discovery. Brielle's tales of their adventures had enthralled Amelie as a child.

She could see that as a refugee in a foreign land, Lord Milverton's offer of marriage must have seemed like a miracle to Louise. He promised happiness and security, a new future for the young, homeless girl. Happiness, though, had been short lived. Louise had been sickly for months after Robert's birth, needing constant nursing, and unable to share in the social flurry of her husband's life. Miles Milverton, having fallen violently in love with a youthful form and a beautiful face, found himself with a wife who had neither.

The constant miscarriages that followed year after year pushed them yet further apart. Amelie's birth and her unexpected survival had brought a small reconciliation, but one that was too brief. Even as a child she had understood the pain written on her mother's face, as her husband left for yet another lengthy stay at a friend's country house, knowing that most of his time would be spent enjoying the company of other women. But that was not going to happen to her! She had her mother's beauty certainly, but also her grandmother's spirit. Louise may have been scared half out of her wits by that flight across France, but Brielle St Clair had thrived on it. Her grandmother's subsequent life would always be a shadow of the excitement she had once known. Understanding this, it seemed, she had deliberately made her new home amid the dull gentility of Bath. Amelie smiled wryly as she imagined the mettlesome old lady daily exchanging vapid gossip at the Pump Room. The last time she had seen Brielle was five years ago at her mother's funeral, a sombre and painful affair.

She stiffened. That was it. She would go to her grandmother. Brielle would be her refuge and would be sure to defend her from Lord Milverton. He was the man Brielle blamed for her own daughter's decline and early death. Her warnings to Louise not to marry had been ignored by a girl desperate for stability.

Amelie got to her feet and straightened the satin ribbons which encircled her waist. Her grandmother would be her champion, she was certain. But how to get to her, how to get to Bath? Deep in thought, she was unaware of the door opening until a tentative voice disturbed the silence. Her maidservant, pale and concerned, white cap slightly askew, hovered in the doorway.

'Oh, miss, is it true? Are you really going to marry Sir Rufus Glyde?'

'No, it's not true.' Her voice was sharp. 'I have no intention of marrying anyone. And I detest Rufus Glyde. He is twice my age and not a fit husband.'

'He's very wealthy, or so Cook says. She says he moves in the best circles.'

Amelie shook her head in frustration. 'No doubt he is invited everywhere but there are whispers about his lifestyle. Even I have heard them. He is a vicious and degenerate man and he repels me.'

Fanny shut the door carefully behind her and said in a conspiratorial voice, 'Mr Simmonds told Cook that Sir Rufus was coming here tomorrow to make you an offer of marriage.'

'You shouldn't listen to gossip,' Amelie chided. 'He may be coming to the house, but I won't be meeting him.'

'But, Miss Amelie, how can that be?' In her abstraction, the maid picked up a stray hairbrush and began to rearrange her mistress's locks.

'I'm going to escape, that's how. I'm going to Bath to be with my grandmother. But mind, not a word to anyone.'

Her maid, brushing Amelie's curls in long, rhythmic strokes, gaped at her open-mouthed. 'However will you get there?'

'I'm not sure at the moment. How would *you* get there, Fanny?'

'On the stage, I suppose, miss, though I wouldn't want to travel all that way on my own. It's sure to take a whole day. Master's old valet used to visit his daughter in Bath sometimes and there was always a fuss about how long he was away.'

'Do you know where he caught the stagecoach?'

'It was from an inn in Fetter Lane. The White Horse? He used to leave first thing in the morning.'

'Then that's what I shall do. You will need to call me early.'

'You're never thinking of taking the common stage?'

'Why ever not? It's a public conveyance. What harm can I come to?'

'But it's not right. All sorts of vulgar people take the

stage – you'll be squashed in with the likes of clerks and pedlars and I don't know what. And I've heard it's dangerous. There are highwaymen on Hounslow Heath and they'll slit your throat for a necklace. And if *they* don't get you, then the coachman will get drunk and land you in a ditch.' Fanny shook her head ominously.

'Nonsense. If other people travel on the stage, I can, too.'

'But, miss, you're Quality,' Fanny maintained stubbornly. 'Quality don't travel on the stage. And you mustn't go alone.'

'I have to and no one must know where I have gone. I need time to reach Lady St Clair and explain the situation to her before my father realises where I am.'

'But you can't have thought. You'll be unchaperoned. You'll receive Unwanted Attentions.' Her horrified whisper capitalised the words.

'In that case, I must blend into my surroundings,' her mistress said practically. She was thoughtful for a moment. 'Who wouldn't be noticed on a stagecoach I wonder? A governess, a servant? A maidservant such as yourself? I will go as a maidservant and you can lend me the clothes.'

'No, miss, that I won't.'

'Fanny, you are the only friend I have in this house. You must help me. No one will know and once I'm established at my grandmother's, I will send for you.'

'But –'

'No buts. We must plan. First we need a ticket.'

She went to the bottom drawer of the walnut chest that had been her mother's and brought out a small tin box.

How lucky it was she still had most of her quarterly allowance. She pulled out a roll of bills and thrust them into Fanny's reluctant hand.

'Here, use this to buy a ticket for the Bath stage tomorrow.'

'But, miss, even if I can buy a ticket, how will you find your way to Fetter Lane? I daren't go with you.'

'I'm sure I will manage. I'll walk until I find a hackney carriage and the driver will know the way to the inn. And once I'm there, I will take care to stay concealed until the coach is ready to leave. There's bound to be a number of travellers and a good deal of activity – I imagine the Bath stage isn't the only one leaving the White Horse in the morning. It should be easy to find a hiding place.

The girl still looked unconvinced and Amelie put her arms around her. 'Don't fret, it's going to work,' she soothed. 'When you return, choose something for me from your wardrobe, but keep the clothes in your own room. And then make sure you are elsewhere for the rest of the day. If we are not together, no one will suspect a thing.'

Fanny seemed rooted to the spot. 'Go on,' her mistress urged when she made no attempt to move. 'Do it quickly before supper and you won't be missed. Bring me the clothes and ticket at dawn tomorrow. I wouldn't ask you, Fanny, if I were not truly desperate. But I am. Somehow I have to escape this nightmare.'

## Chapter Two

In the City some miles from Grosvenor Square, Gareth Denville was also contemplating escape. He sat uncomfortably in the shabby offices which housed Messrs Harben, Wrigley and Spence, solicitors, and wished himself elsewhere. But his demeanour betrayed nothing of his emotions. His straight black brows and hard blue eyes kept the world at bay. He could be accounted a handsome man, thought Mr Spence, who sat opposite him, but for the harshness of that gaze. And the decided lack of fashion he exhibited. He was a well-built man, slightly above average height, with good shoulders and an excellent form for the prevailing fashion of skin-tight pantaloons. But instead he wore buckskins, his coat fitted far too easily across his broad shoulders to be modish and his necktie was negligently arranged. Rather than the gleaming hessians of tonnish fashion, he wore topboots, still dusty from his long journey.

Mr Spence gathered together the papers spread across the huge oak desk and sighed inwardly. The new Lord Denville was likely to find it difficult to adjust to life in the capital. He looked up and encountered Gareth's austere gaze and quickly began the task at hand. Over the next quarter of an hour, Mr Spence carefully enumerated the full extent of Gareth Denville's inheritance while the beneficiary remained unnervingly silent.

The news of his grandfather's death several weeks ago had been accompanied by a polite request from the solicitors for Gareth's immediate return to England. His first reaction to their letter had been to shrug indifferently and carry on with his life, but his grandfather's man of business was nothing if not persistent, and after several summons of increasing urgency, he had bowed to the inevitable. He had been travelling a night and a day without pause, but his powerful frame appeared not greatly fatigued and his air of cool detachment never left him.

The situation was not without its humour, of course, but that did not prevent a slow burning anger eating him from within. He had known, as he travelled to England after seven years' absence, that he was now the Earl of Denville whether he wished it or not. But as Mr Spence dryly read the pages of his grandfather's will, the size of his inheritance astounded him. Infuriated him, too, when he recalled the shifts he had been forced to adopt simply to maintain the appearance of a gentleman. Charles Denville had husbanded his estate well. How ironic that such care and duty should ultimately benefit him, the black sheep, the grandson who could never be spoken of again. His grandfather was unable to deny him the title, but he must have tried and failed to leave his estate elsewhere. Gareth could imagine the old man's fury that such an unworthy successor was about to be crowned.

'Are you sure, Mr Spence, that there are no other legitimate heirs to the estate?' he asked crisply.

'None whatsoever, Lord Denville. Our searches have been diligent, particularly...' and here he coughed delicately '...in the light of the peculiar circumstances surrounding your lordship's inheritance.'

The solicitor was far too circumspect to mention details, but Gareth knew well that Mr Spence referred to his banishment as a young man for the gravest of sins in *ton* circles. He had cheated at cards, or so it was alleged, a transgression that had brought instant shame to him and to his family. His grandfather had bundled him out of the country overnight, refusing to listen to his version of events.

'Like father, like son,' Lord Denville had said. 'I was stupid enough to let your father stay in the hope that he would reform his way of life, but he died in the gutter where he belonged. I will make sure that you at least cannot disgrace the family name further.' And what, thought Gareth, had the family name come to after all?

It had all once been so different. He had been everything to his grandfather, an unexpected light after the black years of his own father's ruin. He remembered his childhood at Denville Abbey, his grandfather teaching him to ride and to shoot, watching over his progress to manhood with pleasure and anticipation. And then disaster, just three months on the town and accused of marking his cards.

That night was etched on his brain. The heat of the room, the guttering candles, the disarray of empty glasses. And the four other men who sat around the table: his dearest friend, Lucas Avery, General Tilney, an old ally of his grandfather's, the languid form of Lord Petersham whose customary lethargy belied a sharp intelligence, and Rufus Glyde, playing recklessly that night, his spiteful tongue unusually stilled. It was the General who had first seen the mark on the card and raised the alarm. He remembered the incredulous stares of his companions as it became obvious to all who had cheated.

But he hadn't cheated. Someone there had done so, but why and how remained impenetrable. The men with whom he'd played were wealthy and had no need to cheat. But he was on a tight allowance and awaiting the next quarter's in some desperation. It was common knowledge that he was short of money. He had vehemently protested his innocence, but his grandfather had been deaf to him and to Lucas's staunch plea that his friend was an honourable man. Lord Denville had listened in stiff silence and remained unmoved. General Tilney's embarrassed account of the evening was the only one his grandfather was willing to countenance. Gareth's disgrace was instant and so was banishment.

'My Lord, if you would be so kind, we will need to go through a number of documents for which I need signatures.'

The solicitor was trying to regain his attention. His mind left that shadowed room in Watier's, and returned to the attorney's untidy office. He felt he was suffocating, yet the window was wide open.

'I need to take a walk,' he said. 'I need to clear my head.'

'Of course, your lordship.' The solicitor rose and bowed

politely. 'I will await your lordship's pleasure.'

'I'm staying at Crillons. I will send from there when I am ready to go through the papers.'

'Certainly, my lord.'

He walked quickly out of the room and down the stairs. The fresh air hit him with welcome relief. Waving away the proffered services of a jarvey, he began to make his way towards the West End of the city. He walked swiftly, street after street, hardly heeding where he went. Inside, he was seething. His fortunes had changed, but his sense of betrayal remained acute. He had no wish to inherit anything that had belonged to his grandfather. Pride made it impossible that he would ever accustom himself to being the Earl of Denville or ever seek to become part of a society he deemed rotten to the core.

Without a glance, he passed the turning for St James's, a thoroughfare housing some of the most famous gentlemen's clubs in London, and continued as if by instinct towards Piccadilly. He came to a halt outside No. 81, Watier's, the Great-Go as it was fondly known to its members. Somehow he had returned to the scene of his disgrace. He walked slowly up the stairs and prepared to confront his demons. The doorman, resplendent in black grosgrain and scarlet silk sash, bowed low.

'Good evening, Lord Denville,' he intoned, 'on behalf of Watier's, may I offer you sincere condolences on your grandfather's death and say how very glad we are to see you again.'

Gareth made no reply, reflecting cynically that commerce knew no moral shades. The doorman handed him on to a footman hovering by the doorway of the salon. He remembered the room immediately. The aubusson carpet, the straw coloured silk hangings and the endless line of blazing chandeliers had not changed.

A group of men nearest the door looked up. They were engaged in a companionable game of faro but at the sight of him the game stopped and for an instant their conversation withered. A man he did not know, and who was evidently in charge of the day's bank, said something in an undervoice which caused a ripple of amusement around the table. Lord Petersham, looking a little thinner and older now, hushed the man and play continued. The incident was over in a moment, but to Gareth it was as though time had stood still. His newly acquired title and wealth might open the doors of society to him, but he would never be allowed to forget the scandal. His fierce reluctance to return to England, even for a few weeks, had been prescient. He had no place here and wanted none.

He blundered down the steps and headed towards the embankment and the river. Its waters were grey and bleak, a true echo of his mood. Defiantly, he decided to drink to the day he would shake the soil of England from his feet for ever and sought out a boozing-ken in a poor area of Vauxhall, known to him from his days of youthful indiscretion. He ordered a brandy and the drink was rough but fiery. He ordered another and tossed it off quickly. He wanted to sink into oblivion. Over the next few hours he drank steadily, as though each drink took him one step further from a hated homeland. It was just short of dawn when he finally lurched to his feet and sought his hotel. His brain, befuddled by brandy, was treacherous and led him in the wrong direction. Very soon he was lost in a labyrinth of unknown streets.

⁓

Fanny woke her mistress at four in the morning. She carried in her arms a set of her own clothes and clutched the stagecoach ticket tightly. She appeared highly nervous, her hands trembling as she gently shook her mistress awake. Her agitation was soon explained.

'Miss Amelie, I don't think you can go. Mr Simmonds is in the hall and he's been sitting there all night. I was so worried I'd oversleep that I woke really early and crept downstairs to see the time. And there he was. You'll have to stay, miss, you'll have to meet Sir Rufus. But mebbe it won't be too bad. You'll be rich and have your own house to manage and plenty of fine clothes and – '

'Do you mean my father has actually set the butler to spy on me?' Amelie was now sitting bolt upright.

'Not exactly spy. But he's there in the hall as right as ninepence and there's no way you're going to get past him unseen.'

'I have to catch that coach, Fanny. I must find another way out. The back door?'

'The scullery maids are already up and working in the kitchen. They'd be bound to report it to Cook and she'll carry it to Mr Simmonds. You'd have to climb over the garden wall to get to the rear alley and they would know of your escape before you'd even got halfway.'

'Then I must go out of the front. Maybe you can distract Simmonds?'

Fanny looked doubtful.

'No? Then there's only one thing for it – I'll have to go out of the window.' She jumped from the bed and ran across the room, looking down on the street below. 'We will need some kind of ladder. A ladder of sheets. That's it. We are on the first floor so we should be able to fashion one long enough for me to reach the ground.'

'You'll never climb out of the window on sheets, Miss Amelie. It's too dangerous. They could give way at any moment.'

'Not if we knot them very carefully. In any case, it's far more dangerous for me to stay. Quick, let's hurry.'

She almost threw on the clothes Fanny had brought, and then sweeping the sheets from the bed, began to knot them one by one. 'We'll need more than these. There should be some in the linen chest.' Fanny obediently ran to the large coffer that lined the bedroom wall and pulled several sheets from its depths. Several minutes later they had fashioned an impressive rope.

'We must make sure we have knotted the sheets as tightly as possible,' Amelie said. 'I don't weigh a lot but it's a fair way to the ground.'

Fanny tightened the last knot and looked anxiously at her mistress. 'It's as safe as I can make it. Safer than for you to be travelling alone all the way to Bath.'

'I don't have a choice. I have to get to my grandmother's. I promise I'll take care. Don't forget,' Amelie tried to reassure her, 'I will be travelling in disguise and nobody will think of looking twice at a maidservant.'

'But you'll still be a very beautiful maidservant, miss,

and people are bound to look at you. Here – wear my cloak and make sure you pull the hood over your head whenever you're in public.'

Her mistress fingered the black velvet robe. 'This is your best cloak. I can't take it.'

'You must, it will make people think you're a very superior lady's maid and they won't bother you! And it will keep you warm. You've never travelled in a stagecoach before Miss Amelie, but I'm told they're the draughtiest vehicles out and you'll be travelling for hours.'

'Fanny, you are the best friend anyone ever had.' The maid blushed with pleasure. 'As soon as I get to Lady St Clair's, I'll make sure she sends for you. Then we will both be safe. My father will never dare to follow us there.'

She slipped the cloak over Fanny's borrowed dress, pulling the hood well down over her tangled curls. A small cloak bag lay ready with just a few of her most treasured possessions. She could take hardly anything with her, but she had no regrets. Once this room had been a beloved haven, but now it was a prison and one that led only to betrothal with a detested man. Sir Rufus Glyde would arrive at noon, but by then she would be miles away and her family confounded. She knew that Fanny would keep her secret, even on pain of dismissal.

She turned to the maid. 'I must be gone. Give me the ticket.'

'When you get to the inn, miss, be sure to hide yourself away until it's time for the coach to leave.'

'You can be certain I will. Once I've gone, Fanny, you must go straight back to your room and not discover my absence until the last possible moment. Please God they won't find out that it was you who helped me.'

'You're not to worry. I'll make sure they won't know where you've gone.' Fanny's face was suffused with tears and her voice cracking. 'Now go quickly, miss.'

## Chapter Three

Amelie deftly tied one end of the ladder to the bedpost and opened the window wide. The sash cord groaned ominously and they both held their breath, but the house was silent except for the distant sounds from the kitchen. They breathed again. Fanny payed out the sheets over the window sill and helped her mistress on to the ledge. The dawn was spreading a grey light over the quiet streets and a fresh breeze fanned Amelie's cheeks. She climbed nimbly over the ledge and began lowering herself down the improvised ladder. The descent wasn't easy. She had to lower herself one movement at a time and the cloak bag, though light, impeded her progress. She wondered if she dared throw it down into the cellar area below the railings, but Simmonds might well hear the noise and come to see what had caused it. So she continued to edge her way carefully downwards, the bag slung over one arm.

Fanny's pale face was at the open window, whispering encouragement. 'You're doing fine, miss. Don't look down, not far to go now.'

But her estimation proved to be optimistic. The sheets,

which had seemed so prolific in the bedroom, suddenly appeared scanty and far too short. They had both forgotten the deep well below the front door steps and had calculated only to the pavement. Amelie was now at the bottom of the ladder, but still at least twelve feet above solid ground. She looked up at the imposing Georgian façade and then down to the terrifying black and gold railings that marched along the pavement. What a horrible fate that would be. She suddenly felt very sick. How on earth was she going to reach the ground? She could jump into the well, but she was more than likely to break a leg or worse. Then all chance of escape would be gone and she would be faced with her father's angry recriminations. She could see him now, his brow furrowed red and his prominent eyes glowering.

As she hung there, her light form bracing itself against the cream stucco of the house, the noise of whistling broke the stillness. Tuneless and somewhat melancholy, the whistling was coming nearer. A late reveller perhaps on his way home? He was almost sure to see her. Fanny had heard the noise too and began desperately trying to haul in the sheets.

'It's no good,' Amelie whispered hoarsely, 'you'll never have the strength to get me back.'

She could only hope that the unknown figure meandering towards her would be too inebriated to notice a young female hanging from a window. That was wishful thinking. The reveller drew near and stood gazing at her for some time, seemingly trying to work out just what he was seeing. Amelie looked down and pulled her cloak tighter. She didn't recognise him and he didn't look like any of the fashionable bloods who ended a riotous evening by staggering home in the dawn air. But there was an indefinable air of authority about him, and she worried that by chance he might remember seeing her at one of the many gatherings of the *ton* this Season. She must avoid discovery at all costs.

Despite having drunk far too much, he seemed alert. His face slowly broke into a derisive smile.

'What have we here then? A mystery indeed. Plainly an escape, but from what? What do maidservants escape from before the household is awake? Have you been stealing and now you are trying to make off with your ill-gotten gains? Should I knock and instantly apprise your employer of your wickedness?'

'No, sir, indeed I am no thief.'

'Well, if you are not a thief, what are you doing climbing out of the window? The house has a door, you know.'

She answered him with as much dignity as she could muster. 'There are circumstances which make it vital for me to escape in this manner.'

She hoped that he would ask no more questions and be on his way, but Gareth Denville's head was still wreathed in brandy fumes. He was indifferent to the fact that he was miles from his hotel and had no idea in which direction it lay. He felt reckless and pleasurably detached from a world he hated. He had no intention of walking away – he was in the mood to enjoy this ridiculous imbroglio.

'But why must you leave unseen? It seems unnecessarily dramatic.'

'I have my reasons,' she replied stiffly. 'Please leave me.'

'By all means, but is that wise? It might be more sensible to ask for my help. Of course, I would need to know just who I am aiding and why.'

'My name is Amelie and I am maid to the young mistress of this house.' She was forced to think quickly. 'I am escaping to avoid the attentions of her brother.'

He caught sight of a chestnut curl and looked intently at the heart-shaped face trying to cower deeper into the enveloping cloak. 'He has good taste,' he admitted. 'But then so do I.' He swayed slightly on his heels and seemed to be thinking things over. 'We will make a bargain,' he finally pronounced. 'I will rescue you, but on one condition.'

'Anything, sir,' she said recklessly. Her arms felt as if they were being torn from their sockets and she knew she would not be able to hold on much longer. The sharp sword points of the railings seemed already to be coming nearer.

'A rather rash promise, but one I shall keep you to. I will help you to the ground and in exchange, you will come with me – as distraction, shall we say.'

'Dear sir, I cannot. I have a journey to make. I am on my way to – Bristol,' she amended, thinking it best not to reveal her plans in their entirety. 'I have to get to the White Horse Inn in Fetter Lane to catch the stage.'

'Excellent. Bristol, why not? There are boats aplenty there,' he added obscurely. 'We will go together.'

He was desperate to get away and he had been intrigued by the glimpse of a beautiful face beneath the cloak. Mr Spence would have to wait for his papers to be signed. Perhaps he would never sign them, never avail himself of his newfound wealth. If so, he would manage – he had for the last seven years.

'A perfect solution then,' he said swiftly. 'I extricate you from your difficulties and we travel to Bristol together.'

He saw her dismayed face. 'You won't have to know me very long. A few hours only. You might even get to like me,' he added harshly. 'I will bespeak a private parlour when we get to the inn. You can have a good breakfast and I can have – well, let us say, I can have the pleasure of your company.'

Amelie heard her maid moan. Fanny had her head below the window sill but could hear all that was being said. This was her worst fear come true but she was powerless to intervene. If she made herself known, the man who ever he was, would discover Amelie's deception. He might spread rumours and society would be sure to shun her mistress for such hoydenish behaviour. She would never find a husband then, not even a degenerate twice her age. As Fanny fidgeted in despair, the decision was made for her.

Her arms breaking, Amelie gasped out, 'Yes, I'll come with you. Just get me down from here, please. Immediately!'

'At your service, madam.' Her knight errant leapt over the railings and down the stairs to the cellar area. Amelie, her hands now nerveless, fell into his arms. He held her to his chest, enjoying for a moment the softness of her young body.

'Let me introduce myself.' He put her down abruptly and cast around in his mind for a name. 'I am Gareth Heywood.'

⌒

She allowed herself to be led up the area steps but once they reached the pavement, she moved to free herself. Her rescuer, though, maintained a tight grip as if to prevent any idea of flight. She looked down at his hands and noticed they were strong and shapely, but tanned as though used to outdoor work. He appeared an enigma. A gentleman, presumably, but one acquainted with manual labour. His earlier nonchalance had disappeared and with it his good humour. A black mood seemed to have descended on him and he strode rapidly along the street, pulling her in his wake. Glancing up at him from beneath her lashes, she saw that his expression had grown forbidding. His chin jutted aggressively and, when he finally turned to her, his eyes were blue steel.

'Why are you dawdling?' he demanded. 'I thought you were desperate to escape.'

'I am.' She was indignant. 'I am walking as fast as I can and you are hurting my arm. I am not a sack to be dragged along the street.'

Ignoring her complaint, he continued to tow her along the road at breakneck speed. 'Come on Amelia – that *was* your name? – try harder. We need to move.'

He must be drunker than she had supposed. His voice was cultured and his clothes, though shabby, were genteel. But his conduct was erratic. One minute he appeared to find her situation a source of laughter, the next he behaved in this surly fashion. He believed her to be a maidservant and had doubtless helped her to escape because of her pretty face. But he had hardly glanced at her since that unfortunate moment when she'd landed in his arms and now he was propelling her along the pavement as though his life depended on it.

Incensed by his treatment, she came to an abrupt halt, almost tripping him up. 'Perhaps you did not hear me. I'm not able to walk faster – and,' she added coldly, 'my name is Amelie, *not* Amelia.'

'However fancy your name, you are still a fugitive, and a fugitive under my command. And my command is to make haste.'

'I will certainly make haste but at a more seemly rate.'

'Seemly – that's an interesting word from a girl who escapes through windows.'

She looked mutinous but was too tired to argue, and submitted once more to being led at a spanking pace through a maze of streets until they came across a hackney carriage waiting for business.

'In you go,' her persecutor said shortly and pushed her into the ill-smelling interior. He uttered a few words to the jarvey and they were off.

It had not been part of her plan to keep company with a man the worst for drink and one who looked as though he had known better days, but he had helped her to escape and now it seemed she was on her way to Fetter Lane. So far, Mr Heywood had been useful and she would stay with him while it suited her purpose. If he could deliver her to the White Horse Inn, she would be set for her journey to Bath. Once in the inn's courtyard, it should be easy to give him the slip and hide away until the stage departed.

They sat opposite in the dingy cab, silently weighing each other up. It was the first time she had been able fully to see her rescuer. He was a powerfully built man, carelessly dressed, but exuding strength and she was acutely conscious of his form as he lay back against the worn swabs. She had no idea who he was, other than the name he had given, and it was evident she would learn nothing more. He sat silent, his gaze intent, assessing her almost as though she were a piece of merchandise he had just purchased, she thought wrathfully. But he would discover that she had other plans; she would leave him as soon as she was able. Doubtless he would start to drink again at the inn and, once fuddled, would not care what happened to her.

In this she was wrong. Gareth had been watching her closely and despite his dazed state, had seen her recoil as she sat down on the stained seat of the cab. A trifle fastidious for a maidservant, he noted. The hood of her cloak obscured much of her face, but what he could see was very beautiful, from the glinting chestnut curls to the fine cheekbones and flawless complexion. A strange maid-servant, indeed, and a strange situation.

As the brandy fumes began to dissolve, he was left with an aching head and a confused mind. What on earth was he doing miles from his hotel, his solicitor and legal papers all but forgotten? How had he embarked on this mad adventure with a woman he didn't know and one who could well be a thief? Perhaps the hue and cry to apprehend her had already started. And he had been the one to make sure she escaped pursuit, rushing her along the streets and away from danger. He must have been very drunk. Was still drunk. He would keep her close until he worked out what to do. In the meantime there would be an hour or so before the Bristol stage left, and he would remind her of her promise. She would provide a pleasant interlude.

There was little traffic and the hackney bounced speedily over the cobbled streets. Much to Amelie's relief, it was only a matter of minutes before they arrived at the White Horse. Her companion helped her down with one hand while paying the jarvey with the other. No escape, she reflected, but she would not panic. Her opportunity would come, she would just have to be a little cleverer.

'I suggest we repair indoors and find some breakfast. A private parlour should give us some respite from this din.'

He had to bend and speak directly into her ear, the noise coming from the courtyard was so great. She could hardly believe how many people were gathered into such a small space. There was luggage scattered everywhere: trunks, cloak bags, sacks of produce, bird cages, heaped up pell-mell. Ostlers ran back and forth leading out teams of fresh horses, coachmen took final draughts of their beer before blowing the horn for departure. Everywhere people yelled instructions and were not heard. It was bedlam, and the relative quiet of the tap room seemed like sanctuary.

The landlord came bustling out, rubbing his hands with pleasure. There was normally little trade at this time of the morning and the most anyone bought was a cup of scalding coffee, to be consumed as quickly as possible. But here was a gentleman and his companion, surely substantial customers, even if the man did look a little the worse for wear and the woman kept her face shrouded.

'A beautiful day!' The landlord beamed ingratiatingly. 'And how can I help you, sir?'

Gareth frowned. 'Prepare a private parlour for myself and the lady,' he said curtly. 'We leave on the Bristol coach, but wish to take some breakfast first.'

'Of course, sir. Right away. If you would care to follow me.'

## Chapter Four

The room the landlord led them to was small and poky with a low window that looked out over the rear garden, but it was mercifully quiet. The curtains were grimy and the furniture looked faded and uninviting. Amelie plumped one of the chair cushions and sent up a cloud of dust. Her rescuer glanced across at her, his expression mocking. 'Shall we defer the housekeeping?'

She glared at him. 'If you don't mind, Mr Heywood, I would prefer to be outside.'

'I am sure you would, but here we'll stay. We will eat breakfast together. Won't that be companionable?'

His tone was ironic, but somehow he made the phrase sound like a caress. The look on his face, though, was calculating. *Weighing me up again*, she thought, *deciding whether or not he made a good bargain.* She was beginning to feel vulnerable, confined as she was to an isolated room with an unknown and unpredictable man. But indignation gave her courage.

'I am unsure what you mean by companionable. I certainly thank you for the service you've rendered me this morning, but I have no need of food and would prefer to wait for my coach in the courtyard. If you allow me to pass, you may enjoy your meal undisturbed.'

'Not so fast. Why would I want to remain undisturbed? On the contrary, I wish very much to be disturbed.' He smiled derisively as he spoke, but his eyes were hard and measuring and she felt bruised by his scrutiny. 'You are mighty proud for a maidservant, are you not? But then a challenge is always welcome.'

She made no reply, for the first time conscious of a shadowy fear. In the gulf of silence that stretched between them the ancient clock in the corner of the room ticked out the minutes. She was very aware of his physical presence. Then without warning, he began to walk towards her. He no longer seemed a harmless reveller. The way those dark blue eyes were looking at her was disquieting, his gaze seeming to drink her in. She was angry that he dared to stare at her so, and angry at the flutter in the pit of her stomach.

Desperately she strove to regain control. 'I don't understand what exactly you want of me.' Even to her ears, she sounded faint and foolish.

'Really? I am surprised. Do they make maidservants that innocent these days? Perhaps I should remind you that we had a bargain. I helped you from your predicament and you promised to stay with me until your – sorry, our – coach left the inn.'

'But why?'

'Come, you cannot be that naïve. Why would any man want a beautiful young woman to stay with him?'

She stepped back hurriedly and collided with the

threadbare sofa. 'You surely cannot pretend any feelings for me.' Her voice was hoarse with alarm. 'You know nothing of me.'

'True, but do I have to? You will be a charming diversion just when I need one. Here, throw off your hood.'

Before she could stop him, Gareth had flung her cloak back to reveal her face fully. He looked at her wonderingly. A tangle of silken curls tumbled around her shoulders. Her eyes, the colour of autumn, were wide and frightened, and the soft cream of her cheeks delicately flushed. It seemed an age that he stood looking at her.

When he finally spoke, his voice was thick with desire. 'You *are* beautiful.'

She flinched and wrapped her cloak more tightly around her body. 'There is no need to be scared,' he murmured. 'I'm sure we will deal well together.'

'Indeed, sir, we will not. I am an honest woman.'

'Honest,' he mused. 'Another interesting word. Honest women hardly choose to escape from their homes at four in the morning. Nor do they come away with men they don't know. Don't play your tricks off on me. Instead, let us be truthful with each other. I am in need of amusement and you, I imagine, are a little adventuress who will take whatever comes her way.'

He grabbed her hand as he spoke and pulled her towards him. In a moment his arms were around her waist, a gesture shocking in its intimacy. She shrunk from him, but his nearness was making her dazed. He pressed closer and she felt her body begin to tingle. For a moment they stayed body to body, then quickly she sprang away.

Her face was pink with vexation. 'How dare you touch me!'

'Very easily, I think you will find. Women are made for pleasure and you'll provide it amply.'

He made as if to recapture her in his arms, but was interrupted by the door opening. The landlord arrived bearing a ham, eggs, some devilled kidneys and toast. A servant followed with a large pot of steaming coffee.

'There we are, sir,' the innkeeper sang out, determinedly ignoring what he had seen as he came in the door. 'Just the job for a fresh May morning. But good travelling weather, I'll be bound.' He continued to spill out words, while Amelie retreated to a corner of the room trying hard to quell a heart that was thudding far too loudly.

When the landlord had left, Gareth sat down at the table and calmly began to carve slices of ham and place them on the two plates.

'Come to the table, Amelie, you must eat,' he coaxed. 'There is no point in starving yourself – you have a long road ahead.'

He had lost the glorious sense of irresponsibility he had known earlier, but he was still enjoying himself. He had no idea who he was with or what would happen, but this beautiful girl had felt warm and tremulous in his arms and he looked forward to repeating the sensation. It was escape that he needed right now and she had literally dropped into his arms, ready to furnish it.

When Amelie refused even to look at the food, his tone changed from coaxing to peremptory. 'Come to the table!'

She remained sitting in the corner of the room. 'I am

not hungry,' she said in a freezing voice.

'Don't be silly. Of course, you are. Come, I wish to eat the ham, not you. Sit down or I will make you.'

Alarmed at the prospect of another close encounter, she abandoned her corner and took her place at the table. She perched on the bench, making sure she was as far from her gaoler as possible, and nibbled at the ham and a slice of bread. The coffee was hot and strong and she downed two cups. The man opposite her ate leisurely, as though he had the entire morning to finish his breakfast. *And when he has eaten his fill*, she thought, *I will be next on the menu.*

She was going to have to make her getaway fast if she were to avoid another dreadful scene. She could not rely on the landlord to arrive so opportunely again. He'd had an unpleasantly knowing look in his eye as he'd laid the food down in front of his patron. It was clear he would do nothing to help her; she would have to save herself.

She cleared her throat. 'Why do you wish to go to Bristol, Mr Heywood?'

'Why should that concern you?'

'If we are to be travelling companions, it might be sensible to know something of each other.' She wondered anxiously if he would take the bait and relax his guard.

'A change of tune? When I tried to get to know *you*, you weren't too keen.' His tone was caustic.

'I'm sorry for that but I find this room a little overheated and when you pulled me towards you...' her voice wavered at the thought... 'I felt faint.'

'Ah, that's how it was. Well, I certainly don't want a fainting woman on my hands, so I'll open this window a little and then we can be comfortable. Come here and let me look at my prize.'

She walked slowly towards him and he stood up to face her, and smiled. She realised with a jolt that when he smiled, his harsh face was transformed into an engaging warmth. His blue eyes lost their steeliness and smiled, too, suggesting humour and good nature. His white teeth were even and his lips full. She stared at him, enjoying the picture he presented.

'I'm not surprised you have had trouble from your employers.' He broke into her rapt contemplation. 'You are far too lovely ever to be let near the average young man.' He laughed softly. 'But I am hardly the average man, so we need have no fears on that score.'

She woke abruptly from her dreamlike state and realised the danger she faced. Picking up her reticule, she fanned herself energetically. 'I am sorry, sir, but I still feel very warm. And I wonder if the ham was all it should be?'

'What exactly do you mean by that?'

'Just that the ham had a slight taint, I thought. But ham never really agrees with me, so it may well have been fine.'

'If it doesn't agree with you, what the devil do you mean by eating it?'

'You insisted, Mr Heywood. I was scared of you, so I ate it. But now I don't feel at all well.' She pressed her handkerchief artistically to her mouth and closed her eyes. 'I think I might really faint this time.'

Gareth cursed under his breath and shouted for the landlord, who came suspiciously quickly. She was sure the salacious old man had been lurking outside the door.

'My companion is unwell, landlord,' Gareth said tersely. 'Your ham seems to be to blame.'

'That can't be right, sir, the ham was freshly cured. Mrs Fawley would be very upset to think that aspersions had been cast on her ham. It's the best in the City. You won't get better anywhere.'

'Yes, yes, that's as may be, but my companion is feeling ill and needs to rest a while. Do you have a bedchamber where she can be accommodated?'

The landlord nodded. 'I'll call my wife and she can help the young lady.'

Mrs Fawley soon appeared on the doorstep with a martial look in her eyes. It was obvious she had overheard the conversation and was ready to defend her ham. But when she saw Amelie, small and white, and looking decidedly unwell, she took pity on her.

'I've got my own opinion as to what's made the young miss faint,' she sniffed, and escorted Amelie to a small but clean bedchamber on the next floor, overlooking the courtyard.

Once on her own, Amelie locked the door and laid down on the bed. She was exhausted by the morning's events. It seemed that she had thwarted one persecutor only to fall into the hands of another – a short while ago, she had only narrowly eluded her would-be ravisher. How stupid she had been in imagining that Gareth Heywood would be no threat. When she'd first seen him, he had appeared no more harmful than a lively reveller returning from a night of pleasure. Untidy and unfashionable, and probably a little the worse for drink, but for some reason she had trusted him. Only after he had used her so roughly, dragging her along the street, throwing her into the hackney and then – certainly best forgotten – pulling her into his arms, had she realised what a foolish mistake she'd made.

And yet even then, she admitted shamefacedly, there had been temptation to remain in his embrace, to let those strong arms encircle her. Of course that was simply a reaction to the alarms of the last few days, but thank goodness the landlord had come in when he had. And now her pretence of illness had saved her again, although for a short while only. She was sure that Gareth would be knocking on the door very soon and demanding admittance. And a bedchamber was an even worse place to meet him than the parlour downstairs. She had to be gone by the time he arrived.

She quickly washed her hands and face, then tidied her hair in the tarnished mirror which hung lopsidedly on one wall. On her way to the room she'd caught sight of a second stairway leading downwards. It was narrow and uncarpeted, obviously a staircase used by the servants. She was sure it would lead to the garden and if she could reach it, she could easily creep unnoticed into the front courtyard.

She glanced at the clock and could hardly believe the time. The coach for Bath would leave in five minutes. Cautiously, she unlocked the door and peered out. All was quiet and she tiptoed as swiftly as she could to the head of the narrow staircase and listened again. The only noise to reach her was the convivial banter from the tap room. She was in luck – no heavy footsteps mounted the stairs to her door. Gareth Heywood would be expecting her to travel to

Bristol and would not know the Bath stage was about to leave. This was her chance.

Regretfully, she would have to leave her cloak bag behind in the parlour below, but at least she had her reticule and in it the precious ticket for the stage. In a minute she was down the stairs and lifting the latch on the door leading to the garden. A female servant suddenly appeared from the kitchen quarters and stared at her uncomprehendingly. Amelie whisked through the door and quickly took the path to the front of the inn.

The scene was a little less chaotic than when she had arrived in the hackney since many of the morning coaches had already departed. She was easily able to identify the coach going to Bath, and once she had shown her ticket to the guard, she was helped aboard. She chose one of the middle seats of the bank of four which lined either side of the carriage. It was likely to be the most uncomfortable, but it would shield her from anyone looking in from the outside. A burly farmer sat to one side and a rotund country woman with an enormous basket on her lap on the other. There was very little room, but Amelie could almost disappear between them.

It seemed a lifetime before the guard blew up the signal to leave and the coach was pulling out of the yard. There was no sign of her tormentor. By now he was sure to have begun drinking again and would hardly miss her absence. Strangely, she did not feel as elated at her escape as she should. It was ridiculous, but she almost fancied that she had let him down in some way. After all, he had shown some care for her. If it weren't for him, she would still be dangling on that rope of sheets or, even worse, impaled on the front railings. He had helped her down, found a cab and escorted her to the inn. He had offered her shelter and refreshment. He had pulled her into his arms and held her in a crushing embrace. Her mind stopped. That was an image she must be sure to leave behind.

They were soon passing through Belgravia and turning out on to the highway which ran westwards. She hoped that her escape had not yet been discovered. She needed to cover as many miles as possible before her family realised she had gone. Fanny would be frantic with worry and the sooner she could let her know that all was well, the better. And all was well, she convinced herself. She'd had a gruelling experience, but she had achieved her aim. She would not be there to greet Rufus Glyde this morning. Instead, she was on her way to her grandmother's and to safety.

## Chapter Five

Gareth drained the last of the coffee pot and decided to go in search of his reluctant travelling companion. He had been unsure whether she was telling the truth about the ham, but she had certainly begun to look very white and he had not wanted to risk any unpleasantness. Truth to tell, she had looked so small and vulnerable that he'd felt a wish to protect rather than pursue her. He shook his head at his stupidity. She was as mercenary as the rest of the world. Her story about escaping from an importuning son probably held a grain of truth, given her undeniable beauty, but he was quite sure there was another tale to tell. Perhaps she really was a thief. Perhaps she had allowed the son too much licence and was now scared to tell her mistress of the inevitable result.

Thanks to the very strong coffee, he had sobered up completely in the hour that she had been gone. He still couldn't understand what had possessed him to get involved. A sense of the ridiculous perhaps? Or a whiff of intrigue – a maid with a French name, finicky manners and a keenness to hide her face – but he felt too weary to puzzle it out. Two sleepless nights had begun to take their toll and he was now eager to wash his hands of her. He would simply put her on the Bristol coach and go back to his hotel. It had been stupid of him to think he could flee his obligations. Tomorrow he would send a message to Mr Spence and sign whatever papers that worthy presented.

He glanced at the cloak bag Amelie had left on the bench. He supposed he had better restore it to its owner and assure her that she had nothing further to fear. He made his way upstairs to the front bedchamber, but found it empty. Thinking he had the wrong room, he looked into the one opposite and surprised the chambermaid who was making up the bed.

'I'm looking for a young lady,' he excused himself. 'She was feeling unwell and came up to rest.'

The maid looked at him blankly. 'She's not 'ere.'

'I can see she's not here,' Gareth returned shortly, 'but have you seen her?'

'I shouldn't think so.' The maid continued smoothing out the bedspread with a bored expression on her face. 'Not many people come up 'ere.' She paused and looked vacantly out of the window. 'There wus a stranger though on the stairs a while ago.'

'A young woman?'

'I couldn't rightly say.'

'Why ever not?'

"Cos of the cloak.'

'A black velvet cloak?' The maid nodded absently.

'That's her. Where is she?'

'How would I know? She went down the stairs and out the door.'

'What door?' Gareth was suddenly alert.

'The back door, o'course.' The maid shook her head at his obtuseness. "Appen she's in the garden taking the air,' she said helpfully.

He swore softly to himself and ran down the stairs two at a time. The garden was empty as he knew it would be, but he saw the path that circled the inn and followed it to the courtyard. The yard was also nearly empty. The last stage of the morning had departed and the inn servants were clearing the considerable mess left by passengers and coachmen.

He accosted a thin, gangling youth who was mournfully sweeping the last of the straw from the cobbles. 'The stage to Bristol?' he enquired curtly.

'There ain't no coach to Bristol, not today.' The boy leant on his broom, happy for an excuse to stop work. 'Bath now, mebbe. And you can allus go on from Bath.'

'Where is the stage to Bath?'

'Where? Somewhere near 'Ounslow I reckon.' The boy grinned cheekily. 'What d'you think, Jem?'

Jem staggered to a halt, bent double under the weight of the saddle he was carrying. 'With ole Tranter driving, probably not yet clear of Kensington,' he jeered.

The other men stopped their work and joined in a chorus of raucous laughter. An elderly ostler leaned lazily against the inn wall and chewed a straw. He smiled widely, evidently enjoying Gareth's discomfort.

'Next one's tomorrow, sir. That's if you don't mind a little wait.' There was a snigger in his voice.

'Move yourself and get me a horse immediately,' Gareth

snapped in response and ran back into the inn. He threw money onto the table in payment of his shot and snatched up Amelie's cloak bag. He had been willing to let her go when he could act the benefactor, but how dare she play him false. A bargain was a bargain and he was going to make her pay.

He stormed back into the inn courtyard and tapped his foot impatiently. It took nearly fifteen minutes for the horse to be ready and by that time he was in a towering rage. He threw the cloak bag across the saddle, then leapt onto the horse's back and wheeled her round to face the courtyard entrance.

"Appen you might catch 'em up,' opined the old ostler, still chewing his straw vigorously, 'but I ain't anyways too sure on it.'

Gareth's reply was to spur his mount forward and out of the courtyard in one bound.

The stage rolled wearily on, but wedged uncomfortably between her fellow passengers, Amelie endured the miles with a happy heart. She had escaped. By now her departure would have been discovered. Her father would be raging through the house, spreading tempest in his wake; he would find it impossible to explain her absence to Rufus Glyde when the latter came calling. For a moment the thought of Glyde's likely retribution made her feel unwell, but she resolutely pushed it from her mind. Lord Milverton would have to find another way of saving the family.

She had no clear idea of the time, but it had to be around noon. Sir Rufus would be stepping up to the front door of the house in Grosvenor Square, expecting to have acquired a bride before he left again. A wave of revulsion passed through her. Anything was better than that, even the harassment she had suffered from Gareth Heywood.

She was glad to be free of him, too, yet she couldn't suppress a twinge of regret. He had behaved abominably, but then her conduct had hardly been that of a delicately raised young woman. If he had realised her true situation, he would not have attempted to make love to her. But that was a nonsense. From the outset he had shown a predilection for seizing her in as close an embrace as possible. Whether she were the daughter of Lord Milverton or the daughter's maid would make no difference to him.

And shamefully, it hadn't mattered to her whether he was Mr Heywood, gentleman, or a choice spirit of dubious origins. She had enjoyed the feeling of being held fast. Even now she was enjoying the memory of a masculine warmth that promised as much excitement as security. How shocking. And how foolish, too. She had escaped one threatened entanglement and must never again find herself at the mercy of a man, particularly one, who by the look of him, could bring her nothing but trouble.

She shifted her position, trying to get more comfortable, but in such a crowded carriage it was difficult. Her feet were already numb from inactivity and her left arm ached with the weight of the portly farmer bunched beside her. A thin-faced clerk in the corner scowled at her attempts to move, but the country woman smiled in sympathy.

'There ain't much room in these coaches, miss, and we large 'uns don't make it any easier.'

The farmer snorted at this and shifted his bulk again, trapping Amelie's arm even more heavily than before. As well as aching from head to toe, she was beginning to feel very hungry. She had hardly eaten a crumb at the inn, so intent had she been on eluding Gareth. Her motherly companion, sensing her thoughts it seemed, reached down to the basket she'd nestled between her feet. She drew out some slices of pie, with a cheese and several apples, and smilingly offered to share her fare. Natural politeness would normally have made Amelie refuse, but her hunger was tormenting and the morning's events had somehow dispensed with normality. She plunged her teeth into the succulent pie just as they left Hounslow Heath.

Her benefactor adjusted her white cotton cap and sighed with relief. 'I'm certain glad we've left that Heath. Terrible things happen there. Just last week my neighbour told me her son was held up in broad daylight and robbed of everything, including his horse. He'd to walk all the way to the City and never a chance of catching the man who robbed him.'

Amelie was as relieved as the woman. Fanny's words still echoed in her mind and a highwayman was at least one danger she had evaded. She reckoned it would take another eight hours or so before the stage reached Bath; if she could catnap a little, the journey would seem less wearisome and, once replete, she found it easy to slip into a doze. She started to rehearse what she would say to her grandmother when she finally arrived and was in the middle of a masterly speech in which she painted a frightening picture of what her life would be like with Rufus

Glyde, when her head began to droop and she drifted gently into a deep sleep. The red-faced farmer beside her also slept, his snores keeping time with the rhythm of the coach, but Amelie heard nothing. Even when the stage came to rest at its designated stops, she remained undisturbed.

⁓

She slept on, mile after mile, until suddenly just past the Chippenham turn-off the coach lurched to an abrupt halt. She was jolted awake and thought at first that they must have reached the small town of Wroxhall, which she had noticed was just twenty miles short of Bath. Hopefully some of the passengers would alight and leave those remaining a little more room. Craning her neck around the still sleeping farmer to look out of the window, she received a shock which sent her senses spinning.

Gareth Heywood wrenched open the doorway of the coach. He was smiling menacingly and in his hand was her forlorn cloak bag. 'You seem to have forgotten something, Amelie.'

The coachman, who had climbed down from his perch, appeared at Gareth's shoulder. 'Ere,'ere, you can't stop a stage on the King's 'ighway to give back a bag,' he blustered.

'It looks very much as if I have,' Gareth said smoothly. 'But do not make the mistake of thinking this is just any cloak bag. Or that I'm returning it. In fact, I have every intention of keeping this bag – as evidence.'

Amelie's fellow passengers were now all wide awake and taking interested note of the proceedings. She heard the word *evidence* being bandied around between them and turned to face her pursuer. His smile had turned positively fiendish.

'You see, my friend,' he continued to address the coachman, 'this bag contains some very expensive trinkets, trinkets filched by this young woman from her employers. In her haste to escape justice, she left the bag behind. But I will make sure she answers for her crime. I intend to deliver her personally to the local magistrate. He is sure to have strong views on dishonest servants.'

There was a gasp from the stout woman who had befriended Amelie. 'Surely not, sir. This young woman can't be a thief.'

'One would not think so, I confess, but appearances can be deceptive. Those we imagine to be young and innocent may harbour evil.'

'How dare you,' spluttered Amelie. 'You are telling a pack of lies, as well you know. The bag is certainly mine, but it contains only a few personal items.'

'Is that so?' Gareth was maddeningly calm. 'Then I suggest, ladies and gentlemen,' this time addressing the inhabitants of the coach who were all now craning forward, intent on the play being enacted before them, 'that you decide whether or not a maid is likely to be carrying these particular personal items.'

And with a flourish he emptied the contents of the bag onto the ground. To her embarrassment a few of her garments spilled out, but her consternation was nothing to the shock when she spied along with them, a diamond brooch, a jewelled tie-pin and a battered but expensive gentleman's timepiece.

'Now what do you think of that?' her tormentor goaded. 'Do they look the kind of things a lady's maid would own? I really don't think so. They do, however, look like items she might have purloined from her employer's bedroom.'

Amelie found her voice at last. 'This is a complete falsehood. I have never seen these things before in my life.'

'And yet somehow they are in your bag. You did say it was your bag, didn't you?'

Her fellow passengers were muttering to themselves, the motherly lady still swearing that she was sure there was some mistake, but the acidic clerk in the corner talking darkly about the declining morals of servants these days. Even the farmer had woken up and was giving his pointed opinion that they were wasting time, and if they didn't get moving soon it would be dark before they could get anywhere near their homes. The rest of the coach nodded in agreement and seemed to lose interest in Amelie's plight.

Gareth reached into the carriage and grasped her arm. 'Now, my dear, I think it time that you came with me.'

Before she could put up a fight, he had pulled her down from the coach and the driver was cracking his whip. Smilingly, Gareth waved the stage on its way. 'Don't worry,' he shouted as the coach began to move, 'I will make sure this young woman gets her just deserts.'

It was all over in seconds. One minute the stage was there, the next Amelie was standing in the middle of a deserted country road, Gareth Heywood at her side and his horse placidly grazing the grass verge.

## Chapter Six

'You are abominable!' she exploded. 'What have I ever done for you to serve me so ill?'

'Desertion perhaps? Have you never been told that it's dishonourable to make a bargain and not keep it? I thought you needed a lesson.'

'I need no lesson on how to conduct myself, particularly from you,' she raged. 'The last time I had the misfortune to be in your company, you behaved intolerably even for someone who was clearly not in their right senses.'

His smile faded. 'I may have been a trifle disguised,' he conceded, 'but my senses were working fine. You are a very beautiful young woman, Amelie, but too spirited by far. As a maidservant, you are in need of schooling.'

She ignored the implied threat. 'How dare you make me out to be a thief? Every feeling is offended.'

'Who is to say you're not a thief? You have behaved most suspiciously.'

She stood erect and looked him squarely in the eyes. 'I have never stolen in my life and I have never seen those articles you tipped out of my cloak bag.'

'No, of course you haven't,' he agreed amiably. 'The

watch and tiepin are mine and the brooch is one that belonged to my mother and that happened to be in my pocket.'

She gaped at him. 'Then why did you make up such a wicked story?'

'To get you off the coach,' he replied blandly. 'What else? I could hardly hold up the stage and demand you dismount. You would have refused and your fellow passengers would have supported you. But thinking you might be a thief, they wanted only to be on their way.'

'You are insufferable. You have stranded me in the middle of nowhere because I refused to keep a shameful bargain. Rest assured that I will still not be keeping it.'

'Now that is where we might disagree.' His tone was unyielding. 'After all, what else can you do? As you so rightly point out, you are stranded in the middle of nowhere, and the only possible transport looks to be that horse over there, and that horse belongs to me. So I think perhaps you might be persuaded to keep your bargain after all.'

'Then you think wrongly. I would rather walk for the rest of the day than be anywhere near you.' And with that, she stuffed her few belongings back into her bag and began marching rapidly along the road.

'It's at least six miles to the nearest village,' he called after her.

'Then I'll walk six miles.'

He swung himself into the saddle and sidled his horse up to her. 'I always get my way, you know. You might as well give in gracefully and enjoy our splendid isolation together. The shoes you are wearing are hardly made for country walking.' The steel had given way to mockery.

She looked down at the dainty pumps, annoyed that she had not thought to change them for Fanny's much stouter shoes. But she would not be beaten. Head held high, she marched onwards, Gareth Heywood walking his horse just a pace behind. We must look like a carnival show, she reflected bitterly.

'Come, Amelie, this is stupid. Get up on the horse and I will engage to take you to the nearest inn.'

'Thank you, sir, but your offer is declined. I am already familiar with the conduct you consider fitting for an inn.'

'You are an obstinate young woman, but I shall win. And if you resign yourself to accompanying me, you will be saved a good deal of discomfort.'

His manner was relaxed and he seemed to have all the time in the world, confident that she would eventually capitulate. Her feet were already pinching badly and she knew that the soles of her shoes would hardly stand up to six miles of rough road, but anger drove her on. The remembered pleasure of his embrace had evaporated without trace. He was a persecutor, there was no doubt. He was as bad in his own way as Rufus Glyde and, just as she had defeated Glyde, she would defeat him, too.

∽

They trudged on in silence. It was pointless trying to persuade her to ride, Gareth decided. He would save his breath. He had been furious when he discovered she had disappeared without a word and had made a snap decision to go after her and wreak his revenge. It was a stupid thing to have done, but he was unused to being bested by a female. From the moment he had met her, he had behaved irrationally. Somehow she had got under his skin and it was a new sensation. Women were for dalliance, passing fancies to be enjoyed lightly before moving on. They were not to be taken seriously, and now he was landed with this ridiculous situation.

He was willing to concede that she had cause to be angry. He had behaved badly but *her* conduct was hardly blameless. She had been lying to him ever since they met, he was certain. And she had made use of him when it suited her. He would show her that no one, least of all a chit of a girl, treated him so and emerged unscathed. Let her walk off her temper and destroy her shoes. She would be all the more acquiescent when he made his next move.

Musing in this way, he was unaware of the distant sounds of an approaching coach. Amelie, far more alert, heard the clatter of wheels seconds before a curricle and four swept around the corner at breakneck speed. She had a terrifying vision of four magnificent greys thundering down on her before she made a dive for cover. Lost in his thoughts, Gareth could take avoiding action only when it was too late. His startled mount reared into the air and he was flung over the horse's head, landing heavily in the ditch. The curricle swept by, its driver, clad in a caped overcoat, according them not a glance.

Cowering in the shelter of the grassy bank, Amelie was certain she had spied a crest on the side of the coach panel. Surely it could not be Rufus Glyde? But she knew that it was. She was all too familiar with that crest. Her flight had been discovered earlier than she'd hoped and he had been sent for, or most probably had taken it on himself, to hunt her down. Her father must have guessed that she had fled to her grandmother – Fanny would never have given her away. Terrified that Glyde might turn the coach and come back to inspect his handiwork, she remained in hiding. There she stayed silent and unmoving for a long time before finding the courage to crawl up the bank to the roadside.

Gareth Heywood was nowhere to be seen. His mount was once more quietly cropping the grass, but there was no sign of the master. A perfect opportunity to escape. The horse was close by and looked biddable. If she led him to the nearest field gate she could manage to clamber into the saddle, then ride to Wroxall, and from there catch the next stage westwards wherever it was going. The sooner she was out of this part of the country, the better. Glyde was not travelling here for his own enjoyment. He was searching for her and he would be back.

A groan sounded from the ditch a few yards away. Tiptoeing to the grass edge, she peered downwards. Gareth was lying on his back, but his foot was at a sickening angle. He had his eyes closed and his face was ashen.

'Are you all right?' She knew it to be an ill-advised question even as she asked.

He opened his eyes and looked directly up into hers. 'Does it look like it? No, I'm not all right, but it's hardly your problem.'

'What has happened to your foot?'

'I may have broken the ankle – I'm not sure. But in any case, I'm not able to move more than a few inches. There's no way I'll walk on it.'

She remained silent and he rasped out, 'Don't mind me, rejoice all you wish. You are free to go. Take the horse and make your escape while you can.'

'But what will you do?'

'Do you really care? I can't imagine so. I shall stay here – I don't have much choice. Someone will come by sooner or later.'

'Let me try to help you up.' She half clambered down the ditch and put her hand under the shoulder that was nearest. At the same time he tried to raise himself to a standing position with his other hand, but the effort was too great. His face turned even whiter.

'I can't do it,' he said, sinking back onto the damp bed of grass once more, 'but thank you for trying. I probably don't deserve it.'

'No, you don't,' she said shortly, 'and this could be just punishment.'

'Spare me the lecture on my morals and go.'

She hesitated but then walked down the road and led the horse forward to the nearby gate. Gareth's last glimpse of her was a mass of chestnut curls flying in the breeze as she disappeared into the distance.

She was an accomplished rider and it took her only a short time to cover the few miles to the nearest inn. As she rode into the deserted courtyard of the George, she called out for help. No one came. She had to dismount and walk into the taproom before she found anyone. An angular woman with a sharp-featured countenance confronted her. Her worn pinafore and rolled-up sleeves suggested that this was the landlord's wife. She barred Amelie's passage, her arms folded pugnaciously, and her eyes snapping.

'And what do you want, missy?' she asked in an ill-tempered voice, looking Amelie up and down with thinly veiled disgust. 'We ain't that sort of place. Off with you. The Cross Keys is where you need to be.'

Amelie was startled. She had never before been spoken to in that fashion. She supposed she must look a fright; she was certainly dishevelled from the long coach journey and her tumble down the bank. The hem of her dress was muddy and her shoes practically falling apart. She rather thought her face was smudged, too. But to judge her a lightskirt!

However she could not afford to alienate the woman further and pinned on her most appealing smile. 'Dear ma'am, I am sorry to disturb you. I'm afraid there has been a riding accident and my disordered appearance is due to having been thrown from my horse.'

Mrs Skinner looked unimpressed. Her arms stayed folded and her expression was grim.

'We, my brother and I, were on a pleasure ride, you see,' Amelie extemporised wildly. 'And my horse went lame, so we had to leave her behind at a farm we passed and we decided to continue home on Gareth's horse. Only then a coach came along at a tremendous speed and the horse reared up and flung us both into the ditch.'

That at least was partly truthful. Mrs Skinner began to look a little more interested, but her arms remained in their fixed position.

'Gareth, my brother, has hurt his ankle – I fear he may have broken it – and I've had to leave him lying in the ditch. I said I would ride to seek help.' She gave a nervous laugh. 'And here I am. Yours was the first inn I came to.'

The landlady continued to maintain an unnerving silence and Amelie cast around for something that would penetrate the woman's reserve. Her eye caught the garish design of what looked to be new curtains.

'Oh, how wonderful!' she exclaimed. 'Such beautiful drapes. I know my mother has been looking everywhere for curtains like these, but she's been unable to find just the right colours.' She prayed fervently for her dead mother's forgiveness.

The praise seemed to be welcome and Mrs Skinner unbent slightly, but it was the thought that she had stolen a march on Amelie's unknown mother that really sealed the matter.

'Where d'you say your brother wus?' she enquired roughly.

'Just a few miles along the road going west,' Amelie said hopefully. 'If we could send an able-bodied man with a horse and cart, we could carry him back here.'

'*We*,' said Mrs Skinner with emphasis, 'can't do nuthin'. You'll 'ave to wait till Mr Skinner gets back from Wroxhall, then we'll see.'

'Yes, of course.' She needed to placate the woman, but wondered anxiously just how long that would be.

⁓

In the event it was two very long hours before she heard the horse and cart pull up in the yard. Two hours of nervously keeping watch at the parlour window, ready to run should Rufus Glyde reappear. And two hours of thinking of Gareth, alone and cold, lying in that ditch. He might be spotted by a labourer returning home from work, but it was unlikely that a passer-by would search the gully without reason. And by now he probably lacked the strength to attract attention. Perhaps she should not have left him? What if he caught a fever or, even worse, died? It would be all her fault. No, that isn't fair, her mind countered angrily – it would be *his* fault. If he hadn't stopped the coach, told such appalling lies about her and forced her to go with him, the accident would never have happened. He wouldn't be lying badly injured and she would be safe with her grandmother instead of stranded in this dreary inn.

'I heer'd you had an accident.' Mr Skinner stood in the doorway. He was as stout as his wife was thin and by good fortune lacked her chronic ill temper. He smiled pleasantly at Amelie. 'I'm sorry I weren't home to help but I've told Will to pack up the cart with blankets and brandy and then go arsk the doctor to come quickly. When the horse is fed, Will and me will be off sharp to look for your brother.'

'Thank you truly, Mr Skinner. I am very worried about him.' And to her astonishment, she shed genuine tears.

'Don't you fret, miss. It'll be all right. It's May and the weather ain't too bad. 'Happen he'll be a little cold and mebbe in pain, but he'll come off fine.'

'Can I come with you?'

'No m'dear – best stay here. It's getting dark and we don't want another accident.'

She had docilely to agree. But now that dusk had fallen,

she worried it would prove difficult for the rescuers to locate the injured man by lantern light. If she had been allowed to accompany them, she was sure she would have found the place easily. Instead she was forced to remain at her post by the window, scanning the darkness with such intensity that it seemed she might cut a path to Gareth through the gloom and rescue him herself.

# Chapter Seven

In the first hour after Amelie left, Gareth remained cheerful. She'd had the chance to break free and he had expected her to desert him. He was surprised that she had even hesitated. He thought of her attempt to help him from the ditch. It had been excruciatingly painful but he had borne with it because she'd cared enough to try – and because she was near. What was it about this girl that led him to behave so rashly? She seemed to exercise a malignant charm over him. By rights he should be at ease in his London hotel, sending a message to his lawyer and planning his escape to the Continent. He supposed wryly that this was a kind of escape although hardly one he would have chosen.

The minutes ticked slowly by and he grew colder as the sun waned and the chill of dusk settled around him. He began to fall into a troubled dream in which a card table and a chandelier swam around the periphery of his vision while a beautiful, chestnut-haired girl danced in front of him. Gradually, he lapsed into a feverish state, the dreams becoming more vivid and frightening. The girl had disappeared and the chandelier was burning his eyes. The cards rose from the table and smacked him hard around the face. Blearily he swam back into consciousness as a hand gently slapped his cheek and a homely country voice encouraged him. 'Come on, sir, time to go. We'll have you in the cart in a twinkling and get you to a warm bed.'

Mr Skinner's plump build belied a strength, every bit of which was needed to raise Gareth from the depths of the gully. Only then could Will reach down to help them both up the steep bank. Gareth was now as weak as a kitten and though he tried manfully to aid their struggle, he had to allow himself to be pulled, pushed and finally lifted from his mossy bed onto the rough boards of the cart. A twinkling had been an exaggeration, he thought, in the throws of extreme pain. At some point he must have passed out. He came to, choking on the brandy that Mr Skinner trickled down his throat. The blankets wrapping him smelt slightly fetid and the jolting of the cart sent shock pains through his leg. At last when he felt he could bear it no longer, they turned into the yard of the George Inn.

The first face he saw was Amelie's. He could hardly believe she was there. He had been too dazed to think how his rescuers had found him, but now he saw he had her to thank.

'You've found my *brother*.'

Amelie ran forward and squeezed Mr Skinner's hand in gratitude. She hoped that Gareth was alert enough to have grasped their supposed relationship. The innkeeper lifted him carefully down from the cart and, with Will's help, carried him up to the spare room. Gareth was no lightweight and Will could only gasp between breaths that the doctor would be with them presently. Once in the room, Gareth sank, pallid-faced, onto the bed.

With difficulty, he turned to Mr Skinner and murmured, 'My sister and I are most grateful for your kindness in coming to our aid.'

Amelie thanked him silently. He had heard her words and was still capable of quick thinking. If he had repudiated their relationship, she was sure that Mrs Skinner would have instantly ejected her from the inn, darkness or no darkness.

⁓

After the doctor had visited his new patient and made his examination, she crept quietly back into Gareth's room.

'What's the verdict?' she asked anxiously.

He looked up slowly and smiled. It was the warm smile she had seen in the London inn. That seemed a million miles away now.

'I haven't broken the ankle, thank the lord, but I have sprained it badly and I'm likely to be laid up for a good few days. The doctor has left me a draught for the pain, and he'll come back the day after tomorrow to change the bandages.'

She could only smile in response. The accident had revealed feelings that she would rather not acknowledge. She felt tongue-tied, badly shaken by the intense relief she had felt when she'd seen Gareth carried into the courtyard. Shaken, too, by how sharp her distress had been at seeing him in pain. There was an awkward silence. The draught was already having its effects and Gareth lay dozing. She was about to tiptoe out of the room, when his voice stopped her in her tracks.

'I should say thank you.'

'There's no need.'

'You could have taken your revenge and left me to my fate.'

'I'm not dishonest,' she said squarely, 'and neither am I heartless. You had suffered a misfortune and needed help. I would have done the same for anyone.'

'You could have told the Skinners of the accident and then gone on your way. You need not have stayed.'

His smile had vanished and his voice was almost brusque. It was as if he resented her help, resented being put in a situation where he was beholden.

'Don't worry, I won't be staying long,' she said in a cool voice. 'Just tonight and then I'll be gone.'

'Where will you sleep? This seems to be the only spare room.'

'I am to share a chamber with Betsy – the kitchen maid.'

'Good,' he said mysteriously.

She couldn't see anything good about it. She had never shared a bedroom in her life and a kitchen maid would not have been her chosen companion. But a more worldly-wise Gareth was satisfied. If she were indeed the innocent young woman she claimed, then Betsy's chaperonage would be invaluable.

'I will see you in the morning before you leave?' His voice was indifferent and it was clear that he wanted to be alone.

'If you wish.' She was equally distant.

He closed his eyes in weariness, looking so ill and worn

that she instantly regretted her coldness. She would have to leave on the morrow as she'd promised, but a small inner voice was urging her to stay and make sure that he recovered fully. The thought was dismissed even as it occurred. It was impossible to remain at the inn. She had spent the entire day evading his unwelcome attentions, so what on earth would he think if she continued by his bedside?

Hours later, she stirred restlessly as the bedroom door shut. There was a thin streak of daylight showing between the badly hung curtain and the window sill, but otherwise the attic room remained dark. Narrowing her eyes, she tried to read the battered clock face on the table beside her and saw that it was only five-thirty. She must have been woken by the maid, leaving for her unenviable duties. She supposed she ought to rise herself and be on her way to Wroxall as early as possible, but they were miles from the town and at this time of day she doubted she would see even a farmer's cart. There would be no way of getting there other than walking and it would take many hours. She would have to beg a strong pair of shoes from Betsy.

She tried to work out what time she would reach Wroxhall and if it would be possible to board a stage that afternoon for Bath. Mail coaches might also stop in the town. They were a good deal faster than the lumbering stage and would get her to Bath well before nightfall, but the cost of a ticket was much higher and her remaining funds were modest. She needed to husband what was left. If she were to miss whatever coaches passed through the town, she would be forced to spend a night there. That was something she dared not contemplate.

She had been nervous embarking on this adventure, but confident that she would reach her grandmother within hours. Complications such as Gareth Heywood had never entered her head. And he *was* a complication. By any measure he had treated her callously and yet she felt a strong thread connecting them, a thread she was finding difficult to break. But there was no doubt he had brought added danger into her life and she was well-advised to be leaving him. Between them, the landlord and the doctor would do all that was necessary to guarantee his well-being. Such a vigorous man would not be laid low for long. And if she left the inn before he woke, she could forgo a farewell visit. It would be unmannerly, but so much easier to walk out of the door right now. If she saw him again, she might be tempted to stay. Her thoughts went round and round in circles until her tired brain gave up the struggle and she once more slept.

⁓

'Miss Heywood, can you hear me?'

The landlord's voice penetrated her slumbers. It sounded an urgent note and she wondered for an instant who he was calling and why, then realised it must be herself. She was the mysterious Miss Heywood.

'Miss Heywood, can you come quickly please?'

She hurried out of bed and hastily donned yesterday's travelling clothes. At the door Mr Skinner looked apologetic, but very worried.

'Sorry to wake you betimes, miss, but Mr Heywood do seem bad. He's feverish for sure and don't respond. Will and me have tried to give him the doctor's medicine but he won't let us near.'

She forgot her resolution to leave the inn as soon as possible and ran down the stairs to Gareth's bedroom. The scene she encountered filled her with dismay. A smoky candle still spluttered on the bedside table, but the curtains remained drawn. In the half-light she could see the bedcovers in disarray, half of them trailing on the floor and the other half heaped untidily on the bed. As for the patient, he was tossing and turning constantly, unable to get comfortable, first throwing off the sheets and then grabbing at them with hot, dry hands while all the time muttering incoherently. She went forwards to the bed and laid her hand on his forehead. It was burning to the touch and his eyes, glancing unrecognisingly at her, were blurred with fever.

'Have you sent for the doctor?' She felt thoroughly alarmed.

'Not yet, miss, we weren't sure to do it, without your say so.'

'Why ever didn't you call me earlier?'

'We did think to,' Mr Skinner conceded, 'but he weren't too bad seemingly.'

'He's certainly bad now.' Her voice was sharp with anxiety.

'Ah, mortal bad.' The landlord looked gloomily down at the threshing figure and shook his head.

She tried to keep a rising irritation from her voice. It looked as though she would need all the help she could get. 'Please send Will for the doctor immediately and ask Mrs

Skinner to bring a sponge and some lavender water.'

'T'would be best if I get it for you, miss.'

'I really don't care who gets it, just bring it please,' she snapped, her nerves frayed by this frightening turn of events.

There was no help for it – she would have to stay. The Skinners believed her to be Gareth's sister and there was no way she could simply up and leave. And seeing him, lying ill and alone, she knew that she couldn't abandon him. When Mr Skinner returned with the bowl of lavender water, she asked him to raise the patient up while she attempted to plump the lumpy pillows into a more comfortable resting place. Then she sat down by the bedside and gently sponged his face. This seemed to soothe the fretting man and for a while he became calmer. But when she rose to move away from the bed, his hand which had been aimlessly brushing the sheet, shot out and grasped her wrist.

'Don't leave me!' he muttered fiercely.

～

The doctor was not long in coming and did not seem overly surprised that his patient had developed a fever. He had, after all, been lying in a wet ditch for a number of hours and, by the look of him, Dr Fennimore judged, he had already travelled a considerable distance and spent much of his strength. But his agitation appeared extreme.

The doctor rose from the bedside and looked at Amelie, his face shrewd and enquiring. 'His fever is unusually severe. Apart from his physical ills, he seems unquiet in his mind. You wouldn't know, I suppose, if there is something disturbing him?'

She shook her head. She could not imagine that the events of the previous day had seriously bothered such a cool, audacious man. But Gareth Heywood was certainly a mystery and she sensed there were dark shadows in his life which might complicate his recovery. She sat down by the rickety table, troubled and very pale.

The doctor clasped her hand warmly. 'Don't worry, Miss Heywood. I'm sure this fever is only temporary. Your brother looks a tough man, certainly not one that a few hours in a ditch will finish off. I'll leave you with a stronger remedy,' he continued bluffly. 'Give it to him every three hours and if his condition worsens, send for me immediately. Hopefully, he should regain his normal strength within a few days. His ankle is already showing signs of improvement.'

As Gareth's supposed sister, Amelie had also to be his nurse. Pitchforked into intimacy with a man she hardly knew, she could not protest without drawing attention to their false relationship. Fanny's horror would know no bounds, she reflected, but this was no time to be missish. Gareth needed her constant attention.

Throughout the next two days, she bathed his forehead, administered medicine and kept his bedclothes as comfortable as possible. All the time his fevered ramblings punctuated the endless routine. He seemed greatly exercised about escaping from a room and needing to find a boat, but none of it made any sense to Amelie and she was too busy to worry over his words.

Mrs Skinner was invariably difficult, grumbling incessantly about the additional work Gareth occasioned. At times Amelie nearly came to blows with her. Fortunately, her husband was of a different disposition. He took Amelie's place by the bedside at breakfast and dinner to allow her to eat and to stretch her limbs. During the night he insisted on taking over Gareth's care and sent her to bed in the early hours of each morning. By then she was too tired to protest and retired gratefully to the little attic room, not caring that Betsy beside her was snoring heavily. She was so weary that she could have slept in Gareth's ditch.

On the third morning Mr Skinner reported that the fever had broken around dawn and that the patient was at last sleeping peacefully. After a hasty breakfast, she tiptoed quietly into Gareth's room with a bowl of chicken broth that the formidable Mrs Skinner had been persuaded to make. He lay supine, a still powerful figure, but the days of fighting fever had taken their toll. She felt a surge of tenderness as she saw the leanness of his face and the pallor beneath the tanned skin.

At her approach, he opened his eyes and a puzzled look flitted across his face. He appeared to be in a bedroom, but it was certainly nowhere he recognised. He felt amazingly tired and cursed himself for his weakness. The events of recent days slowly began to percolate his mind – a nightmarish cart ride, exquisite pain and a pair of gentle, soothing hands. Some kind of accident an age ago, or so it seemed. This ravishing girl had been there, she had ridden away on his horse, so what was she doing in this room? For a while, he considered the matter dispassionately but it remained inexplicable.

'You're still here,' he murmured.

She bent over him, gently arranging the pillows to support his shoulders. He was aware of her soft warmth and of a fragrance that drifted in the air.

'Take some of this excellent broth Mrs Skinner has made for you. You haven't eaten for days.'

He gave up the challenge of trying to make sense of the world and meekly sipped from the spoon she held out to him.

# Chapter Eight

A few days later he was well enough to leave the stuffy bedchamber and make his way with Will's help down the stairs to the garden at the back of the inn. Amelie brought up the rear of the procession with a stool and blankets in case it was chilly. But the sun shone blithely from a cloudless blue sky and Gareth, his ankle supported by the stool, laid back in his chair and soaked up the warmth. Beside him Amelie savoured the scent of apple blossom and the rich smell of new grass.

He looked disparagingly at the glass she handed him.

'The doctor said you should drink as much milk as you can,' she chided. 'It will help you regain your strength.'

'You need strength to drink the stuff,' he protested. 'I think I'll settle for my present state of health.'

'You are a stubborn man.'

'And you're a stubborn woman. Why are you still here? I seem to remember sending you on your way.'

'You did and more than once, but it would be strange behaviour for a sister to abandon her brother.'

'Ah, yes, I'd forgotten that I had acquired a sister. Quite a surprise for me – though entirely beneficial.' His blue eyes held the warm glow that she found so unsettling, but instinctively she returned his smile.

'It can't have been pleasant for you, forced to attend a sick man you barely knew and with no help from that bracket-faced termagant.'

She wanted to say that she knew him a great deal better now, but instead chose safety. 'Even less pleasant for you, I fear. But Mr Skinner has been so helpful. He's watched over you constantly and even persuaded his wife to cook for us.'

'Has she been very tiresome?'

'Shall we say she is not best pleased to be entertaining two vagrants.' Amelie grinned, remembering the skirmishes she had endured while Gareth lay helpless above.

'One thing does occur to me,' he said thoughtfully. 'The Skinners must be wondering why no one has come from our supposed home to look for us.'

'I told them that I'd sent the local carrier with a message when he passed here the day before yesterday.'

'And they believed you?'

'Mrs Skinner probably didn't, but then she wouldn't believe anything. She decided from the outset that we were imposters, and of course she's right.'

For a moment he looked startled. 'I mean,' she explained, seeing the surprise on his face, 'that we are playing this charade of being brother and sister.' She looked at him enquiringly. 'Do you have a sister, in fact?'

'No.'

'Do you have any family? Will they not be wondering where you are?'

'No and no,' he said shortly. Then added in a more conciliatory tone, 'My only relative was my grandfather and he is dead.'

'I'm sorry.'

The compassion in her voice touched him on the raw. 'Don't be. It's a matter of indifference to me.'

He sounded prickly but she wasn't deterred. 'If you have no family in Bristol, why do you want to go there?'

He shifted his position but said nothing.

'While you were suffering from the fever you mentioned taking a boat and escaping,' she persevered. 'What did you mean?'

'I have no idea. When people are feverish, they talk a lot of nonsense.'

She had the distinct impression of an iron gate clanging shut; she would learn no more. And in a trice he had deftly turned the tables and begun to probe her own story.

'And why were *you* determined on travelling to Bristol?'

He must know that she had been less than honest with him, at the very least that she had lied about her destination. 'A family there were advertising for a lady's maid, and I intended to apply for the position.'

'That must have been days ago. By now the situation could be filled.' He had evidently decided to maintain the pretence.

'I daresay you're right,' she replied airily. 'They are sure to have hired another girl.'

'So when you get to Bristol, what will you do?'

'I think, in fact, I'll try my luck in Bath.' She was picking her words carefully. 'There are any number of retired dowagers living there and one of them is bound to need assistance.'

'I wish you good fortune. Would you like a testimonial from me?' It was a joke, but then his face took on a more serious air. 'Without a reference from your previous family, you will find it difficult to get work.'

'I shall manage. I have no reason to feel ashamed. I shall tell the truth about why I had to leave.'

'Will they believe you though? As an employer, I might find it difficult to accept your situation was so desperate that you had to climb out of a window. Things like that happen only in novels. If you had simply told your mistress what her son was up to, she would have intervened.'

'No, she wouldn't. He is spoilt and pampered and no one gainsays him, least of all his adoring mother. She would never have believed me. She would have accused me of plotting to ensnare him and turned me off without notice.'

'But how has your situation improved? You are still without a job and still without references.'

'Maybe, but I haven't had to endure lies and false accusations.'

He looked a little conscious at this. 'Until you met me, I suppose.'

'Until I met you.'

She was looking directly at him and he was caught by her gaze. How could a pair of eyes sparkle with such militancy and yet drown a man in their depths. 'Was there nobody else in the family you could turn to?' he said quickly. 'What about your young mistress?'

'She was a good friend to me,' Amelie admitted, happily weaving her fantasy, 'but she is to be married to a wealthy man against her wishes. She is powerless to offer me protection.'

'*You* could always marry. You would receive ample protection then. And I'm sure you've enjoyed plenty of attention from your fellows – beautiful and intelligent maidservants are not two a penny.'

'I will never marry,' she declared resolutely.

Gareth's smile was indulgent. 'You are not much more than a child – far too young to know how you will feel in the future.'

She was nettled by his patronising tone and her response was sharp. 'On the contrary, I shall feel in the future just as I do now. I intend to stay a single woman – if I can.'

'Then you are vastly unlike the rest of your sex. Why so definite?'

'I have no wish to be subject to a man.'

'The right man would not subject you, but would be a powerful defender.'

'Not those I have known. They have been either dissolute or vain and shallow.'

'There are men who are none of those things.'

She raised her eyebrows sceptically. 'You, for instance?'

Damn her, he thought, why was she forever putting him in the wrong? He had behaved appallingly, he knew, and for no other reason than a desire to master her, to ruffle that beautiful surface. She was just too lovely.

Aloud he admitted to his offence. 'I behaved stupidly when we first met, more than stupidly.' He shook his head at his folly. 'I made a bad situation worse by getting extremely drunk.'

She looked enquiringly at him, but it was evident he had no intention of explaining his erratic conduct. She wondered if it had anything to do with the grandfather for whom he had just professed the utmost indifference. She wanted to know more and tried another tack.

'You may not have relatives in England, but what about friends?'

'None of those either,' he muttered roughly. 'I am a wanderer, Amelie, and friends and family play no part in my life.'

She was certain that beneath his harsh detachment, there lurked a vulnerability he would not admit. Her eyes clouded with sympathy and without thinking she reached out and stroked the tanned forearm that showed beneath his rolled-up sleeves.

His hand closed over hers and held it tightly. He looked directly into her concerned face, hard blue eyes meeting soft brown, his gaze intent and wondering. For a long moment they sat thus. Then he reached out and slowly caressed her cheek. Her pulse began an erratic dance as his touch warmed her face. He let his hand slide from her cheek to tangle itself in the glossy curls which tumbled to her shoulders. Turning his body towards her, he cupped her face in both his hands and tilted it upwards. She watched as his mouth came closer and without thinking offered up her lips. His kiss was hard and warm and lingered long.

How long they would have kissed she had no idea, if Mr Skinner had not suddenly appeared from the depths of the inn leading the doctor behind him. She sprang back, flushed. Gareth looked annoyed. If Mr Skinner had seen that embrace, they would be in trouble. How to explain when they were brother and sister! Jumping up from her seat, she nodded briefly to Dr Fennimore and quickly ran up the stairs to her bedroom in the eaves. She poured water from the jug into the chipped white basin and bathed her heated cheeks. She must truly have run mad. What on earth was she doing kissing a man of whom she knew nothing or at least nothing creditable. She sat down on her bed and stayed there for a very long time, trying hard to still her heart and erase the feeling of Gareth's hard, warm mouth on hers.

The doctor's visit was brief. He was evidently well-satisfied with his patient and needed to come no more. She heard him call out his farewells followed by the sound of Will helping Gareth up the stairs to his room. Until she could leave the inn, she must make sure they were rarely alone together. He could not be trusted. She had allowed herself to show sympathy and his response had been immediate – an assault. An assault that she had made no attempt to escape. She could not trust herself either. His gaze had sent her heart thudding, a simple touch had left her breathless. And that kiss. No, she would not think of that kiss.

∽

As the sun slipped from the sky, Mr Skinner appeared at her door with a message. 'Your brother would like to know if you will dine with him tonight. He is feeling a good deal better and would like to celebrate his recovery.' The landlord enunciated the phrases painstakingly, relieved that he had remembered Gareth's precise words.

*I'm sure he would*, she thought crossly, *and I can imagine the kind of celebration he intends*. 'Tell my brother that I regret I have the headache and will not be dining tonight.' Then more diffidently she added, 'It would be very kind of you, Mr Skinner, if you could bring a bowl of soup to my room.'

For the first time since she had come to the George, she found it difficult to sleep that night, her mind endlessly roaming the day's events, but finding no peace. She could not banish the attraction she felt for Gareth Heywood. Her heart was forever pulling her towards a man with whom it was madness to embroil herself. He was arrogant and capricious. He was reserved and unforthcoming and she strongly suspected that unfortunate secrets lay hidden in his past. Yet she, too, was equally guilty of dissembling. From the outset she had told him a pack of lies and ever since had spent considerable effort in embroidering them.

It was clear now she must leave for Bath as soon as she could and avoid any further entanglement. Certainly, she must not fall in love with him. If ever she were forced to marry, Lord Milverton's daughter would be expected to look a great deal higher than a mere Mr Heywood of unknown and possibly disreputable lineage. But she *wasn't* going to be forced to marry. She would not emulate her mother's sad fate. Her security and peace of mind lay in a solitary life and that meant eschewing dalliance, no matter how attractive the man.

⁓

After breakfast she repaired to Gareth's bedroom to tell him she was leaving. It was another beautiful May morning and the leaded windows were flung wide to welcome the sun. A warm breeze gently lifted the curtains. He was sitting by the window fully dressed and smiled mockingly as she came through the door.

'I hope I find you recovered?'

She looked blank for a moment.

'The headache? I understand it was so painful that you could manage only a bowl of soup for dinner.'

'I am well, thank you.' She did not meet his eyes. 'And you?'

'I am well, too. Almost my old self. Does that strike terror into your heart?'

'Indeed no, why should it? I am well able to defend myself.'

He shook his head in irritation. 'Let us stop sparring, Amelie. Come and sit with me instead.'

She moved towards the window and the empty chair. For the first time that morning she looked directly at him and it was not a comfortable experience. She felt her body warm beneath his gaze and it took considerable effort to ignore the answering pull. She was still on dangerous territory and must step carefully.

He stretched out his hand to her but she disregarded it. 'When do you intend to leave for Bristol?' she asked. 'I presume you are still going there.'

'Maybe.' His tone was curt. 'I haven't yet made up my mind.

'If you don't continue to Bristol, where else will you go? Back to London?'

'Possibly.'

'So you are as free as a bird?'

'It would appear so.'

Frustrated at his stonewalling, she went on the offensive. 'Are you saying that nobody in the entire world will miss you, if you don't soon put in an appearance?'

'That about sums it up.'

She didn't understand him. Her questions were innocent enough, but his bald refusal to answer made it clear that he didn't trust her. She was fine to kiss but not to confide in. He must have sensed her anger because his face lit with the smile that disarmed her.

'Why don't we just enjoy this morning? I imagine you've come to tell me you are leaving soon.'

'Now that your ankle is better, I must be on my way.' She was annoyed with herself that she sounded almost apologetic.

'Of course you must, and I cannot detain you. You have kept your bargain, after all.'

For a moment she looked befuddled – she had completely forgotten their old quarrel. Then she gave a smile herself. 'Yes, I have kept it, though not quite as you planned.'

'Better, in fact. You have seen me through some difficult days, so don't let's spend our last few hours brangling.'

She remained mute and stared fixedly through the window at the untended orchard beyond. When he spoke again his voice was subtly different. Tender, she thought, and it caught at her heart.

'I have you to thank for the good shape I'm in. You must know I am deeply grateful.'

'I don't want your gratitude.'

'What do you want?' Again he reached out for her hand.

Mindful of her overnight resolution, she jumped up and walked to the door. 'What I want is to leave tomorrow. But in the meantime I am sure the George can supply us with some entertainment. I'll go downstairs and see what they have to offer.'

And with that she disappeared rapidly from view. Gareth looked after her, a slight flush creeping into his lean cheek. Offering his hand in friendship to a woman was a new experience for him and being rejected was equally novel.

# Chapter Nine

She returned half an hour later, having searched high and low for dominoes or Chinese chequers. Will had helped her for a while until Mrs Skinner, catching sight of the two of them, had snapped at him to fetch water from the pump. Then she had stood coldly over Amelie and demanded just what Miss might be wanting. Her attitude was one of unconcealed hostility. Amelie was sure now that the landlord had seen her spring back from Gareth's kiss yesterday and had confided this unsettling news to his wife. She blushed deeply at the thought of their conversation.

'I'm looking for dominoes or chequers,' she said as calmly as she could. 'My brother is feeling a good deal better and it will be a way of passing the hours.'

Mrs Skinner snorted as though she knew well enough how they intended to pass the hours, but reluctantly led the way into an inner sanctum, opened a tall oak dresser in the corner of the room and shuffled around inside. The reek of mothballs filled the already malodorous room.

'There's some cards and a game of spillikins.' The landlady thrust the items at Amelie and stood glaring at her.

Understanding that she was dismissed, Amelie made

to leave. The pack of cards would be a diversion, but she found it impossible to picture Gareth playing the child's game. She would leave the spillikins in her bedroom. With hurried thanks, she gathered the items together and ran up the stairs.

'I've found something,' she called out gaily. 'A pack of cards. Or rather Mrs Skinner found them, tucked at the back of an enormous dresser, which I doubt she has opened for at least thirty years. Unfortunately, they smell of mothballs, but then this room isn't exactly fresh, is it? Even with the window wide open.'

As she was speaking, she cleared the small table of empty glasses and medicine bottles. 'There, a perfect card table. What shall we play? I only know one game, but I imagine you can teach me others.'

'No.' The brusque monosyllable startled her.

'I beg your pardon?'

'I said no. I cannot teach you any card games, nor do I wish to play.'

She looked puzzled. 'How difficult am I to understand?' he said sharply. 'I don't wish to play.'

'But it's only a game of cards – an amusing diversion.'

'For the last time, I don't wish to play.'

The familiar bleak expression had returned to Gareth's face. His eyes were once more stony and the straight night-black brows threatening. He leaned back in his chair, detaching himself from the proceedings and refusing to look at her.

'That's fine,' she said a little uncertainly. 'I didn't mean to upset you.'

'You didn't. Just learn to take a refusal when it is given.'

She bit back a retort. After tomorrow she would never see Gareth Heywood again. It was hardly worth quarrelling with him despite his extraordinary rudeness. But it was difficult to believe that he was the same man who had kissed her with such ardour only yesterday. She felt deeply wounded by the change.

'I'll find something else to play,' she stammered.

Minutes later she returned with the spillikins. The hard look on Gareth's face had disappeared and when he saw the spillikins he laughed out loud. 'I know you have been my nursemaid these past few days, but have I regressed that badly that you need to play a child's game with me?'

'It's all the Skinners have and we must make the best of it.'

She held the bunch of thin sticks upright, then allowed them to fall at will. They scattered untidily across the table top.

'The sticks coloured blue score most highly, red next, then yellow, and green are the most lowly,' she explained.

'I shall be lucky to pick up one stick cleanly, never mind its colour. I've suffered an accident, after all.'

'You have sprained your ankle, not your wrist.'

'But women are so much more dextrous, it's hardly fair.'

'Surely, Mr Heywood, you are not saying that a woman can outdo you.'

'Gareth, please. If we are to be serious competitors, we must be on first name terms. That way when insults fly, they will be nicely personal.'

'I have no intention of trading insults. It's a game, not a competition.'

She had spoken carelessly but nevertheless tried very hard to win. She took minutes to weigh up the arrangement of sticks before deciding which one she would extricate from its place without dislodging the others. Gareth had gone first and could begin with the most accessible, but once into the thick of the game, they were both forced to concentrate intently. At one point, he appeared to disturb one of the sticks he was trying to avoid and she called foul.

'I merely breathed on it and the stick moved of its own accord.' He shook his head in pretend bewilderment.

She burst out laughing. 'That's certainly original. I'll give you the excuse if only for sheer invention.'

So the game went on until there was just a small pile of sticks left in the middle of the table, all thickly entangled. They were neck and neck in the number they had managed to acquire and, faced now with the most difficult moves, they both studied the table keenly trying to decide their best approach. In the event it was Gareth who managed to extricate his last spill without disturbing the one other that was left.

'*Voila!*' he exclaimed.

'*Magnifique*,' she unconsciously rejoined, responding spontaneously to his skilful play.

'A maidservant who speaks French as well as having a French name. It becomes more and more intriguing.' He looked searchingly at her.

'I would hardly say that I spoke French.' She was desperate to move the conversation on to less dangerous ground.

'Still, it's an unusual maid who knows any French. And you *are* an unusual maid, aren't you? You are proud and independent, you speak genteelly and hold yourself like a lady. If it were not for your clothes, I would take you for a lady.'

From the bottom of her heart, she thanked the absent Fanny for her wardrobe, then set about allaying his suspicions.

'My young mistress made a great friend of me and I learned from her how to go on.'

He considered this for a moment. 'You may have learned conduct from her, but not, I think, your courage.'

'What do you mean?' She was disconcerted.

'Did you not say that your mistress was being married off against her will?'

'She is, but courage won't help her. Her brother has gambled away the family's fortune and this marriage is the only way to restore it. She is expected to make a sacrifice for her family.'

'Quite a sacrifice. Would you make it, I wonder?'

'I would not,' she declared with a vehemence that surprised them both.

He looked at her as she sat across the table. Her creamy skin glowed translucent in the sunlight that filled the room and the velvet brown of her eyes held fire. She had never looked more enchanting.

'Nor should you.' His voice was husky with feeling.

The atmosphere had suddenly become charged, their bantering mood forgotten. He should defuse the moment, he thought, make a joke, turn away. Instead, he rose quickly from his chair, taking no heed of the damaged ankle, and took both her hands in his. Slowly he raised her up and encircled her in his arms. She was crushed against his hard frame and he felt her tremble beneath his hands. Very gently he kissed her hair, her ears, her cheek. In a moment his tongue had parted her lips and was slowly exploring the softness of her mouth. His body moved against her and he heard her groan with pleasure.

Could it really be she who was groaning? She was dissolving into this nameless delight, yet some voice of wisdom pulled her back to consciousness. This was a man who came from nowhere and would go to nowhere. She would never see him again once they parted. He had made her vulnerable, created a desire in her that she had never before known. And desire meant weakness. She had only to think of her mother's fate to know that. Impelled by a new urgency, she pushed him away with force and began to tidy the scattered sticks, barely able to see them for the feelings raging within.

'That shouldn't have happened.' He was still standing close to her, his breathing ragged and his voice rough. He seemed furious with himself. 'After yesterday I vowed I would never again touch you.'

Distractedly, she smoothed her tumbled hair and then began to pack the last of the spillikins in their box.

'Forgive me if I've distressed you.' His harsh tones broke through her silence.

'It's of no importance and I have no wish to talk of it.' Her outward calm belied her turmoil. 'It must be time for nuncheon. I'll fetch some refreshment from the kitchen.'

As she turned to leave, she gave a fleeting glance out of the window. A carriage had pulled up at the entrance to the building. In itself that was unusual but this was not any carriage. It was a lightly built curricle drawn by four high-stepping greys and the curricle door had a well-known crest on its panel. It was Rufus Glyde. He was here. He had traced her after all. She turned sheet-white and the box dropped from her suddenly lifeless hand.

'Excuse me,' she gasped. 'I have to go.'

And with that she dashed from the room, leaving Gareth baffled and infuriated.

~

Rufus Glyde was in no pleasant mood. He had been driving almost continuously for two days without ever once sighting his quarry. In addition he'd had to endure the sharp tongue of Brielle St Clair when he had dared to enquire for her granddaughter at the Bath house. It had been a terse encounter on both sides, but he had definitely come off worse, told in no uncertain terms that his intervention in family affairs was not welcome. It had been the first intimation for Brielle that all was not well with her granddaughter. She was furious that Lord Milverton had not come himself to tell her of Amelie's flight, but instead left it to this patronising stranger to break the news. Most of all she was desperately worried. She felt sick when she thought of what might have befallen the young girl. Her dread fuelled a naturally acerbic tongue and Glyde was still smarting from his dismissal.

As he entered the George the idea that he was on a wild goose chase became insistent. For a while he had thought that he might be on Amelie's trail. At Reading where he'd stopped for the night, he had overheard a conversation between two travellers that gave him pause. One of them had told the strange story of a stage held up on the Bath road, not for jewellery or money, but for a young woman travelling in the coach. It had caused something of a sensation when the passengers had disembarked in Bath and begun to tell their tale.

He had been sufficiently intrigued by the news to abandon his return to London and head once more in the direction of Bath. By dint of questioning everyone he met – and most of these he castigated as ignorant bumpkins – he had managed to discover the district in which the hold-up had occurred and then begun to cast around at various inns for news of the errant Amelie. So far it had proved a fruitless task and the George looked no more promising.

Entering the taproom, he was greeted by drab, outmoded furnishings and the stale odour of old beer and tobacco. He turned round full circle. The afternoon sunlight in its attempt to pierce the dirty windows only served to emphasise the dilapidation within. Surely Amelie Milverton would not be residing here. The inhabitants, if there were any, were either dead or asleep. Nothing stirred. Irritably, he rang the bell on the counter and when there was no response, rang it again more loudly. Mrs Skinner appeared from the top of the cellar steps and scowled at him.

'Did you want somethin'?'

Her voice was not encouraging. Glyde looked the woman up and down. She was gaunt, badly dressed and with a face marked by ill temper. 'It would appear so since I rang the bell,' he countered acidly.

'What is it then? I'm busy.'

He tried to keep the rising anger from his voice – he needed this woman's help – then began on the same story that he'd told at the other dozen inns he had visited. He had been travelling with a friend, he said, but they had become separated. He was careful to avoid mentioning the sex of his companion. His friend had not appeared at the rendezvous on which they'd agreed, and he, Glyde, feared that his comrade had met with an accident. Did the good lady have anyone staying at the inn who might be his friend?

'Nobody you'd know,' she sniffed.

'But you do have someone staying?'

Mrs Skinner grudgingly admitted the fact but added, "E ain't your friend, 'e ain't a top-lofty gent like you.'

'My friend is hardly top-lofty. May I ask who this person is?'

'You can arsk, but mebbe I ain't of a mind to tell you.'

Again he had visibly to control his anger. 'I am sure we can remedy your lack of memory.' A sneer disfigured the thin white face.

He took out his bill folder and extracted a note of some considerable value. Mrs Skinner blinked at this unexpected largesse and thought of extending her prize curtains to the rooms above.

"Is name's Heywood and I've told you 'e ain't a gent, not with 'is scruffy clothes.'

Glyde's hopes withered. For a moment he had thought he might finally be close to success, but a male resident who wore scruffy clothes and wasn't a 'gent' as Mrs Skinner put it, was not someone who could be of any interest.

'And he is your only guest?'

'You're a nosy one, ain't you?' Mrs Skinner's hand closed over the tantalising money bill. 'As it 'appens, 'is sister's staying with 'im. They 'ad an accident, too. Funny, the number of accidents round 'ere these days.'

Glyde ignored the witticism, but his mind was working rapidly. A sister of Mr Heywood might mean a young woman, and this young woman could just be the prey he sought. It was a chance in a thousand, but he had to know. He cast around for a way of distracting Mrs Skinner, who appeared to have taken root in front of her benefactor. His luck suddenly took a turn for the better. Will, who had been working in the cellar alongside his mistress, appeared at the top of the stairs.

'Mrs Skinner, ma'am, where d'you want the new barrels put?'

'Where d'you think, you numbskull?'

'There's not enough room behind the old barrels,' Will continued bravely.

'Dratted men,' she muttered, 'can't be relied on to do anythin',' and giving Glyde a last withering glance, she disappeared back down the cellar steps.

Her head had hardly faded from view before he made his move. In a few seconds he had reached the stairway leading to the top of the house and readied himself to search for Mr Heywood and his mysterious sister.

## Chapter Ten

Gareth stared blankly through the window at the curricle as it disappeared towards the stables. From the rear it looked to be a nobleman's carriage, but he had no idea to whom it belonged or why it was at the George. Amelie had evidently gained a better view and she *had* recognised it. The thought came to him that this might be her previous employer, enraged by her questionable departure. He realised with a jolt that his initial suspicions had been completely lulled and now his mind could no longer think of her as a deceiver. He dismissed the idea even as it came into his head. And common sense soon reasserted itself. Whatever she may have done and however furious her noble employer, the possibility of his seeking out a delinquent maid in a rundown country inn was extremely unlikely. So there must be some other explanation, but what? What on earth had a maidservant, no matter how beautiful, to do with such a carriage or its inhabitant?

His annoyance at Amelie's abrupt departure mingled with feelings of self-reproach. He had spoiled the companionship of the morning. One minute they had been laughing, joking, funning with each other, and then everything had changed. He had touched her and he shouldn't have. She was irresistible, but he should have resisted. God knew he'd had enough experience in escaping amorous situations, so why was this so different? He could not account for it. Her indignation that she might sacrifice herself for her family had lent her skin an ardent glow and her eyes a sparkle of molten brown. In that moment her beauty had been overwhelming, but it was more than physical allure. In that moment, too, it seemed her very soul had been laid bare and spoken unmistakeably to his. He gave himself a mental shake: such fanciful nonsense! But whatever the reason, he had not been able to stop himself from touching. Even now he could feel her mouth, soft but eager, opening delicately to his.

When he heard the bedroom door open, he rose to his feet, a contrite expression on his face, but instead of the woman he'd expected, he was confronted by Rufus Glyde, a man he had not seen for seven long years. Both men stared at each other in amazement. Glyde was the first to find his voice.

'Surely,' he jeered, 'it cannot be Gareth Denville. Are you not supposed to be 'resting' on the Continent? You cannot have returned to claim your father's earldom? Even the blackest sheep might be expected to do the decent thing and stay away.'

Gareth remained silent, his face impassive and his darkened eyes unreadable. For years unfounded suspicions had plagued his mind over Glyde's role in that ill-fated card game.

'Are you not going to invite me to sit down, Mr Heywood?' Glyde tormented. 'I'm presuming it *is* Mr Heywood? Why the false name, I wonder? A silly question no doubt. I imagine you would prefer to keep your identity hidden for all kinds of reasons. And staying in a place like this!' The smirk became more pronounced.

Gareth remained standing. His voice was cold and curt. 'State your business. Mine is none of yours.'

'Still hot-tempered, I see. Some things never change. Though it's true you have aged – not quite as fresh faced as when I saw you last. Now when was that? Ah yes, the Great-Go. Quite a night, quite a sensation, I recall.'

'Cut to the chase, Glyde, what do you want?'

'Not you, for sure. Keeping company with the flotsam of society is not really my custom. But I am rather interested in the sister you appear to have acquired. If my memory serves me right – and, of course, I could be wrong, family genealogy was never my strong point – your father, another unfortunate I believe, had only one child and that child was you. So a sister?'

'It's none of your affair and I'll thank you to leave.'

'Now that is where we might disagree. I feel it could well be my affair.'

'I have nothing further to say to you. Leave of your own free will or at the end of my boot. It's your choice.'

'Proud crowing from someone plainly unable to enforce his threat.' He gestured at Gareth's bandaged ankle. 'Tell me what I want to know and I will leave as quickly as you could want. What about this sister?'

Gareth weighed up the odds of forcibly removing his

antagonist from the room and decided it was not worth the pain. He would give him the minimum of information and speed him on his way.

'She is merely an acquaintance who happens to be staying at the inn.'

'An acquaintance you call a sister. Come, Denville, that won't wash. Who is she?'

'She is a maidservant, no one you know and no one of any interest.'

'A maidservant? Pitching it rather low even for you. A maidservant – and your doxy, I presume.'

Gareth's knuckles tightened until they were white. 'Get out!'

'Dear, dear, that temper again. Yes, I see, your doxy, and to pacify that dreadful harpy downstairs, you pass her off as your sister. You are right, of course, I have no interest in her. The woman I seek would not pass the time of day with you, and as for impersonating a maidservant and sharing this vile refuge, the idea is laughable.'

'Now that you've had your laugh, you are at liberty to leave.'

'Indeed, and I shall do so very shortly. But first, tell me – how does the cardsharping business prosper? Do you make a living?' Glyde glanced down at his own elegant coat of superfine and then at Gareth's outfit, daily looking more frayed.

'And I always thought such practised tricksters went on prosperously,' he murmured, 'but it would seem not.'

Ignoring the intense pain in his ankle, Gareth moved with unexpected swiftness towards his enemy and clasped him violently round the throat.

'If ever you call me a cheat again, you will not live,' he ground out.

The door had remained open throughout their acrimonious exchange and with his hands still wrapped around Glyde's neck, Gareth thrust his adversary through the doorway and down the stairs.

∽

At the moment Glyde had dismounted from his carriage, Amelie had escaped through the back entrance of the inn. She bolted past the crumbling outbuildings and through the small wicket gate which led to open pasture. Terrified at the turn of events, she ran without thinking where she was going. Her mind was in chaos, refusing to accept that Sir Rufus had tracked her to this remote place. It was impossible. Nobody except Gareth Heywood knew her whereabouts and he was ignorant of her true identity.

Slowly through the confused toss and tumble of thoughts, a chilling idea began to emerge. Was it possible that they were in alliance together, that Gareth knew who she was and had been Glyde's accomplice all this time? Was it coincidence that Rufus Glyde had appeared out of nowhere, just after she had been abducted from the stagecoach? The fact that his carriage had mown Gareth down and thrown him into a ditch could have been a simple misjudgement. Was that why Gareth had refused point blank to tell her anything about himself, in case she unmasked him before Glyde could catch up with them? And to think that she had so nearly succumbed to his charm.

By now breathless, she was forced to come to a stop. In

any case it was pointless running farther across the fields. She had no idea where she was going and if she turned back again to regain the road, Glyde could overtake her in his curricle at any moment. A nearby clump of trees would provide shelter and from this vantage point she could observe the inn from a distance. She settled herself beneath an old oak, her back against its sturdy trunk. The gentle summer sun filtered through the leaves above and birdsong filled the air. It was hard to imagine there was anything wrong with the world.

Gradually her breathing returned to normal and her disordered thoughts began to settle. It was madness to imagine that Gareth was in league with the man who was hunting her. How could he have arranged to be outside her house at the precise moment she had climbed from the bedroom window? It was ridiculous. Even more ridiculous to think him an accomplice. She knew, as well as she knew herself, that he would loathe and despise a creature such as Glyde.

The time passed tantalisingly slowly. She told herself that her pursuer would not be at the inn long. Even if he ran into Gareth, he would not know him and any description of Miss Heywood's appearance was unlikely to match that of the aristocratic woman Glyde sought. He would be eager to leave an inn as insalubrious as the George and would make again for the pleasures of London. And once he had driven away, she could take shelter for one more night. Tomorrow morning she would get her lift to Wroxall and be on the stage to Bath and safety.

She waited for what seemed an age, although in reality

only half an hour had passed since she'd fled the inn so precipitately. In that time she had neither glimpsed any activity nor heard a sound from the distant building. Maybe her hiding place was too far away to hear the noise of any departure? She debated what to do. At this rate she could be sitting under the oak tree until nightfall. Gathering her courage, she decided to chance a return. With some stealth she began slowly to approach the inn and, meeting nobody, crept through the back entrance into the passage which ran the length of the building to the open front door.

Almost immediately she became aware of Glyde's carriage being led back into the courtyard and turned to flee again. But at the same time raised voices sounded above and she was sure one of them was Gareth's. She strained to hear what was being said, but the voices were too indistinct. As she listened, there was a sudden noisy creak of bedroom floorboards overhead. In a trice she had whisked herself into the shadows beneath the stairs. Just in time. Rufus Glyde clattered down the staircase, his face twisted in fury. He was so close that had she reached out her arm, she could have touched him. She remained frozen to the spot as he stormed past and out into the sunlit yard, throwing himself onto the driving seat of the carriage and frenziedly whipping his horses.

She found she was shaking uncontrollably and her first thought was to seek the sanctuary of her bedchamber. But there were questions burning through her brain that needed answers. The angry scene she had come upon in its dying moments made no sense. Her former suspicions began to return; there was a connection between these two men and she needed to know what it was.

~

Gareth's ankle throbbed angrily, but it had been worth the pain to knock the sneering smile from his enemy's face. Glyde would be forever associated with the scene of his disgrace and his heart rejoiced that he had routed the man so completely. But if he were honest, it was the idea of Glyde and Amelie together that had spurred him to extreme action. The image was seared on his mind's eye, even stronger for being intangible. He had no idea why Glyde had turned up at this remote inn or what connection he had to the girl, but suspicion gnawed at him. He doubted he would ever get the truth from her – he had been a fool to believe that she was trustworthy.

When she came in, he was standing by the window, exactly where she had left him. If his mind were not teeming from that furious altercation, he might have imagined she'd been away for only a few minutes and the intervening time a bad dream. But he knew his face must tell another story. He turned as he heard her footsteps, his eyes blue flint and his mouth close-gripped. She started to speak but he cut her off.

'Why did you leave like that? What is that man to you?'

He could see she was distressed but her voice was even when she answered him. 'He is nothing to me. I ran away because I feared being discovered.'

'Why should it matter that he saw you?'

'I told you. I feared being seen – by anyone.'

'Anyone? Do you take me for a fool? He came looking for a woman and I think that woman was you. You turned white when you saw his carriage in the yard. You fled. Can you really expect me to believe that it was because some stranger had suddenly arrived?'

'You may believe what you wish. I ran away because I was scared of being found here. I am an unmarried woman and for the last week have been living under the same roof as you.'

'You would have me accept that a girl who thinks nothing of throwing her lot in with a man she has never before met is worried that others will see her with him?'

'I did not throw my lot in with you. You forced me to accompany you.'

'It does not seem to have pained your sense of propriety too greatly.'

'You may mock all you wish. You may not have a reputation to defend, but I do. I must earn my living and I cannot afford to attract gossip.'

She hoped this would prove an inspired invention, but instead Gareth pounced on her words and shredded them to pieces.

'If you don't know this man, then how could his seeing you affect your reputation one way or another?'

'I did not say I didn't know him,' she was forced to concede.

'At last,' he muttered, 'we are getting near the truth or as near as we're ever likely to.'

'And what do you mean by that?'

He could feel her anger slice through the airless room, but it didn't stop him. 'What do I mean? Simply that you appear to have a slippery relationship with the truth.'

'If we are to call each other liars, you fare no better.

What of the lie you told my fellow passengers? That was blatant.'

'And this isn't?'

'I was telling the truth when I said I was fearful of being discovered. The man is an intimate of my young mistress's brother and visits the house regularly. I was worried he might recognise me and report my situation to the family.'

Gareth was silent, seeming to turn this over in his mind. She was unsure he believed her and, to deflect him further, renewed her attack. 'I have told you how *I* know him, though I can't understand why it's any business of yours. But perhaps now you will tell me how *you're* acquainted with him.'

He stared sightlessly through the window, once more in that overheated, overfurnished salon. The babble of rich men intent on their pleasure filled his ears, then the sudden silence, the incredulous stares, the shuffling of feet and finally the cool withdrawal of the well-bred from the social disaster in their midst.

Amelie waited for his response, never taking her eyes from his face. Aware at last of her scrutiny, he looked up at her, his expression bleak. 'My acquaintance with him is very slight.'

His discomfort was palpable and she pressed home her advantage. 'You were quarrelling,' she insisted. 'You must know the man well enough to quarrel.'

'He angered me. He invaded my room without permission and then refused to leave.'

'And that was enough for you to throw him down the stairs?'

'Something of an exaggeration. He is a particularly obnoxious man and I didn't care for his tone.'

'You seem to have argued for a long time. Why did you not rid yourself of him earlier?'

'You may not have noticed,' he replied scathingly, 'but I have sustained an injury. You had fled and I was left alone to deal with him. I got tired of his importuning and decided to risk the ankle. It hurt like hell, but I'm glad I assisted him on his way.'

He seemed to have regained something of his poise and his face no longer bore the icy expression she had come to dread. She was almost encouraged to tell him her true situation. Almost, but not quite. To do so might jeopardise her plans entirely. If Gareth were the man she hoped he was, he would feel impelled to pursue Glyde when he knew the full extent of his infamy. That would cause a scandal she would never live down. And if he were not that man, if he were as untrustworthy as she had recently speculated, she might fall into in real peril. Once he knew her true identity, she could be in danger of kidnap or blackmail.

'Does he know that you have a sister staying here?' she ventured. She was reluctant to talk more of Glyde, but she needed to know what she was facing.

'He knows,' came the short reply.

'You didn't tell him my name?'

'No.' His voice had become distant again. 'Your fears are unfounded, my dear, your identity is safe. I doubt that a man of Glyde's position would consider it interesting or worthwhile to spread scandal about a maidservant, even if he knew her name.'

Euphoric at her escape, Amelie hardly noticed the caustic tone and unwisely pushed onwards. 'Thank you for not giving me away.' And when he didn't reply, she said again, 'Thank you.'

'Spare me the gratitude.'

There was a pause as he looked her fully in the face, wondering how he had allowed himself to be taken in by a girl so adept at lying. He had begun to believe his judgement of womankind faulty, but it seemed that Amelie shared generously in the attributes of her sisters. She was no different from any of the women who had passed through his life.

'He thinks you are my doxy,' he said deliberately, and then added with undisguised bitterness, 'And who could blame him? You behave like one – scuttling for cover instead of facing him honestly.'

The words came out of nowhere and fell like hammer blows on her ears. Scarlet with mortification, she ran from the room. How could he throw such a vile insult at her? Even if she were the simple maidservant she purported to be, she would be justified in protecting her good name. Yet by his reckoning, she had committed an unforgivable offence. She was no better than Haymarket ware.

Once in her bedroom, she grabbed the faithful cloak bag and hurriedly packed the few items she still possessed. Then she ran down the stairs and out into the back yard. Will was busy washing the cobbles.

'Will, come here,' she called urgently to him. 'Mr Heywood has taken a turn for the worst. He needs the medicine the doctor prescribed in an emergency. I must get to Wroxhall.'

Will rested from his labours, leaning on the broom with one hand and scratching his head with the other. 'Mr Heywood were fine this morning. 'Happen he'll come about again soon.'

'No, Will, he won't. He has been feeling poorly for hours but did not like to complain. Now his fever seems to have returned. We must get to Wroxall.'

'I'd like to help, Miss Heywood,' he said doubtfully, 'but I'll have to ask the missus. Mrs Skinner do like to know where I am. And she don't like it if the horse is taken without her permission.'

'Mrs Skinner is out,' Amelie lied recklessly. 'And Mr Skinner, too. I saw them on their way to visit neighbours.'

Will slowly shook his head. The image of the Skinners visiting their neighbours was one he was having difficulty with.

'Please help me,' she pleaded. 'You don't want Mr Heywood to become really ill again, do you?'

Will once more shook his head, but still looked unhappy.

'It could be a matter of life or death. I wouldn't ask you otherwise.'

She felt guilty at deceiving him, but refused to think of his likely punishment for helping her. She had to get away. Unwillingly, Will put down his bucket and brush and went towards the trap which stood backed into the corner of the rear yard. He carefully moved it into the centre and arranged the leather ties. The mare had then to be led from her stable and harnessed. For Amelie, desperate to leave the inn behind, every minute seemed an impossible age. One or other of the Skinners could put in an appearance at any time and ruin her escape.

Will might be slow, but he was methodical. Finally the trap was ready and she jumped up on to the passenger seat.

'Please make haste,' she enjoined him as they turned out of the yard onto the highway.

Will, who had begun to enjoy his freedom from cobble washing and enter into the spirit of the adventure, whipped the placid bay into something approaching a trot. They were soon out of sight of the inn and she allowed herself to breathe. She would never see Gareth Heywood again. His words flung at her so bitterly had cut whatever cord existed between them.

## *Chapter Eleven*

She stood beneath the white portico of her grandmother's house. The rain had been falling in torrents ever since she'd alighted at the White Lion Inn and she was soaked to the skin from the brief walk to Laura Place. The weeping skies seemed an echo of her present mood. After all the obstacles and alarms she had encountered since leaving London, the final leg of her journey had been deceptively simple. Once in Wroxall, she had given Will the slip with only a few pangs of conscience. There was less than an hour to pass before her coach departed and she had found it easy to hide herself away until she boarded the stage with minutes to spare. Now her escape plan was complete and she should be flushed with excitement. Instead, she felt a dawning fear. What if her grandmother were out of town? What if Brielle were so outraged by her granddaughter's conduct that she refused to receive her?

She stared at the ebony door with its brass lion's head. It seemed to challenge her right to be there and she had to summon all her resolution to lift the knocker. The resulting clatter reverberated through the hall beyond. Tense minutes of silence followed. She was just lifting her hand to knock again when she heard footsteps coming towards the door and the butler's familiar person was there before her. Horrocks was looking at her strangely, seemingly trying to puzzle out just what or who had arrived on the front steps.

'You should go to the back entrance,' he said reprovingly, as he took in the bedraggled figure in front of him.

'Horrocks, it's me, Amelie.' She pushed back the hood of her cloak to reveal her face fully.

'Miss Amelie?' Horrocks stared in disbelief. 'Whatever are you doing here? Her ladyship said nothing of your coming. And where is your escort? You surely cannot be alone.'

He peered up and down the empty street in a vain search. Then, recalled to his duties, he ushered her quickly into the house and she slipped past him into the warmth of the hall. The house looked little different from the last time she had seen it as a child, perhaps a little smaller, a little less grand.

'Her ladyship is out this evening, Miss Amelie, but I can send a messenger to fetch her home. She is only a few minutes away.'

'No, don't do that Horrocks,' she was quick to say. 'I will wait until she gets back. I don't imagine she keeps very late hours.'

The butler looked grateful. 'No, indeed. But you should get out of those wet clothes straightaway. I will send Miss Repton to you.'

This was the first time she had heard of Miss Repton. The woman was evidently a new addition to the household and must be her grandmother's dresser. Horrocks led the way upstairs to the small sitting room overlooking Laura Place. This was Brielle's favourite retreat, even though she had a far more elegant drawing room at the rear of the house with views over a surprisingly large and immaculate garden.

Miss Repton turned out to be a disapproving middle-aged woman, manicured to within an inch of her life. She looked Amelie up and down in disbelief.

'You will need a change of clothes, miss.' She sniffed. 'Where is your valise?'

Amelie adopted what she hoped was a careless tone. 'My luggage was mislaid during my journey. It will be coming on later.'

The lie did not appear to satisfy and the dresser continued to gaze at the girl with barely concealed disdain. 'I will try to find something of milady's to fit you, but it won't be easy.'

Unused to such disrespect, Amelie spoke sharply. 'It really doesn't matter. If you will be so kind as to take my cloak, I will dry my dress by the fire.'

Miss Repton looked scandalised and even more so when the discarded cloak revealed Fanny's plain, and by now, severely dilapidated dress. Amelie looked the woman in the eyes, challenging her to make a comment. But the dresser remained mute and made for the door, pointedly holding the sodden cloak at arms length.

'I will ask Horrocks to send up tea, miss,' she said tonelessly.

The door closed behind her and Amelie sank deep into

a velvet covered chair. A fire was burning brightly in the grate and her chilled body relaxed in its warmth. She closed her eyes and gradually the peace of the room soothed her nerves so that by the time Horrocks brought tea and toast, she was in a fair way to thinking that all would be well once her grandmother returned. But as the minutes ticked by and there was no sign of Brielle, tormenting thoughts once more began to possess her. Her grandmother might have led an unconventional life, but she was a stickler for propriety. She would be greatly disturbed by her granddaughter's flight from home. Somehow she must be won over, made to understand the nightmare that was in store for Amelie if she were forced into marriage with Rufus Glyde. Perhaps that would not be too difficult – Glyde was an objectionable man. But how to explain where she had been since leaving London, how to gloss over all that had happened this last week?

She suddenly felt very alone and a little scared. With a start she realised that she had rarely felt this vulnerable during the time she had been at the George. Her mind drifted to Gareth and she wondered what he was doing. Was he thinking of her, too? What nonsense, of course he wasn't. He would never have spoken so shockingly if he'd had an ounce of feeling for her. From the start he had made it clear that she was simply entertainment and when she'd refused that role, he had pursued her out of pique. Any fleeting moments of tenderness were just that, fleeting. He was a loner, happy to use a woman if she crossed his path, but as happy to dismiss her from his mind if she ceased to be of interest.

The noise of the front door opening and closing drifted up the stairs. She heard voices below and her stomach churned. Suddenly, her grandmother was there, and she was swept up in a warm, perfumed embrace.

'Amelie, dear child, what is this that Horrocks is telling me? Let me look at you, you poor little thing.' Brielle held her granddaughter at arms' length, her gaze taking in the drab dress, its creases now dried hard by the fire's heat, and the sadly bedraggled curls that framed a white, pinched face.

'You are in a sad way, my dear, but I cannot tell you how relieved I am that you are safe. I have been out of my mind with worry. This evening was the first invitation I've accepted since I knew that you had left your home. And this is the very evening you arrive on my doorstep! But I thank God for that.'

And once more Amelie found herself pulled into the jasmine-scented embrace she remembered so well from childhood. Whether her grandmother approved her conduct or not, it didn't matter. Brielle loved her and would care for her. She bit back the treacherous tears.

'I'm so sorry to have worried you needlessly, but I can explain.'

Brielle took her granddaughter's hands in hers and squeezed them lovingly. 'I am sure you can, but first we must make you comfortable. I really don't understand why you are wearing that dreadful dress. You should have changed it immediately. I cannot think what my woman is about. Why did she not find you a dressing robe at the least and order your bedchamber to be made up?'

'It doesn't matter. I was comfortable here and Horrocks brought me tea.'

'Tea! What are my servants thinking of? What you need is a decent meal and to get out of those clothes or the next thing we'll know is that you are running a fever.'

She rang the bell energetically and her butler appeared rather too quickly. Like the rest of the household, he had been greatly intrigued by Miss Milverton's dramatic and unexpected arrival and hovering by the sitting-room door, had been hopeful of learning more.

'Horrocks, ask the housekeeper to make up Miss Amelie's bedchamber immediately, and get Cook to put together a tray of something nourishing, and I don't mean just soup.'

'Yes, milady, immediately,' the butler murmured, suitably abashed by his mistress's sharp tone.

Brielle was still fiery, Amelie observed, even though the years had begun to take their toll. Her grandmother, elegant in dove-grey Italian crepe, seemed smaller and frailer than when she had last seen her.

'Horrocks is getting old. He no longer thinks very clearly.'

'He looked after me very well,' Amelie declared loyally, making ready to accompany the housekeeper upstairs.

She recognised the room instantly. Eau-de-nil hangings and bedcovers created shadows of pale green, her mother's favourite colour. A photograph of Louise was displayed prominently on the dainty cherrywood writing desk. To one side, a deep tub was even now being filled with hot water by one of the housemaids. As soon as the servants had left, she stripped off the despised dress and dropped it in a heap on the floor. The bath was blissful – how could hot water feel so good? Nevertheless, she thought it best not to linger and by the time her grandmother rejoined her, she was sat in an easy chair and wearing a wrapper of the finest chenille silk.

'This robe is far too beautiful for me to wear, Grandmama. Miss Repton must be in anguish.'

'Never mind about her. She has far too high an opinion of herself. Though she does have a way with my hair and makes her own complexion cream from crushed strawberries. Otherwise I would never keep the creature.'

Her grandmother put down the tray she was carrying. 'I've brought your food myself so we can be quiet together. Make sure you dine well. You look as though you have barely eaten all day.'

It was true. A sparse breakfast had not been followed by lunch. She had been too busy hiding from Rufus Glyde to think of eating, and then Gareth's unexpected abuse had sent her flying from the inn to Wroxall and finally to Bath. She attacked the cold chicken with relish.

While she ate, Brielle kept her amused with stories of Bath life. It was clear she viewed English provincial society with some irony, but she had put down secure roots and now had many friends and acquaintances in the locality. The quintessential French woman had become almost English.

She let her granddaughter finish her meal before saying, 'Now what is this nonsense I have been hearing?'

'Nonsense?' Amelie's stomach clenched. The inevitable

moment had arrived.

'About a week ago I received a most unwelcome visitor. His name was Hyde or Glyde or some such. He told me some faradiddle about your being pledged to him in marriage.'

'He was lying,' Amelie said quietly. 'I never agreed to marry.'

'Then why did he think you had?'

'It was Papa who decided I should marry him. I decided I would not.'

'But why should your father wish you to marry a man you so clearly dislike?'

'Sir Rufus Glyde is very rich. Papa thought to help the family by marrying me to him.'

'The family, perhaps, but not you it would seem. Your father is a selfish man and I won't hide from you that I do not hold him in a great deal of affection. But I have always thought his love for you showed him at his best. Why would he try to force such a marriage, knowing how you felt?'

She had no idea how much her grandmother knew of the Milvertons' financial difficulties and did not want to alarm her unnecessarily, so she said as nonchalantly as she could, 'We have a few money problems.'

Brielle looked at her straitly. 'Your father has always lived high, that is certain, but surely the income from the estates he holds must be sufficient to cover even his expenditure.'

'There are other problems,' Amelie began awkwardly. 'Robert...' And her voice tailed off.

'Ah, Robert, an unfortunate boy by all accounts. Even in

this backwater we have heard tales of his foolish gambling.' She fixed her granddaughter with an acute eye. 'Exactly how bad is the situation? Tell me the truth.'

'Sir Rufus holds the mortgage on the house in Grosvenor Square and the property is all we have left.'

Brielle let out an audible gasp. 'I know your father and brother to be foolishly extravagant, but I had no idea that things had come to this pass.'

'Grandmama, I cannot marry Rufus Glyde. Please help me.'

'My darling, you shall not marry a man you hate. Your father will have to think again. And until he does, you will stay with me here in Bath.'

Amelie's brown eyes sparkled through a mist of tears. She launched herself at her grandmother, hugging her so tightly that the older woman was almost crushed.

'Hush child, you have squeezed the breath out of me. You are a loving and beautiful young woman. You deserve better. We may even find you a Bath beau to take the place of this Glyde person.'

Amelie's smile faltered a little. 'I'm not looking for any other man. I don't wish to marry. If you'll let me stay here with you, I am sure I can be useful – even more as you get older.'

'What nonsense is this? To waste your youth and beauty on running errands for an old woman. Certainly not! Why are you so opposed to the idea of matrimony? It is every woman's destiny, after all.'

'I don't think it mine,' she retorted. 'The men I've met are either frivolous and foolish or they feel compelled to dominate. I've no wish to be either the master or the mastered.'

'You have been unlucky then in those you have met. But that's not to say that a strong man with the confidence to allow you independence does not exist, or that you won't encounter him.'

'Even if I were to meet such a paragon, how could I ever be sure that he would remain so? Mama...' And she allowed the rest of her sentence to fade into the air.

Her grandmother gazed unseeingly into the fire, and it was a while before she spoke. 'You must not allow your mother's difficult life to determine your choices,' she said at last. 'A woman's duty is to marry. But we will say no more for now. I shall introduce you to Bath society while you are with me and who knows, the right person might just appear on the threshold.'

Brielle's thoughts were already ranging across the eligible males she knew and had begun to centre on the one name she thought might just alter Amelie's mind. But for now she was content to change the subject.

'You haven't told me yet how you escaped from Grosvenor Square.'

Amelie recounted the tale of the sheets and the stagecoach, carefully omitting the entrance of Gareth Heywood into her life. Brielle enjoyed the story immensely, even more so because it was a rebuke to a son-in-law she did not trust and a suitor she had disliked on sight.

'Grandmama, can we send for Fanny, please? I promised her I would do so as soon as I could.'

'I am not at all sure that we should, my love. Fanny aided you in what was a foolish and dangerous escapade. I have been enjoying your tale, but that is because you are safe here with me. When I think what might have befallen you! And Fanny would have borne a grave responsibility for it.'

'That is unfair,' her granddaughter cried hotly. 'Fanny tried to persuade me not to escape, but I made her help me. And no doubt she has suffered for her loyalty. I cannot make her suffer doubly.'

Brielle blinked with surprise at this passionate outburst. 'You are far too hot at hand, my dear, and I am not surprised you emerged from your first Season unwed. A fiery temper is not perhaps the best asset a young woman can possess.'

'Forgive me, ma'am. I did not mean to be discourteous, but I owe Fanny so much.'

'Including a dress by the look of it,' her grandmother remarked drily. She looked askance at the miserable heap of cloth lying abandoned in the corner. 'I was about to send a message to your father to assure him of your safety, and when I do I will ask him to despatch Fanny to us. We must hope that he has not already discovered her perfidy and sent her packing.'

Amelie's smile was wide, but she had gently to stifle a yawn. Hopefully, Brielle would take the hint and leave her to sleep. So far she had managed to evade all mention of her stay at the George, but as she had foreseen, her grandmother was not so easily satisfied. The stagecoach had left the White Horse Inn in London over a week ago – so where had Amelie been in the interval?

'The stage had an accident,' she lied, 'and we had to find accommodation at a local inn. One of the passengers was hurt and I stayed to care for them. As soon as they were better, I finished the journey to Bath.' How glib that sounded and how very far from the truth.

'And were you the only two passengers at this inn?' Brielle questioned shrewdly.

'There were only a few other people on the stage. And they lived a short distance away and were able to finish their journey on horseback.' More lies, she thought guiltily.

'Was there no one else who could have offered to nurse?'

'I felt obliged. The person had been very kind to me.'

'But who was this passenger you were so devoted to?'

This was the question Amelie had been dreading. 'An elderly gentleman.' Age is relative, she told herself. 'You wouldn't know his name. He was actually on his way to Bristol, so he's not local.'

'A gentleman? You were looking after a gentleman? Surely that cannot be right.'

'I had to help. There was no one else who could devote the time to nursing him. The doctor called a few times and the landlord assisted when he could.'

Her grandmother was silent for a moment. 'Just how old was this gentleman?'

'I'm not very good at ages,' she prevaricated. 'A good deal older than me.'

'And who else was at the inn with you?'

'The landlord and his wife, and some of their serving staff. I shared a bedchamber with the kitchen maid.'

Brielle felt relieved and decided not to probe any further for the moment. Amelie was looking tired and distressed. But she sensed her granddaughter was not being entirely truthful and was determined in the next few days to get to the bottom of whatever mystery there was.

'You must sleep now. Tomorrow we will put your wardrobe to rights. I understand from Horrocks that you arrived with only a cloak bag.'

'I'm afraid so. It will be wonderful to wear a dress other than Fanny's.'

'I should think so indeed. After breakfast, we will be off to the modiste. In the meantime I'll make sure that Repton looks out a dress from my younger years and alters it to fit you.'

'Thank you. You are too kind. I don't know how I can ever repay you.'

'I'm sure I shall think of something,' Brielle replied, her mind firmly fixed on the man she intended to present once the girl was looking her best.

## Chapter Twelve

Gareth was finding it difficult to sleep. His anger still burned brightly, but he knew that he'd offended Amelie beyond pardon. His deep suspicion of her relationship with Glyde was justified, he was sure, but to call her a doxy had been inexcusable. She was no such thing as he knew to his cost. Countless women of his acquaintance perfectly satisfied that description, but not Amelie. Even so, she was as cunning and manipulative as any of her sex.

He had known plenty of women in his years of wandering and learned his lesson well; a woman was worth only the pleasure she gave. Amelie had given him pleasure, it was true, but not as he had expected. It had been something altogether deeper, more exciting and more disturbing – a dangerous delight. It was as well that she'd left when she had. There was no place in his life for loyalty or love, even if he could be sure of her. And he couldn't.

He would leave her in peace to find a new situation and be on his way. Within the next day or so his ankle would be strong enough for travel, but to where he knew not. He was close to Bristol. A journey to the port would take half a day at most and once there he could book a passage to France. It would be easy enough to resume his old life at the tables of less respectable gaming houses or take whatever menial work was offered. That way he would never touch a penny of the inheritance so long denied him.

But why should he not enjoy his legacy? Would it not be sweet revenge to plunder the fortune his grandfather had so carefully conserved? Perhaps he would travel back to London after all, deal with Mr Spence and his formalities, and ensure a constant flow of funds to his pocket over the years to come. That would certainly spare him the discomfort of living off his wits as he wandered Europe. But what an existence. The one thing that had sustained him in seven long years of exile was the excitement and intrigue of a life on the edge. Take that away and what was left? A tedious round of places he didn't know, people he would never see again, and plans that held no interest.

One way or another, though, he would leave England and this time willingly and for good. There was nobody to mourn his going – except perhaps Lucas Avery. Lucas had been his one true friend and he knew him to be living in Bath, a short distance away, with a wife and children that Gareth had never met. He wondered if he dared risk calling on him before he boarded the ship, or whether Lucas might have changed his mind about his old friend in the years since that fateful evening. The unknown wife, too, might not welcome a convicted card cheat into her home. But he would like to have bid the man a final goodbye.

And Amelie, he suspected, was also in Bath. If he chose to make the journey, he might even see her there.

If he chose! In his heart he knew that the decision had already been made. Of course he would make the journey, of course he would see her. Be truthful with yourself, he thought savagely. She was dangerous to him, a threat to his plans and to his peace of mind, but somehow he couldn't keep away. He might try to justify the trip to Bath in a dozen ways, but he was going there for one reason alone. He had willed himself to forget this girl, but he could not. She was a constant refrain singing in his mind. London or France – they would both have to wait.

Amelie, too, stayed awake longer than she expected. Her body was exhausted, but her mind would not be still. How was she to avoid telling her grandmother the true nature of her stay at the inn, for she knew that Brielle would not be content to leave the matter to rest? She smiled reminiscently at the description she had given of Gareth – he was neither elderly nor a gentleman! – but somehow she must maintain this fiction. Her smile died as suddenly as it had come. She must not think of him ever again. It had been foolish of her to allow an early attraction to melt her reserve and flourish unchecked. She had grown far too close to him. When he'd kissed her, she had felt a longing she had never known before, but was left now bruised and baffled.

The insults Gareth had flung at her should have crushed such troublesome feelings. But apparently that wasn't so. As she drifted half in and half out of sleep, his powerful frame invaded the room. It was as though he were there with her. If she reached out, she could trace the outline of his smile with her finger. If she reached out, she could feel the strength of his embrace. Shaken by her need for him, she buried her head in the pillow.

∼

She awoke to the swish of heavy silk curtains being drawn and felt the warmth of the mid-morning sun streaming across her bed. She had not heard the maid's light footfall, but when she turned her head, she saw that a cup of steaming chocolate sat waiting and a large jug of hot water was already on the washstand. A refashioned dress of her grandmother's was draped across the armchair, hardly the height of fashion but acceptable enough for this one day. Miss Repton had been busy. She supposed she must thank her.

She lay back on the pillows and stretched lazily. When eventually she had closed her eyes last night, she'd slept long and deep, cocooned in the comfort of the four-poster, a far cry from the straw mattress of recent days. At last she was at her grandmother's. She had succeeded in what she'd set out to do and the world felt good. Or rather, a part of it did. Gareth's figure once more crept unbidden to mind. His ankle would soon be mended and he would be preparing to leave the George. What would he do? Where would he go? Whatever his decision, she scolded herself, it concerned her no longer.

This morning she was intent on pleasure for she knew it would be fleeting. She had no false expectations that Brielle would agree with her wish to remain single. For a woman of her grandmother's generation, indeed for a woman of her own, marriage must be the goal of life and any female who rejected it was either unwanted or eccentric. How much better, though, to live alone than be chained to a man with whom she shared nothing but a roof. But living alone was likely to remain a dream. Even so, there was one thing of which she *was* sure: her heart would stay her own. It would not be a difficult vow to keep. Until now she had felt nothing for any man she had ever met. Until now. But Gareth Heywood was clearly ineligible and destined to travel through life alone. A misguided passion for him would ensure the very unhappiness she was trying to escape.

The bedroom door opened and her grandmother came into the room fully dressed and looking business-like. 'Good, you're awake. Are you well rested?'

Amelie smiled her assent.

'That's as well since we have much to do today. I will see you in the breakfast room in thirty minutes.'

Brielle's brisk commands were diverting. Her grandmother might be approaching old age, but she was as sprightly as ever and it was clear that she had risen betimes to plan the day ahead. Amelie made haste to comply.

The carriage arrived at the front door immediately after breakfast and they were very soon bowling along Bath's main thoroughfare. Brielle's destination was the small but elegant shop of a highly talented modiste. She had heard on the grapevine that this new young seamstress had the originality and skill of many a more expensive establishment and had decided she would be the very person to suit her granddaughter – something in the French style, she thought, beautifully cut and simply adorned, to flatter the young woman's budding figure.

It seemed to Amelie that the next few hours were spent in a fantasy of fashion. There were outfits for every occasion: braided, embroidered, some adorned with knots of ribbon, others with spangled rosettes and silver fringes. Walking dresses, riding costumes, day *toilettes* and ball gowns floated past on a wave of elegance. She tried hard to keep her feet on the ground, worrying about the mounting cost and how she could ever repay her grandmother even a fraction of the staggering bill for this dazzling wardrobe. Frantically, she tried to catch sight of the price tags as the dresses were brought forward for her inspection. An evening gown in sea-green tulle made her gasp in wonder at her reflection in the mirror – she hardly recognized the modish young woman looking back at her.

'How much did you say this gown was?' she asked the seamstress tentatively.

'That is one of our newest creations, *mademoiselle*, and made from the finest silk tulle. A very reasonable hundred guineas. It suits *mademoiselle* to perfection.'

Shocked by the price, Amelie began reluctantly to take off the charming creation when the modiste, catching a minatory look from Brielle, coughed apologetically and decided that she had made a mistake.

'Of course, for such a beautiful young lady, we can come to an agreeable arrangement, I am sure. You will wear the dress with a distinction that will bring honour to our small salon and build our reputation.'

After that colours and fabrics flew past her eyes like a moving kaleidoscope and she gave up trying to keep count of the ever-increasing total. It was all way beyond anything she could ever have afforded from her allowance. To the pile of dresses were added fur-trimmed pelisses, tiny pearl-stitched slippers, long white leather gloves and a Norwich silk shawl, all apparently necessities for a protracted stay in Bath. By the time they left the salon, the carriage was brimming with boxes and packages and had to be sent back to Laura Place while they made their way to Milsom Street to pay a call on Brielle's favourite milliner.

Amelie, who owned precisely two hats, was amazed by the information that she would need no fewer than six if she were to grace the Bath social scene successfully. One extraordinary confection followed another as Madame Charcot laid before them the finest of her wares. Amelie's London Season had been notable for its modesty. Lord Milverton had neither the money nor the wish to expend large sums on his daughter's coming-out and expected her natural beauty to be sufficient to win a husband. An old acquaintance of his youth had acted as chaperone, and since she also had a daughter to launch, she had shown little interest in her new protégée or her clothes. Amelie had chosen almost single-handedly the restricted wardrobe her father had permitted for the three months of her London Season. Now Brielle, with her highly developed fashion sense, was intent on giving as much enjoyment as possible to her granddaughter.

Seated amidst a tower of hat boxes, waiting for the carriage to return, she revealed that she had been busy first thing that morning putting together a guest list for a small evening party the following day.

'It will be more comfortable for you to meet a few people before going into society properly,' Brielle explained.

Amelie made haste to reassure her. 'I won't be uncomfortable, Grandmama, not with you by my side.'

'That's as may be. I'm an old woman now. You need to meet younger people. It will be just a small, informal party. Nothing too overwhelming. But when we visit the Pump Room or the Assembly Rooms for the first time, you will already know a few faces.'

Amelie was unsure. She had expected to live quietly in Bath, but it was evident from the morning's shopping that this was not what Brielle had in mind. She was grateful for her grandmother's unstinting kindness and she would try her best to behave conformably, but she had little desire to socialise. That, though, was something best left unsaid.

Like her granddaughter, Brielle decided on silence. It had been difficult to conjure up interesting guests at such short notice, but she'd felt it essential to introduce Amelie as swiftly as possible to many of those the girl would see in the coming weeks. It was important to establish the notion that her granddaughter was paying a protracted visit and one that had been planned for many months. That should limit any damage rumour might do.

This morning while her granddaughter slept, she had briefly surveyed the people she might invite, those who would not be offended by the very short notice. Celine Charpentier for one, a fellow *emigrée* and friend since the time they had left France together for exile. Celine would support her in whatever plan she was hatching, Brielle knew. Then there was Major Radcliffe, a genial soul always ready to add his bonhomie to any party. Unfortunately she would also have to invite Miss Scarsdale. Letitia Scarsdale was a permanent fixture at all her parties, a difficult neighbour in constant need of placating.

But one particular guest would more than earn his place. Brielle had high hopes of him. Sir Peregrine Latham was well-known in Bath, a handsome man and delightful companion. Perry was no country bumpkin, either. He preferred a quieter pace of life, dividing his time between his Bath mansion and a Somerset estate, but he visited London regularly and was not devoid of town bronze. He was well into his thirties now and, gossip had it, the victim of a sad history. The story went that he had lost his fiancée when a very young man and had never recovered from the blow. Nevertheless, Brielle reckoned he might be persuaded to think again by the sight of her enchanting granddaughter.

# Chapter Thirteen

The following day brought with it another whirl of activity. The hairdresser called early to trim Amelie's chestnut locks into submission. Her shining curls were artlessly twisted into a knot on the top of her head and then allowed to cascade down the sides of her face in loose ringlets. Before she had time to properly admire this transformation, it was the turn of the dressmaker. Hours the previous evening had been spent thumbing the latest editions of *La Belle Assemblée* to decide on suitable styles. For several uncomfortable hours she was draped with muslin and stuck with pins. The dressmaker, she was told, would make her gowns for wearing at home when no one of any importance was expected. She began to wonder when she would ever have time to don even half of the wardrobe she had so suddenly acquired.

Shortly before their guests arrived that evening, Brielle appeared with a pearl necklace and earrings which had belonged to Amelie's mother. They were the perfect accompaniment to the simple pink crêpe-de-Chine gown she had chosen for her first party.

'Wear them for Louise,' her grandmother said with

a catch in her voice, the closest she would ever come to expressing the pain she still felt.

Now that the evening was here, Amelie determined to take pleasure in it, if only for Brielle's sake. It was true that the guests assembled in the elegant drawing room were something of a motley crowd, but they were all evidently well-wishers. All except Lady Lampeter, who had two very plain daughters of Amelie's age and who was furious to discover that her acceptance of such a late invitation had been pointless. Not even the fondest of mamas could expect the Lampeter girls to compete with Amelie's beauty.

'Claudia Lampeter will come at short notice,' Brielle had confidently predicted to Celine. 'She has a mountain to climb with those girls of hers. One has spots and the other a sad figure. She will take them anywhere in the hope of finding a marriageable man.'

Knowing nothing of her grandmother's wiles, Amelie remained serene, cutting a path through the mingled guests and attracting admiring looks as she moved from one chattering group to another. Brielle was delighted to see that in company her granddaughter was both modest and assured.

'She does you credit,' Celine remarked. 'She is a beautiful and unaffected girl.'

The Major took a long pinch of snuff and gave his considered opinion. 'With those looks and that charm she will take Bath by storm.'

As the evening proceeded, Amelie began to appreciate the gentle rhythm of Bath social life. The great society gatherings of her London Season had been a strain but here she felt unruffled. Even the man she imagined had been invited to partner her was unexceptional.

'And how do you like Bath, Miss Milverton?' Perry Latham began as an opening gambit.

He had been stunned by the beauty of this new young woman and was eager to see whether her intelligence matched her looks.

'So far, Sir Peregrine, I've seen only the inside of dress shops, but I am sure I shall enjoy it immensely.'

'And Bath will enjoy you, too,' he rejoined gallantly. 'Can we hope to see you at the Pump Room shortly?'

'Indeed, yes. I understand my grandmother is planning our first visit tomorrow.'

'Excellent. I will make sure I attend. But I'm afraid you may find the town a little dull. You will see many of the same faces at the Pump Room as are here tonight.'

'I shan't mind that. I find familiarity comforting.'

'I'm not sure you will think so once you have met the same set of people a dozen times.'

Privately, Amelie thought that was more than likely, looking around at the less than stimulating collection of people who shared the room with her. She couldn't stop herself smiling at the thought of what Gareth would make of the company. 'An assortment of gargoyles,' she could hear him say. One of the older women, the scrawny Miss Scarsdale, bore an uncanny resemblance to Mrs Skinner.

'You smile.' Perry Latham had been watching her closely. 'You see, Miss Milverton, you are already beginning to have doubts.'

'No, Sir Peregrine. I was smiling at how very pleasant it

is to be among friends.'

Diplomatic as well as intelligent and beautiful, he thought, already half smitten with this entrancing girl who had appeared so suddenly in his world.

'Please call me Perry. I hope you will count me as one of those friends.'

The last guest departed well before eleven. She wasn't sorry that Bath inhabitants seemed to keep early hours. The party had been convivial and undemanding, but it had still cost an effort to play the role expected of her.

'I saw you talking to Perry Latham,' her grandmother remarked casually. 'He is a good-looking fellow, don't you think?'

'Very presentable.'

'A thorough gentleman, too.'

'Indeed, yes.'

And not without town bronze,' Brielle pursued. Amelie smiled warmly back at her. 'He is a veritable pattern card of all the virtues,' she replied laughingly, while her thoughts roved dangerously elsewhere.

∽

The next morning dawned fair, a perfect day Brielle declared for her granddaughter's first visit to the Pump Room. Amelie felt little enthusiasm, but knew that her grandmother had been delighted by the success of yesterday's small party and was now eager to introduce her to wider Bath society. Brielle did not herself take the famous waters, which she privately considered disgusting, but many of her friends drank a daily glass for a variety of complaints, imagined or otherwise. And she made sure that she attended the Pump Room regularly as a way of keeping in touch with what was going on in Bath. It was said that a morning spent there would vouchsafe the visitor all the current gossip of the town.

The room they entered was spacious with a wall of tall windows giving on to carefully tended lawns. A richly moulded azure ceiling was hung with ornate chandeliers glittering with light even on this bright morning. Small golden chairs were positioned around the edges of the room or marshalled by visitors into friendship or family circles. The salon emanated wealth and leisure, capturing the essence of Bath as a town of affluence and pleasure.

Almost immediately they spotted Celine Charpentier, who had just procured a glass of water from the pumper and was busy wending her way through knots of people deep in conversation. Brielle began to follow in her wake, zigzagging to avoid the couples who slowly paraded around the room, arm in arm, intent on seeing and being seen. Amelie was acutely conscious of the many pairs of eyes staring at her, some curious, some measuring and some frankly admiring. She gave thanks for the familiar faces already gathered at the far end of the room. As her grandmother had predicted, it was comforting to recognise acquaintances among a sea of unknowns. As she drew nearer, Perry Latham's sunny smile beamed across at her.

But before they could reach him, they were intercepted by a very thin, richly clad figure. Amelie caught her breath – the man bowing profusely before her grandmother was none other than Rufus Glyde! He had returned not to London, but to Bath. He must have suspected that she would eventually find her way here.

'Lady St Clair,' he purred, 'my most humble apologies for intruding, but allow me to say how delighted I am to see that your granddaughter is safely restored to you.'

Brielle nodded briefly and went to move on, but Glyde was intent on detaining them.

'My lady, if I could beg a few minutes of your time... May I tender my heartfelt regrets for any misunderstanding that may have occurred when we last met.'

'I am not aware of any misunderstanding, *monsieur*,' Brielle said stiffly.

'I mean only that my motives for seeking your charming granddaughter were not clear and I fear may have been misinterpreted.'

'On the contrary, I understand perfectly your wish to pursue my granddaughter and since we are being frank, I will tell you now that your pursuit is unwelcome. Miss Milverton stays with me for the forseeable future. I am to be responsible for her welfare.'

Amelie felt a glow of satisfaction. Surely that would put an end to his attentions.

'Naturally I am delighted that Miss Milverton has found sanctuary with a loved one. It is right and proper that she should do so.' Glyde's voice was smoothly persistent. 'My pursuit, as you term it, was a wish only to be of assistance to a young woman I had reason to believe was happy to become my wife.'

Unsure of precisely what Miles Milverton had promised, Brielle was forced to concede the point. Emboldened, Glyde continued, 'Now that the position is clear to me,

Miss Milverton may rest assured that I will in no way incommode her in the future. Indeed, I wish her very well whatever that future may be.'

Her grandmother had begun to look a little more gratified and answered neutrally, 'We thank you for your good wishes, sir, and for your reassurance.'

His thin lips arranged themselves into a tight smile, the sunken lines on either side of his mouth becoming more deeply etched. Amelie recoiled in distaste, but was forced to remain by her grandmother's side.

'In that case I hope that we may continue to enjoy a pleasant association. I had just begun a visit to friends here when I felt it necessary to interrupt my stay to search for Miss Milverton. Now that the matter is happily concluded, I can look forward to enjoying the delights of Bath more thoroughly.'

'I hope the town will live up to your expectations,' Brielle murmured.

'I am sure it will and if not, I have always the pleasures of my country estate – it lies nearby. But I cannot imagine Bath will pall with two such charming ladies at the forefront of its society. I trust I am forgiven sufficiently to be included in your personal group of acquaintances.'

Brielle inclined her head slightly. 'Naturally, we are bound to encounter each other on occasions, Sir Rufus.'

'I look forward to meeting you and your granddaughter frequently. Bath is such a small society that I imagine it to be inevitable.'

Amelie had managed to put on a brave face during this interchange, but her heart plummeted at these words. She the large palm trees that graced either side of the doorway.

In an instant Gareth Heywood stood before her. She had a fleeting glimpse of his muscular figure, clothed now in a perfectly fitting coat of blue superfine, his shapely legs encased in skin-tight pantaloons of the palest fawn. Hardly had she absorbed his new image, when he advanced menacingly towards her and grabbed her roughly by the wrist.

'It's evident you have managed to acquire a very liberal employer since we met last.' His voice was a snarl. 'Such elegance, Amelie, such a taking coiffure, but hardly fitting for a maidservant.' She saw his lips curl with disdain.

'Or a doxy, I imagine.' Her retort was swift and equally angry.

His face shadowed and he let go of her arm. He should apologise, but he was damned if he would. She had utterly deceived him. The girl standing before him, so beautiful he could devour her on the spot, was thoroughly false. She had lied and lied again to him.

'Would it be too much to enquire exactly who or what you are?'

She replied with as much dignity as she could. 'My name is Amelie Milverton. My father is Lord Milverton.'

'Well, well, a poor little rich girl. Wasn't being Miss Milverton exciting enough for you? Did you get some shabby thrill from dressing up as your maid?'

'There was no thrill, I assure you. Disguising myself as a maid was the safest way to travel, or at least it would have been if I had not been unlucky enough to meet you.'

'Not that unlucky, as I recall. You might still be dangling on the end of a rope if it were not for me. Or were you was sure they carried an implicit threat and, glancing up at his thin, white face, she saw the wolfish eyes staring out at her from behind the social mask. Her grandmother, though, seemed to sense nothing amiss and, with another bow in his direction, moved towards her group of friends.

Glyde turned swiftly on his heel and left the Pump Room. Now that he was gone, Amelie found her limbs were trembling and she had to fight to calm her breathing. His trite commonplaces had cloaked his true intent, she was sure. He had not given up his intention to marry her, whatever platitudes he mouthed to her grandmother. And Brielle appeared to have been completely taken in. With a sickening jolt Amelie realised that the sanctuary she had sought and found with so much difficulty might now prove as dangerous as her London home. Glyde's strategy was becoming clear. He would make sure that he was constantly in her grandmother's company, presenting himself as a loyal and dependable friend. Gradually he would chip away at her grandmother's suspicion until Brielle began to wonder why her granddaughter had taken such a dislike to him. There would be nowhere else then for her to run and little by little she would be coerced into an appalling marriage.

Her grandmother was already deep in conversation with the Major, and she saw with dismay that Perry Latham ha begun to walk towards her. Unable to face him imme ately, she fled towards the entrance hall, intending to s in the cool, fresh air until she regained her comp Looking straight ahead, she moved swiftly towar goal, barely noticing the figure standing in the sh hoping your friend Glyde would happen by and execute a magnificent rescue? Was it a ploy to reel in a reluctant suitor?'

'How can you be so stupid! I was escaping from Rufus Glyde.'

'Another fantasy? Or worse, another lie. A minute ago, I saw with my own eyes on what familiar terms you stand with the man.' His tone was scathing.

'Then your eyes tell you false. Sir Rufus has designs of his own and wishes to ingratiate himself with my grandmother.'

'For what purpose?' With an impatient gesture, he pushed back the dark hair that had fallen across his brow.

'I don't see that it is any business of yours.'

'Really? You don't consider your constant lies give me any reason to demand the truth from you?'

She bowed her head slightly and said in a voice he could hardly hear, 'He wishes to marry me.'

'And...?'

'He hopes my grandmother will persuade me to agree.'

'How much persuasion will that take, I wonder?'

'I detest him,' she burst out. 'He is a vicious and depraved man. He has followed me here when I thought I was safe and is plotting against me still.'

'He is certainly vicious,' Gareth said measuringly. 'But why are you running from him? You have only to tell your father that he is plaguing you and you will be free of his demands.'

'I wish that were true, but my father has decided that Sir Rufus is the suitor he wishes me to accept.'

'The last time I looked we were living in the nineteenth century. Forced marriages no longer happen. You must have given your consent or at least appeared to do so.'

'I did not. I tell you I hate the man, but my father is adamant. I cannot speak of my family's difficulties, but Glyde wields considerable power over us.'

Gareth considered this for a moment, his long limbed figure reclining against a carved pillar.

'So you were the mistress who was being forced to marry for money? And the maid's defiant independence a mere charade, I imagine.'

Amelie flushed, but said nothing.

'And why go to so much trouble to deceive me? Why couldn't you have told me the truth and asked for help? Did you not trust me?'

She swallowed uncomfortably. 'I was worried you might react unthinkingly. You might have chased after him and caused an even greater scandal.'

'Chased after him? With an injured ankle? You can do better than that.' His tone hardened. 'Wasn't it rather that you thought I might use the situation for my own benefit?'

She blushed. That was precisely what she had thought, imagining if only in fancy that he might be capable of blackmail or kidnap. He saw the telltale flush and drew his own conclusions. 'You didn't trust me,' he said bitterly, 'and only now that I've exposed your deception are you willing to be honest.'

'You shouldn't judge me harshly. You cannot know what it feels like to be so besieged, without a friend in the world.'

His smile was crooked. 'Can I not?'

'It is different for men – you make your own rules. A woman is always subject to others. Even a strong woman,' she added.

'You must have known I would stand your friend, yet you disappeared from the inn without a word.'

'I had to – you treated me abominably.'

'I regret my intemperance,' he muttered unwillingly. 'It was unfair, but Glyde provoked me and I knew you were lying.'

'It was more than unfair. You insulted me vilely. I wanted never to see you again.'

'Nor I you.'

They stood facing each other, their figures tense, the air between them scorched. Then quite suddenly his expression relaxed and he said lightly, 'But here I am.'

'And why exactly are you here? I thought you were going to Bristol, or was it London? It seems to me, Mr Heywood, that you also have some explaining to do.'

'I have a particular friend in Bath. I wanted to say goodbye to him before I sail for France.'

She digested the news. 'You never mentioned this friend before. In fact, you were adamant you had no friends.'

'He slipped my mind.'

'Or maybe he is simply a figment of your imagination?'

'Like Amelie, the maidservant, you mean? No, he exists all right. His name is Lucas Avery and I am staying in his house.'

'Even so, I'm not sure I believe you. Why suddenly do you wish to say goodbye? You weren't intending to do so. You had no plans to come to Bath.'

'I have determined to quit England for good and since

our little adventure brought me close by, it seemed right to say a final farewell.'

'And that is the truth?'

'Not quite.' She looked up into the blue eyes and felt their disturbing gaze. 'I needed to see you again. I needed to say a proper goodbye.'

For a moment the warmth of his glance took her breath away. She felt a flutter of panic. She must remember her doubts, she told herself, remember his insults, stay angry. She must not allow herself to falter.

'You have seen me now and said goodbye.' Her voice was barely above a whisper. 'Let us end this chapter and wish each other good fortune.'

He made no reply, but took hold of her wrist again, this time with gentleness. Her heart turned a small somersault. Oblivious to the scandalised looks of people passing into the main room, he pulled her towards him and encircled her waist. His mouth brushed her forehead and smoothed her hair. Crushed against his hard frame, she felt her body once more dissolve. But the embrace was over in a moment.

Breaking from her, Gareth took her hands and held them to his lips. 'We are deceivers both, Amelie. In another world we would belong together.'

Through a hot veil of desire, she became aware of the murmurs around her and blushed deeply. Quickly, she disentangled her hands.

'I must go,' she managed in a constricted voice. 'My grandmother will be wondering where I am.'

And with that she turned and walked swiftly away.

## Chapter Fourteen

As Gareth made his way back to Lucas Avery's house, his mind was a battleground. He had gone to the Pump Room that morning in the slender hope of finding Amelie in attendance on a new mistress. When he had glimpsed her across the room, he could hardly believe his eyes – no longer the beautiful but simple maidservant that he had come to know, but a modish creature, moving effortlessly in the highest circles.

Transformed she might be, but she was still the same girl who had stirred his senses so fervidly, and anger over her deception fought with desire. Then Glyde had appeared and all his questions over their relationship were answered. It seemed that Amelie Milverton was indeed a true daughter of Eve. She had lied and deceived as expertly as any of the harpies from his past. His anger had exploded into blind fury. He could have run the man through if he'd had a sword. *And* in the back. Glyde's ingratiating smiles announced clearly that Amelie was destined for a man Gareth held in the deepest contempt. He had been sickened by what he saw and was about to leave when Glyde had hurried from the room. When Amelie had followed suit, he had been unable to stop himself. He'd had to confront her.

But now it seemed he might have read the picture wrongly. According to Amelie she was escaping Rufus Glyde, not embracing him. Did he believe her? If she were in truth being pursued by the scoundrel, why hadn't she confessed her troubles at the inn and enlisted his aid? In his heart he knew why not. She mistrusted him and she was right to. He had told her as many lies as she had told him. If not lies, then omissions, and even now she was still ignorant of his true situation.

∽

Lucas was at home when he knocked for admittance. From the moment he had arrived in Bath, he'd been welcomed with open arms. His fear that Lord Avery was no longer the friend he remembered had vanished with the first emotional clasp of their hands.

'Did you enjoy an invigorating morning with the old tabbies?' his friend greeted him gaily.

'Not exactly. I didn't make it into the Pump Room.'

'Was it that daunting?'

'It was singular, shall we say.'

And Gareth, who had earlier sketched for his friend the details of his stay at the George, told him of that morning's meeting with Amelie and the very different circumstances he had found her in.

'But that's wonderful,' Lucas enthused.

'How is that?'

'A maidservant was an impossibility, but Lord Milverton's daughter will make the perfect partner for the Earl of Denville.'

'Hold on a minute.' Gareth was only half laughing. 'You go too fast. For one thing I have no intention of playing the Earl of Denville and for another I'm not in the market to become leg-shackled.'

'Tell me, why *did* you come to Bath? I am quite sure it wasn't just to meet your new godson!'

His friend maintained a discouraging silence, but Lucas persisted. 'We may not have seen each other for the past seven years, Gareth, but I know you as myself. In fact, I may know you even better.'

Gareth was goaded into a response. 'I came to say a final goodbye – you know that – and if Amelie Milverton has crossed my path, it's pure chance.'

'Doing it much too brown!' his friend said crudely. 'You've just returned from the Pump Room, the Pump Room for Heaven's sake! Why ever else would you visit such a place?'

'I admit that I had it in mind to seek her out. I wanted to make peace with her before I left. But that was before I realised I had nothing to apologise for. She is as much a jade as any woman I've known.'

Lucas looked thoughtful and it was a while before he replied. 'Do you know that when you speak of her, your eyes say something quite different?'

'Do they say that she has been thoroughly dishonest with me?'

'If she's deceived you, I can understand your anger, but you are equally to blame. Have you confided your troubles to her?' He looked searchingly at his companion. 'No, I thought not. Neither of you have been honest with the other.'

There was a long silence until Lucas once more broke it. 'Face it my friend.' His voice was amused but sympathetic. 'She has got under your skin. Whether you like it or not, love is in the air.'

'I know nothing of love,' Gareth countered lightly. 'Now dalliance, that's different. Dalliance is where I'm an expert!'

⁓

During the following days Amelie was caught up in a whirl of social activity, a round of dance classes, supper parties and recitals which left little time to think of her recent meeting with Gareth. Only at night, when she escaped to the solitude of her room, was her mind free to roam over their brief, angry encounter. She had been astonished to see him at the Pump Room and looking every inch a gentleman. Where had this sudden wealth come from and who was his supposed friend in Bath? She wasn't at all sure that either existed.

His anger at her deception had been real enough, but he was surely as guilty – she knew no more about him now than when they had first met. Yet he seemed compelled to seek her out; she knew without being told that she was the real reason for his presence in Bath. If she had needed confirmation, his scandalous embrace in that shockingly public place had been proof enough. But what had he meant by saying that in another world they should be together?

She had little time to puzzle over his words. Every day her grandmother chaperoned her to what seemed a dozen different engagements and every day she was forced to appear unconcerned and happy. The week sped past, a constant bustle of movement, culminating in her first ball at the Upper Assembly Rooms. Its Master of Ceremonies had visited the ladies early in Amelie's stay. Mr King was a man who took his duties seriously and it was clear he was determined to introduce Miss Milverton to any and every suitable young man he could find. The advent of a splendid evening of dancing promised him even greater scope. Amelie's lessons in the waltz, a daring new dance for Bath, were to be put to the test.

Her interest in attending the ball was mild, but the minute she was ushered through the classical columns of the Assembly Room to its richly hung interior ablaze with light, she found herself responding to the colour and movement all around. Brightly clothed young women floated past on the arms of their black-suited escorts, while their chaperones lined the walls of the ballroom enjoying the opportunity for an agreeable exchange of news.

As she and Brielle entered the room, they were besieged. Within a very few minutes every slot on her dance card was filled; all the young men present, it seemed, wanted to dance with this beautiful new addition to Bath society. She couldn't help but give herself up to enjoyment. The sensation of being twirled around the highly polished floor in the arms of one admiring partner after another, and of knowing she was the toast of the evening, was gratifying. Perry Latham, revealing himself to be an excellent dancer, took the floor with her twice, much to the delight of the Bath gossips.

It was certainly pleasurable to be the most sought after girl in the room, but the froth and glamour of the night could not disguise the truth of her situation. This ball, like so many others, was part of an elaborate ritual which must lead eventually to the altar. It was a path she was desperate not to tread, even as she realised her chances of escape were slim. And now it was more imperative than ever that she stay true to herself. It was since meeting Gareth, of course. He was rude and overbearing, duplicitous, too, but he had lit a flame within her that made it impossible to settle for the good enough. She had believed herself to be cool, rational, even passionless. And yet within a few short weeks he had destroyed that belief, but offered nothing in return. In the last moments of their meeting at the Pump Room, he had shown her tenderness, but that altered nothing. He was getting ready to move on and tenderness had simply been a prelude to his leaving.

Knowing nothing of what was passing in her granddaughter's mind, Brielle looked on complacently, secure in the knowledge that Amelie was the most beautiful girl in the room. Dressed in a gown of white sarsnet over a white satin petticoat with pearl fastenings and a circlet of pearls in her hair, she looked every inch a fairy-tale princess.

~

Halfway through the evening, when the gentlemen's starched shirt points had begun to wilt from the heat of the hundreds of wax candles burning in the wall-sconces, the orchestra took their break and everyone began to make their way towards the refreshments laid out in the adjoining room. Amelie had been dancing constantly and was grateful for the chance to sit down. As she went towards the door, Brielle following, Mr King caught up with them, clearly wishing to introduce an escort for the buffet which lay beyond. It was Rufus Glyde.

'Miss Milverton, how very good to meet you again and in such pleasant surroundings. I hope you have enjoyed the dancing?'

The white mask of Glyde's face leaned towards her while his eyes ran lightly over her body. She felt herself squirming, but managed a brief curtsy without meeting his predatory gaze.

'Thank you, Sir Rufus, I have.'

'I wonder if you would be willing to add to my enjoyment by allowing me the pleasure of escorting you to tea?'

She looked desperately around for Brielle, who was now inconveniently deep in conversation with her neighbour. Following her glance, he said silkily, 'I have already asked your grandmother for permission and she is more than happy to entrust you to my care for half an hour.'

She was left with no alternative than to agree. She felt the loathsome touch on her arm and stifled her repulsion, allowing Glyde to lead her through to the adjoining room. Here he found her a chair and went in search of food and drink. Escape was impossible.

In a very short while he was back and handing her a small gold rimmed plate. 'I hope I may have gauged your tastes correctly, but tell me, please, if you would care for anything else.'

'This will do very well, thank you, Sir Rufus.

'Please, Rufus. I feel we know each other sufficiently

well to be on first-name terms. Do you not?'

'I would prefer our acquaintance to remain formal. I am sure you will appreciate my reasons.'

'I'm not sure I do. I am a little disappointed that you feel unable to trust me. Your father evidently does or he would not have wished me to make you an offer of marriage.'

'My father has nothing to say in the matter. And I beg you to refrain from mentioning your proposal.'

'As to that, I would think your father has everything to say, notwithstanding your temporary stay in Bath. And I do trust that it is temporary.'

'I am unsure of how long I shall be here, but certainly for some considerable time.'

'We shall have to see.' His voice held a dark edge. 'In any contest of wills, Miss Milverton, I think I might back your father.'

'Sir, I find the tone of your conversation not to my taste and I beg you to cease harassing me.'

'I see that I must mend my tone. I have no wish to upset you unnecessarily. Be assured that I will make no further request for your hand. I am not, after all, in the habit of requesting – as you will come to know.'

'If you will excuse me, I must find my grandmother.'

Unable to stifle her disgust any longer, she snatched up her reticule and fled back into the ballroom. Brielle was nowhere to be seen, but she knew that even if her grandmother were to materialise in that instant, she would not tell her of Glyde's menaces. What could she say? He was far too clever to issue direct threats. There was nothing she could pin down. Nevertheless she was aware that she had just been issued with a warning. Glyde was planning his revenge and it would be coming soon.

Scared that he might follow her, she ran towards the long French windows which stood open to the garden. The damask drapes, drawn back to welcome the night air, scarcely stirred. Very quickly she made her way out onto the terrace that ran the length of the building and descended a shallow flight of steps to one of the many paths that bisected the gardens, making sure she could not be seen from the lighted room behind. The night was still, as if holding its breath, the crunch of her slippers on gravel the only sound to disturb the warm peace.

The smell of lilac newly in flower floated towards her. Ahead the trees were motionless, a black mass silhouetted against the pale night sky. Her eyes gradually adapted to the darkness and now she could see shades of grey emerging from the shadows and close by, a pinprick of glowing red. The tip of a cigar, she realised with a start, and turned to flee back into the Assembly Rooms where the musicians had once more begun to play. A sardonic voice sounded softly in her ear.

'Tired of dancing so soon, Miss Milverton?'

# Chapter Fifteen

She spun round and saw in the muted light Gareth Heywood's derisive smile. 'As the belle of the ball, you surely cannot be leaving already?'

'I was merely taking the air. It's a beautiful evening.'

'It is. Shall we take the air together?' he suggested in a voice that brooked no refusal.

Not wishing to draw unwanted attention – from where they stood, they were clearly visible from the ballroom – she laid her hand lightly on the arm he proffered and retraced her steps along the pathway towards the knot of trees in the distance. The moon, which had been hovering behind clouds, swam free and the garden was suddenly bathed in silver. For the first time she saw her companion clearly. The white frilled shirt and black tailcoat and knee breeches deemed necessary for a formal occasion set off his body to perfection. He looked magnificent and she was bewitched, her eyes longing to linger on the seductive picture he presented. Hastily, she averted her gaze. She had no wish to advertise the effect he was having on her.

'I see you have reacquainted yourself with your friend?'

'You have been spying on me.'

'Hardly.'

'Then why are you here?'

'I'm here because the Averys wished to attend the dance and I accompanied them.'

'I didn't see you dancing.'

'I prefer to watch. One notices all kinds of interesting things. Rufus Glyde, for example, your sworn enemy.'

'You don't believe that he is my enemy,' she said flatly.

'From where I was standing, it looked unlikely. That was a cosy little tête à tête – what did you enjoy most, tasting the sweetmeats or listening to sweet nothings?'

'I was forced into taking tea with him. They were threats he was uttering.'

'Forced? Threats?' Gareth looked quizzically at her.

'Hints then that I had better do as he wishes and accept him as a suitor.'

'And do you intend to?'

'How can you ask me that?'

He gave a slight shrug of his shoulders. 'Your family is keen for you to make the match. Your life might be easier if you were to agree.'

'My life would be monstrous.'

Standing motionless in the cold, bright moonlight, her shoulders suddenly crumpled into defeat. She looked very young and very vulnerable and his heart missed a beat.

'If you need help, you have only to ask.' He stopped beneath the broad leaves of a chestnut tree and turned to face her.

'Thank you, but I doubt you can aid me.'

'You could be wrong.' He reached out to trace the line

of her cheek with one finger.

She took an involuntary step backwards. His brief touch had sent a shiver dancing the length of her spine.

'You are leaving England very shortly and I would be unwise to rely on your assistance.'

His smile was lazy and assured. 'If you asked nicely, I might delay my journey.'

'Why would you do that? You believe me a trickster, the perfect deceiver.'

'You are certainly artful – like every woman I have known.'

'I bow to your limitless experience,' she said caustically.

'You should – it's been hard won and generally unrewarding.'

'If I'm no different from every other woman, why offer me help?'

'Maybe because you *are* perfect as well as a deceiver. And because you need help. It seems to me the net is closing in.'

She shivered and he moved closer to her. Then, tipping up her chin, he kissed her gently on the lips. She should break away, ask him to escort her back to the ballroom. Already she had sufficient menace in her life without struggling against such dangerous temptation. But the taste of his mouth was something she needed to know again and her lips opened unresistingly to his. He kissed her long and deep until she was soft and pliant in his arms. The hard planes of his body pressed against her while his hands slowly and expertly caressed her bare skin. She was inundated by a wave of desire that permeated every fibre of her being. The small pearl buttons of her dress were soon undone and the white flesh of her breasts exposed to his touch. His kisses became hotter and more urgent with every moment.

Somewhere an owl hooted and for an instant they were stilled, listening to the sounds of the night. Brusquely, he pulled away.

'You should go back and find your grandmother.' His voice was rough with suppressed passion.

With shaking fingers she began to put her dress to rights while he watched her from a short distance, his expression impossible to read.

'You should be married, Amelie,' he said at last. 'And quickly. Surely there must be a suitor in the wings other than Rufus Glyde.'

She felt the anger exploding within her. How dare he use her in such fashion and then suggest she marry another man? Was this simply a new version of the old insult? Did he indeed think of her as a doxy, permanently in a state of heat for any man who came her way?

She marched past him with her head high, but he caught her by the arm and pulled her back. 'I meant it, you know. If you are in trouble, send for me.'

She shook off his restraint and ran swiftly towards the ballroom. Thankfully, Brielle was seated near the window and alone.

'I'm afraid I cannot dance any more, Grandmama, I have the most dreadful headache.'

Looking at her granddaughter's drawn face and hearing the agitation in her voice, Brielle hesitated only long enough to gather her belongings. Once they were seated side by side in the town coach, her grandmother took her hands in a warm clasp and stroked them comfortingly. 'You are fagged to death, my dear. We shall have a few quiet days and then you will be more than ready to socialise again.'

If only she knew, Amelie thought, but she dared not mention the existence of Gareth or, even worse, her own impropriety. She needed to push the incident into the furthest recesses of her mind. She had behaved as unchastely as it was possible and with a man who cared nothing for her. It was obvious he viewed her as an amusement, to be enjoyed when it suited. He had awoken the most frenzied desire and then walked away. As she thought of their encounter, her face blazed scarlet and her body was suffused with shame. But she must not think of it, she must not.

˜

'I admire your choice. A diamond of the first water!' Lucas grinned as Gareth entered the Avery family carriage. 'We caught a glimpse of her returning from your moonlight tryst.'

'She is a most beautiful girl,' his wife interjected. 'No wonder you are in love with her.'

Gareth glared at his friend. 'I won't ask who put that notion into your head, Katherine, but you have it wrong.'

She wrinkled her nose. 'I wonder,' she said gently.

'Admit it, you're in love, just as I said.' Lucas was jubilant. 'And what could be better? I was worried when I thought you had fallen for a girl who was completely ineligible, but it turns out the situation is very different.'

'No, it isn't,' was the terse reply, as the coach trundled a slow passage over the darkened cobbles.

When they reached the house, Lucas took his friend

by the arm and ushered him into his den. No one ever entered this room except by invitation. He poured two glasses of brandy and handed one to Gareth.

'I may be stupid,' he began, 'so explain to me exactly why you are determined to walk away from this stunning girl?'

'Amelie *is* a beautiful young woman and I'm as red blooded as the next man. But there it stays.'

'Why though?

'Women are a complication I can do without.'

'Women, maybe, but forget all the others who have flitted through your life – this girl is different.'

'I don't see that.'

'You said yourself that you can't lose her from your mind.'

'I have to and I will.'

He glanced across at his friend and saw the perturbed expression. 'I'm not looking for a bride. I'm not even looking for love. That would involve trust and I don't have trust to give.'

Lucas's eyes were troubled. 'Trust can grow – if you give it a chance.'

'I did. Once. But we both know the end of that story.'

'It's a story from the past,' his friend argued. 'It doesn't mean you can't start again.'

'There is no starting again. I chose my path years ago and I can't now unchoose it.'

'It wasn't a choice, it was forced on you. I'm reluctant to speak ill of your family and of someone who isn't here to defend himself, but your grandfather treated you shabbily.'

Gareth gave a small, mirthless laugh and his friend continued, 'I can see you're a changed man, but don't let that accursed scandal ruin the rest of your life. You are innocent of any wrongdoing.'

'I know that and, thank God, so do you. But to the rest of the world I am a guilty man and always will be. I can never ask anyone to marry me – even if I wanted to. It's as well that I don't.'

His companion gave a sigh of frustration. 'If we could discover what really happened that night... Have you any idea who might have cheated? If it wasn't you, and it wasn't me, then it was one of the other three people around that table. General Tilney is an impossibility and Petersham is so wealthy it would be laughable to suggest his cheating. But Glyde? He is a man steeped in all kinds of murk.'

'Of course I've thought about who cheated that night. I've thought about nothing else for seven long years. It could only be Glyde. But what would he have to gain? The stakes were not that high and in any case he is a rich man. Not in Petersham's league, I grant you, but rich enough.'

'I'm not sure he's as well-breeched as he appears. There are tales that every so often he is forced to sell property and some of his horses. Then he has a lucky streak and all is well again. He replenishes his stables and says he merely fancied a change of cattle.'

'So where does that get us?'

'It means that Glyde might have had a motive after all – money. There's been a good deal of whispering lately about his keenness to play with very young men. Those who have little experience but are plump in the pocket.'

'I was certainly not one of those. Wet behind the ears, it's true, but I didn't have a fortune to lose. You know as well as I how stringent my grandfather was. I received a very small allowance, hardly worth Glyde's effort if that was the plan.'

Lucas sat thinking for several minutes. 'It's true he wouldn't have fleeced you of a great deal,' he said at last, 'but the man is spiteful and has a thoroughly malicious nature. He might just have wanted to destroy a young man with a golden future – good looks, charm, a title in waiting and a grandfather who loved and respected him.'

'It's not enough. It has never been enough. If there had been a motive and concrete evidence of his wrongdoing, I would have confronted him years ago, exiled and penniless though I was.'

'I think you may be underestimating our friend Glyde. He would destroy anyone. For a wager perhaps, or even for fun. His kind of fun.'

Gareth said nothing for a while and when he broke the silence, his voice was harsh. 'And now the man is hanging around Amelie Milverton. I thought at first that she was playing games, pretending to dislike his overtures while angling to become the next Lady Glyde. But she appears to detest him. Despite that, he is determined to pursue her. First in London, then at the George and now here.'

'Then if you have a care for the girl – I won't call it love,' Lucas said hastily as he saw his friend's face, 'you must look out for her.'

'That won't be easy. She doesn't trust me and she is right not to.'

'Tell her the truth about yourself, then she will.'

'I doubt it. She is far more likely to turn away in disgust.'

'But she needs to know the lengths to which Glyde will go. She needs to understand what she is facing if she acts against him.'

Gareth stood up abruptly and began to pace the floor of the den. 'You're right,' he pronounced minutes later. 'I need to warn her. France will have to wait. And defeating Glyde's plans would certainly bring me pleasure.'

'Don't underestimate him, Gareth. He can be a dangerous man.'

'That I can believe, but – *I* can be even more dangerous.'

## Chapter Sixteen

It was the small hours before Amelie slept. Try as she might, she could not erase that evening's stolen meeting from her mind. The scene constantly replayed itself and every repetition made her feel worse. She knew she had behaved recklessly and immodestly. Yet what had she really been guilty of? Showing her true feelings, allowing herself to trust? In return she had suffered a savage humiliation. Years ago, witnessing her mother's distress, she had made a vow never to allow herself to feel too much for any man. This evening she had broken that vow and now she was paying the price. Her only hope was that Gareth Heywood would very soon leave Bath and she would never have to meet him again. Never have to see in his face the easy contempt he must feel.

∽

A troubled sleep left her tired and dispirited and it was with reluctance that she agreed to take a walk in the Sydney Gardens the next morning. Her grandmother had set time aside to wrestle with the household accounts and Fanny, newly arrived at Laura Place, was deputed to accompany her mistress. Amelie had no wish to burden the girl with her wretchedness, nor with her worries over Rufus Glyde. The maid had received a severe scolding for her part in her mistress's flight and the last thing Amelie wanted was to revive bad memories for her. It was best that Fanny thought her perfectly happy.

The gardens were looking particularly inviting. An overnight shower had polished the leaves and encouraged the flowers to put on their most vivid colours. The two women strolled at a leisurely pace along pathways which criss-crossed the well-kept lawns, making their way slowly around the grounds and back into Great Pulteney Street. Fanny was eager to hear the details of last night's ball and her mistress was occupied trying to paint a cheerful picture. Neither saw the clouds gather and the sky begin to darken until the rain started to pour in earnest. Snatching up their skirts, they ran for cover. A small wooden summer house at the end of the gardens offered what little shelter there was. They arrived there breathless and not a little wet.

'We should have brought our umbrellas, Miss Amelie. Bath weather is that changeable.'

The maid began to shake off the large drops of water that clung to her skirt and then turned to Amelie to help her do the same. But her mistress did not respond even when Fanny asked with some puzzlement, 'Is everything all right, miss?'

Amelie was standing motionless, seemingly welded to the wooden floor of the hut and staring at the man who shared their shelter. Fate could not have been more unkind; Gareth Heywood was the last man in the world that she wanted to see. He bowed slightly to the two women, but remained silent. His blue eyes gazed into the distance and a lock of wet hair shadowed his brow. The rain had moulded his coat of superfine to his form and the feelings Amelie had willed herself to suppress began to throb back into life. Dumbly, she looked out at the teeming rain, unable to say a word. He was the one to break the silence.

'I trust I see you well this morning, Miss Milverton?' His black brows were raised in enquiry.

She made an enormous effort to gather her wandering wits. 'I thank you, sir. I am well.'

'And fully recovered from the exertions of the last evening, I hope?'

His words provoked an anger that was incandescent. Not content with mortifying her, he must now seek her out and taunt her with her shame.

'I am not such a poor creature that dancing a few cotillions exhausts me, Mr Heywood,' she snapped.

'Ah, *dancing*, naturally not.' He wore the slightest suggestion of a grin.

'You are unhandsome, sir.'

'How is that?'

'I may be forced to take shelter here, but I should not be forced to suffer your mockery.'

He looked genuinely surprised. 'That's far from my intention.'

'I find that difficult to believe. From our first meeting you have treated me with contempt and last night you excelled yourself.'

Fanny gasped. The mention of Heywood had revived a distant memory. She gazed in astonishment, first at her mistress and then at the man who bore this disquieting name. In an attempt to capture Amelie's attention, she shuffled her feet noisily on the bare wooden boards. Her mistress, reminded for the first time of her presence, made haste to send her away.

'Go back to the house, Fanny, and find our umbrellas.'

'But, miss, the rain has almost stopped.'

'Don't argue. The weather looks like to remain inclement and I have no wish to get any wetter than I am.'

Fanny looked doubtful, but her mistress wore such a severe look that she scurried away with hardly a backwards glance.

Gareth watched the maid out of sight, then began to move closer. She held up her hand, stopping him in his tracks.

'I don't know if you have happened here by accident or if you've followed me. It matters not. You have taunted me for the last time. I wish never to see you again. Nor speak to you or even hear of you.'

A frown creased his brow. 'I have no idea why you should be so angry, but I am sorry to be the cause.'

'No idea! When all you have ever done is play games with me. Save them for the women you meet and discard on your travels. I'm sure they will be more appreciative. I am not one of them.'

'As I know to my cost,' he murmured wryly. 'And I have never suggested you were.'

'No? Then how do you account for your despicable conduct last night?'

'I should not have made love to you, I agree, but how

was that despicable?'

'You were trifling with me.'

'Believe me, Amelie, I was far from trifling.' He smiled reminiscently.

She found herself remembering, too. Recalling his smell, his touch, the feel of his body, and desperately sought to stoke her anger.

'You cannot help yourself. You are so used to treating women as trophies that you think it your right to appropriate any female that comes your way.'

He shrugged his shoulders. 'It's true that plenty of women have passed through my life and true that I've let them go without regret. But they have hardly been trophies. Merely ragged comfort along a stony path.'

'Very poetic, but it doesn't disguise the fact that you lured me into a compromising situation and then humiliated me.'

'You have a taste for the poetic, too, I see. I admit I should have resisted temptation, but you make that very difficult.'

He smiled down at her in a way that made her body crumple with desire. Alarmed by her response to him, she sprang away, leaving as much distance between them as possible.

His expression turned wrathful. 'If you must cast blame, look to yourself. You are angry because last night you surrendered to your feelings. Be grateful that I saved you from betraying yourself further.'

Amelie choked. The man's effrontery knew no bounds. 'Naturally you are my knight errant, always rescuing me from disaster. I had forgot. How painful last night's episode must have been for you.'

'Inconvenient, shall we say. Such moments can benefit neither of us and you should have a care for your future. You do not want to hear it, but your best route out of the dangers that beset you is to find a good man to marry.'

'I shall never marry.'

'Ah, the old refrain, but why ever not? There *are* decent men in the world.'

'Perhaps, but few women find them or, if they do, manage to keep them. My mama did not,' she added in a subdued voice.

He looked at her for a long time and his expression softened slightly. 'Whatever your mother's plight, you are not destined to repeat it.'

'Except that my experience of life tells me otherwise. Did *you* play the decent man last night?'

'I tried my best. Do you really think I wanted to lose control?' His voice was harsh. 'Of course I did not. I have survived a brutal world by making sure I am never slave to my emotions.'

'But today you are here, exposing yourself to the same peril. How is that? Or are you about to claim it was an accident that you happened by?' Even if his lovemaking had not been a deliberate ploy to humiliate her, it was at best an aberration, an inconvenience. And which was worse?

'No accident. I sought you out this morning. I saw you leave Laura Place and hoped to overtake you on your walk. It was fortunate that the rain brought us together.'

'*Fortunate* is not the word I would use. Last night you

denied spying on me, but spying is exactly what you are doing.'

'I sought you out,' he said deliberately, 'because I have something I must say. But don't fret, you will be free of my presence very shortly.'

'That is good news,' she retorted childishly. 'I cannot imagine why you are still in Bath. How long does it take to bid your friend goodbye?'

He ignored her pointed rudeness. 'I've stayed because I have business to complete. When I go depends on you.'

'How very surprising.' Her voice sliced through the dank air. 'And there was I thinking you were a law unto yourself.'

'I need only a few minutes of your time, then you may be on your way. And I will be on mine.' His expression was impossible to read, but his tone was unusually serious.

'A few minutes then, Mr Heywood, although I cannot imagine you have sought me out to exchange confidences. You have always delighted in being a figure of mystery.'

His face relaxed and he smiled. Once more the blue eyes were alight with warmth and, despite herself, she felt drawn into their gaze. He had moved very close and was looking at her intently. She realised that just as his rain-soaked clothes had displayed his muscular form, hers were revealing of her figure. The sheer sprig muslin clung sensuously to her curves and he was clearly enjoying the sight.

'I am glad you find it amusing,' she snapped, annoyed that her heart should be in such disorder.

'A figure of mystery sounds flatteringly enigmatic. My smile was only for that.'

'And are you about to cease being a mystery? Do you

intend to tell your secrets?'

'Yes,' he said unexpectedly.

'Now?'

'Yes.'

'You are going to be honest with me at last?' she persisted.

'I am going to be honest with you,' he replied solemnly. 'For your own sake, I need you to trust me. When you have heard what I have to say, you may choose to disown my acquaintance, but I still have to say it.'

The light had gone out of his eyes and his face was grave. She began to feel nervous. She had always wanted to know his true history, but how troubling were the revelations he was about to make?

He remained standing close to her, their bodies almost touching, but not quite. He made no attempt to possess himself of her hands, no attempt to kiss her. She felt real fear of what he was about to recount.

'Miss Milverton, what on earth are you doing out in this dreadful weather?'

It was Perry Latham. He bounded up the steps of the summerhouse, a large umbrella above his head. 'I met Fanny a while back and assured her that she could go home to dry and I would come to your rescue.'

'Thank you, Sir Peregrine.' She knew she sounded flustered and tried hard to calm her voice. 'That is most kind of you.'

'I am delighted to be of assistance. I am, in any case, a messenger from your grandmother.'

He caught sight of Gareth, standing still as a statue.

'Your servant, sir.' He made an awkward bob with his umbrella as a token of courtesy.

'Yours, sir,' Gareth replied stiffly. Amelie made haste to introduce the two men, but Gareth was in no mood for social niceties. 'If you will excuse me, I have a number of calls to make. You have an escort now, Miss Milverton, and will have no further need of my company.'

'But...' began Amelie.

'It was good to make your acquaintance,' Perry called after the rapidly disappearing figure, as Gareth strode towards the gates across one of the Chinese style bridges that dotted the gardens. 'A pleasant fellow,' he said, turning to Amelie. 'At least, I think so.'

'What message did you have from my grandmother, Sir Peregrine?'

'Perry, please.' He beamed at her. 'I must tell you that a splendid excursion is arranged for tomorrow. A picnic to Severn Abbey. Always providing the weather changes for the better.'

'A picnic tomorrow? How can that be? We were not to have any social engagements for several days. It seems strange that Lady St Clair should arrange it without consulting me.'

'Oh, it is not her ladyship who has arranged it. No, far from it. Everything is taken out of her hands.'

'*You* have planned it?'

'Nor me either, I fear. I did think of it, but I was pipped at the post. Some chap called Hyde, I believe.'

'Glyde?' Amelie faltered.

'Yes, that's the fellow. Good natured of him, don't you

think? He's gone to a lot of trouble apparently. Invited a large crowd and even booked musicians.'

She had the presence of mind to pin on a smile of pleasure, but her heart was beating uncomfortably fast. This was the first strike in Glyde's renewed campaign. She must return home immediately and speak to her grandmother. Brielle must be made to understand Glyde's true purpose.

'Sir Peregrine – Perry, I was intending to visit the haberdashers after my walk, but I have just now realised I have left behind the ribbon I wished to match. I will have to return home for it.'

'Then you must let me accompany you.'

'No, indeed, there is no need. The rain has stopped. Please don't let me keep you from your business. I will see you tomorrow, no doubt.'

And with that rapid dismissal, Perry Latham had nothing to do but bow politely and walk away in the opposite direction.

## Chapter Seventeen

'Why are you so upset?' Brielle was clearly bewildered by her granddaughter's response to the invitation. 'It is simply a picnic, my dear. I shall be there and a good many other people that you know.'

'But so will Sir Rufus Glyde. The last thing I want is to be in that man's company. Why did you accept? Why did you not ask me first when you know how I feel?'

'Dear child, strive for a little common sense. I accepted because to refuse would have been churlish. Sir Rufus has gone to considerable trouble organizing this expedition – he made it plain to me that it was to compensate in some small way for the unpleasantness he unknowingly subjected you to. In those circumstances it was impossible to refuse.'

Amelie looked mulish. 'You could have said I was unwell and gone by yourself.'

'How could I have done that without appearing to lie? How many people have seen you today in the full bloom of health? You are refining too much on what has gone before. I do not believe that in the past Sir Rufus fully understood your feelings, but now that he does, he simply wishes to be a friend.'

'I love and respect you, Grandmama, but in this I believe you are judging wrongly.'

Brielle's expression was stern. 'You must allow me to know a little more of the world. I will hear no more of this nonsense. The invitation is unexceptional, certainly nothing you need fear.'

'I do fear it. I loathe the man. I want nothing from him except his absence.'

'You are being unnecessarily alarmist. Whatever harm can come to you from going on a picnic?'

She had no answer and her grandmother continued smoothly, 'I am sure that Sir Rufus means well. The trip to Severn Abbey is a kind thought on his part and will give you the chance of getting to know him better. It might even encourage you to change your mind.'

Horrified, she burst out, 'I will never change my mind as long as I live. The idea of marriage to such a man is abhorrent.'

'And yet you seem not at all interested in marriage to anyone else, despite having been introduced to some of the most eligible bachelors living in Bath. Perry Latham is clearly entranced and one small sign from you would produce an offer of marriage, I feel sure.'

'When I said I never wanted to marry, I spoke the truth.'

'I also spoke the truth, Amelie, when I said that you will have to marry, unless you are content to beg shelter as a poor relation for the rest of your life.' But not unsympathetic to her granddaughter's plight, Brielle tried to coax her towards accepting the inevitable. 'If you have no preferences, would it not be sensible to go along with your father's wishes for the time being? You may even come to think he has chosen wisely for you.'

'Never, never, never!'

'No histrionics. You must begin to think sensibly. I accept that Rufus Glyde may not be the partner for you, but you cannot dismiss marriage entirely. Take heed of the fact that once you are wed, you will no longer be under your father's control. It will be your husband's duty to protect you from any interference from your family. If you choose a man like Perry, mature, independent and wealthy in his own right, he will have the power to do that. He would make you a good husband.'

'I don't want a good husband,' Amelie found herself saying while Brielle looked aghast.

In the silence that followed, her mind was a maelstrom, chasing itself from thought to thought, but returning always to that small insistent voice which would not be banished. What she wanted, she was learning, was a man who would possess her utterly, body and soul.

In the reaches of the night, she knew that man and he looked uncommonly like Gareth Heywood. But he was the last person who could feature as an eligible husband: marriage would never be for him. He desired her, that was obvious, and he would take her with a passion she dared not imagine. The thought torched her body, but in an instant she plummeted to earth. After the passion, what then? He would love her certainly, but just as certainly he would leave. He would cut loose with barely a backward glance.

Once again she lay awake for hours, her mind agitated and circling, Gareth always at its centre. His last words to her had been disturbing. What was it that he had wanted to say so urgently? She had seen him angry, bitter, laughing and loving, but never before so serious as the moment when Perry Latham had interrupted their conversation. He had followed her quite deliberately this morning, but what was he about to confide and why now? Did it flow from that shared moment in the moonlit garden? Did his feelings go more deeply than she suspected? Even if they did, he would not acknowledge them. He had made it plain that emotion was a weakness he could not afford; the moment's pleasure was his only interest. And yet... She longed to be able to seek him out on the morrow and know the answers. But convention decreed that a single woman must be sought rather than do the seeking. And in any case the day was not even hers – it would be filled by an excursion she longed to forgo.

⌒

The heavy overnight rain cleared towards dawn and by the time ten o'clock struck the next morning, the sky had mellowed to a clear blue, streaked with wisps of white. It seemed there was to be no reprieve from the weather. She had decided on the plainest of dresses, but her grandmother dismissed this plan immediately and insisted she put on one of the most fetching of the modiste's creations, a soft green lustring and matching cape. Miss Repton was sent to dress her hair. Her grandmother's maid had unbent slightly over time, Amelie's natural beauty providing her with the best opportunity she had ever enjoyed to display her professional skills. Her protegée acknowledged her efforts with courtesy, but with little interest. This was a day to be got through as quickly as possible.

From the outset it was clear that Sir Rufus had spared no effort or expense on the planning of his excursion. A cavalcade of carriages set off from Laura Place just before noon, the last two filled with servants, blankets, sunshades and hampers containing every conceivable kind of food and drink. It took only a short time before they were in the countryside, the morning bathed in mellow sunshine and stretching fresh and green before them. The delicate scent of wild flowers on either side wafted into their carriage as they swished through the narrow lanes. Amelie saw and felt none of it. This day was a prison sentence, the outing a part of Glyde's plan to bend her to his will. Miserably, she recognized that her grandmother could no longer be counted as her ally in the battle against him.

Sir Peregrine, dapper in dove grey pantaloons and claret waistcoat, shared their carriage and maintained an able flow of chatter. He tried and failed on several occasions to draw her into the conversation.

'Do you know the countryside around here, Miss Milverton?'

'I regret that I don't. As a child, I never went beyond the town.'

'There are a great many local places of interest, you know.'

'I am sure.'

'The Abbey we are visiting today for instance? Do you

know anything of its past?'

'I am afraid not.'

He fell quiet, evidently deciding against regaling her with his potted history of Severn Abbey. Instead he said, 'You might be interested in the legend that surrounds the building.' Her smile had him plunging into a confused account which interweaved a mad monk, a black crow and a murdered spouse who was forever dressed in white. Amelie listened with what she hoped was an expression of interest, but his words went unheard, dissolving into the air above without trace.

They arrived at the Abbey far too soon for her comfort and, once the carriages had disgorged their occupants, she and Brielle joined the whole party in a walk around the ruins. Perry Latham as an acknowledged expert on the Abbey's history entertained the small crowd with anecdotes of its past. The most popular proved to be that of the ghost, although the story had grown even more confused in the retelling. Until called to order by their formidable mama, the Misses Lampeter giggled in nervous excitement at his description of the lady in white who floated through the ruins at full moon. Rufus Glyde pointedly ignored the storytelling, deciding instead to play the perfect host. He darted here and there, at one moment mingling with his guests and at the next snapping out commands to his servants. At his insistence the musical trio positioned a little way off struck up a cheerful air.

'This seems a little excessive for a simple picnic,' Amelie remarked to her grandmother.

'Don't be ungrateful,' Brielle chided. 'If the event is a little extravagant, I am quite sure it has been done for your benefit.'

'I think it more likely that it satisfies our host's love of ostentation.'

'You are unfair, Amelie, and unrealistic. It is clear to me that Sir Rufus cares for you and still wishes to marry, despite your rejection. You are not interested in Perry – I saw how you treated him in the carriage. If you won't take him, then you should seriously consider the very advantageous offer that has been made to you by your father's choice of suitor.'

Before she could respond, they were interrupted by Glyde himself, who appeared without warning at their side. Summoning up his most amiable smile, he turned to face Amelie.

'I hope you are enjoying our impromptu little affair, Miss Milverton, and that all is to your satisfaction. Sir Peregrine's little stories, I feel, have given the event an added *frisson*. Or perhaps, unlike the Misses Lampeter, you don't enjoy tales of ghostly visitations?'

'I have more interest in the present than the past, Sir Rufus.'

'How very sensible, although one must never entirely forget the future.'

'That is something I'm not like to forget, sir.'

'Exactly so. When one is young, the future is an exciting blank, is it not, just waiting to be filled?'

'Indeed it is. And waiting to be filled as one wishes.'

She sounded defiant but Glyde remained unruffled. 'He will be a lucky man who helps you.'

'I said nothing of any man. My future is mine alone.

Brielle looked sharply at her granddaughter. 'Sir Rufus is surely right to suggest that the most satisfying future is a shared one.'

'That is a matter of opinion,' Amelie replied, turning her head away.

Brielle's seeming change of heart was lacerating. If she could not depend on her grandmother, she was lost. This excursion was always a trial to be endured, but now it had become a monster. When the picnic lunch was served in the shade of the chapel ruins, she could not bring herself to eat a mouthful. As well as folding tables and chairs scattered across the close-cropped green, blankets had been spread for those who preferred the informality of eating close to nature. Servants circulated busily among the guests, offering platters spilling over with the finest food, followed by tray after tray of cool champagne in crystal glasses. Glyde hovered around their table, constantly offering Amelie a variety of delicacies, to which her reply was just as constant. 'Thank you, but, no.'

'In this heat I eat very little.'

'I really am not hungry.'

And as for champagne, 'I rarely drink wine and never during the daytime.'

As Amelie parried her enemy's advances, Brielle became more and more incensed with her wayward granddaughter. Here was Sir Rufus making a concerted effort to give the girl an enjoyable day and Amelie appeared intent on treating him with an indifference that bordered on rudeness. Over the past week Brielle had come to think that Glyde's proposal should not be dismissed out of hand. He appeared to be a man deep in love, but he had shown a restraint and courtesy that she had not expected of him. It was true that he was considerably older than Amelie, but that was no bad thing in Brielle's view. He was wealthy, a necessity now that the Milvertons' fortune was in such a parlous state. It was a little worrying to be sure that he had acquired the mortgage over the house in Grosvenor Square, but Brielle thought that her granddaughter had perhaps misunderstood the nature of the transaction and that it had not been used as a threat, but as a way of helping a family with whom Glyde evidently wished to ally himself.

It was with relief that Amelie saw the servants at last begin to pile blankets and hampers back into the carriages and thought thankfully of the return to Bath. But the end of her misery was not yet in sight.

'Lady St Clair, I wonder if I might be permitted to drive your granddaughter?' Glyde had detached himself from the crowd of picnickers and was now bowing graciously to Brielle. 'I will undertake to deliver her safely to Laura Place.'

Brielle ignored her granddaughter's pleading look and gave her assent. It would be a chance for them to talk together without interruption. Perhaps they could sort through their differences, and if not, nothing had been lost.

'Grandmama, why don't you accompany Sir Rufus yourself?' Amelie appealed. 'I can drive home with Perry.' She had a desperate hope that Brielle would be content if she accompanied at least one of her potential suitors.

'I have already arranged with Perry to return with him, my dear.' Her grandmother neatly cut the ground from beneath her feet. 'And since Sir Rufus has been good enough to organize this wonderful excursion with you in mind, it would be fitting that you accompany him.'

This was the nearest Brielle had come to a public rebuke all day and it was one that Amelie could not ignore. Her face burning, she climbed into Glyde's carriage without another word.

# Chapter Eighteen

For the first few miles they drove in silence. She had no intention of playing the gracious guest and Rufus Glyde was evidently biding his time. They were halfway back to Bath before he broke the ominous quiet.

'I am so glad you felt able to accompany me, Miss Milverton. I fear our acquaintance began badly and I've had no real chance to remedy this. You have given me the opportunity now to plead my true feelings for you.'

She fixed her gaze on the blur of trees as they sped headlong through the country lanes. She was his quarry, hunted and cornered. She could escape ensnarement only by jumping from the curricle and that could mean injury for life, or worse.

Undeterred by her silence, Glyde began again. 'I would like to use this moment to tell you how much I hope you will consent to be my wife.'

That brought a response from her. 'Did you not say, Sir Rufus, just one week ago, that you would not be renewing your proposal?'

'That is true, dear lady, but I think perhaps that I was a little premature. I find my feelings for you are stronger than ever and I am looking forward to making you Lady Glyde.'

'Then I regret I must once more decline your kind offer. I am unable to return your affections.' She delivered her words as calmly as she was able.

'I hope you may be brought to change your mind.'

'I shall never change my mind.'

'Never is a very long time. You may think differently once you know me.'

'I know all I need to know, I assure you, and I will never wish to be your wife. I have no desire to hurt your feelings, but please accept my decision.'

'You do not hurt my feelings, Miss Milverton. Very little does. But I have decided that you are the woman I shall wed. Your opposition merely adds spice to the conquest.'

'If you persist in your delusion, there is nothing more I can say.'

'There is one word and that is yes.'

'I will never say yes.'

'I think you will. I have powerful forces on my side. You see, I know you took at least a week from London to reach your grandmother's house and I ask myself just where you were. And what you were doing during that time. Others might start to wonder, too, if they knew of your long absence from the protection of your relatives. I might even suggest to the inveterate gossips among us that you were up to no good. A possible love tryst? A scandal at all events. How would the *ton* react to that, I wonder? I imagine it might prove the end of all your hopes to shine in society, certainly all your hopes of a prestigious marriage.'

'I have no wish to shine in society. Nor any wish to make

a marriage, prestigious or otherwise. Your threats leave me unmoved.'

They had reached the outskirts of Bath and Amelie, her hands tightly clasped to prevent them from shaking, could only hope she would get to Laura Place with her dignity preserved. Her tormentor continued to drive at a spanking pace through the town's streets, seemingly undisturbed by her intransigence.

They had begun to approach the busier part of town, when she gave an abrupt start. A familiar figure, his back turned, was walking purposefully along the pavement. It was Gareth. During the long day's ordeal, she had thought of him constantly – yearned for him, she admitted shamefacedly to herself. And suddenly here he was, longing transformed into reality.

Her start had not gone unnoticed by Glyde. He looked long and hard at the figure striding along the road, scarcely able to believe his eyes. 'And how do you know that fine gentleman?' he asked sharply.

'That is no concern of yours, but since you ask, I believe I met him a few days ago at the Pump Room with my grandmother.' She was aware that this sounded less than convincing.

'Drinking the waters? Evidently, a new come-out for him.'

'Whatever do you mean?'

'I interest you at last! Strange, when the subject is a man you only *believe* you met.'

'He is of no interest to me. I simply did not understand your meaning.'

'Then allow me to explain. The man we have just passed is a low scoundrel. A sharp, to be precise.'

'A sharp?'

'As a young lady of impeccable background, I doubt you will know the term. A sharp is a cheat who lives by his skill at manipulating the cards or dice. In effect, a thief.'

Her face paled, but she said in a voice that hardly wavered, 'I don't believe that he is any such thing.'

'Why not? Is your knowledge of the gentleman so much greater than mine?'

'On what grounds do you accuse him of such base behaviour?'

'I saw him cheat with my own eyes. Pretty good grounds, wouldn't you agree, my dear?'

She sat rigid, in a state of shock. Glyde turned to her, a malicious smile on his face. 'The man is not suitable company for any woman of quality.'

When she said nothing, he continued to taunt. 'You seem a trifle upset at my revelation. Could it be that the gentleman is a little more to you than the casual acquaintance you claim?' And then slyly, delivering his crushing blow, 'So, we may have an answer to where you were for that missing week. With *that* man? And you refuse *me*!'

'I told you,' she said desperately, 'I hardly know him. And I doubt that you know him much better.'

She was far from feeling the certainty she expressed, haunted as she was by the remembrance of the quarrel she had witnessed between the two men at the George.

'I hate to contradict a lady, but today I will make an exception. I know a great deal of him. He has recently returned from the Continent where I believe he has been pursuing his vocation with mixed success. He appears to have enjoyed better luck here. You are the first bird to be plucked, my dear, if not at cards.'

'How dare you! Kindly set me down. I will not stay a minute longer in your company. I shall walk the rest of the way.'

'As you wish. But you are naive if you think you can flout society's rules and go unpunished. That is a grave error. If I know the truth, how long before others do, too? You will learn your mistake soon enough. Your biggest mistake by far is to tangle with me.'

༄

She ran blindly towards her grandmother's house. Passers-by turned to stare at the young woman hastening past them, bonnet untied and hair flying free. Once in the house she rushed up the stairs to her bedroom and locked the door. She needed time and solitude to make sense of what she had just heard. Glyde's threats had hardly registered. She had always known him a vicious man who would stop at nothing to gain what he wanted. But what he had said of Gareth had turned her world upside down. It cannot be true, it cannot be true, echoed over and over again in her mind. Rufus Glyde would not hesitate to denigrate any man he thought might be a rival, but the confidence with which he had delivered his damning judgement on Gareth had had its effect.

With all her heart she wanted to repudiate his words, but the fact that they accorded all too easily with what she already knew gave them a dreadful ring of truth. So many details fitted: Gareth's estrangement from his grandfather, his shabby clothes when she had first met him and his air of having known better times, his wish to leave England and return to the Continent. The silence about his background was readily explained if he were the disgraced man that Glyde intimated. It would explain the way he had constantly deflected her questions and his anger when she had continued to probe. And explain all too evidently why he had looked so grave when she had encountered him yesterday in the Sydney Gardens. He had something to tell her, he'd said, the truth about himself at last. Was that what he was about to confess when Perry Latham had interrupted them so inopportunely?

Perhaps after all not so inopportunely. If Gareth didn't say the words, then maybe they wouldn't be true. She had no wish to hear such things from his lips, from the lips of the man she had come to love. There it was... and she could no longer deny it. She had fought hard to preserve her heart, but in vain. She had lost it to a man who cared for nothing and nobody, whose tenderness was a fleeting caress and who, it now transpired, was an outcast from society. She lay down on the silk bedspread and closed her eyes. She was too deeply upset to cry, but her head thudded painfully. Her mind darted here and there, going over and over all the conversations she'd had with Gareth, trying to find a chink of light, trying to find a different interpretation. But the dreadful realisation dawned that there was no other.

How long she lay there she had no idea, but a discreet knock on the door brought her off the bed instantly. It was Fanny.

'Milady wants to speak to you, Miss Amelie,' she said softly.

'Tell her I am indisposed. Tell her I have the headache.'

'I think you should see her now, miss, then I'll brew you something for the pain.'

'My grandmother will understand if you say I'm not well.'

'I don't think she will. She's in a rage and ringing a peal over everyone who dares come near. Best to go down.'

Why was Brielle in such a temper? She had obeyed her grandmother's wishes and suffered a hateful journey for her pains. What, then, could be wrong? Lady St Clair's inexplicable mood seemed the final straw for a day so wretched that she wished to blot it from memory for ever. Reluctantly, she combed her hair, smoothed out her dress and made her way to the library.

'There you are at last.' Brielle greeted her impatiently. 'That girl of yours takes her time.'

Amelie bridled. 'Fanny came as quickly as she could. I was lying down, Grandmama. I have a monstrously bad headache.'

'Another one? This seems to be getting a habit with you. Though after what I have heard today, it hardly surprises me.'

She stared at her grandmother uncomprehendingly.

'Yes, you may stare. I have never been more mortified. To think I should hear of my granddaughter's appalling conduct from a man who, as yet, has no connection to the family.'

'I don't understand,' she murmured in a dazed voice,

but her bewilderment did nothing to appease her grandmother's fury.

'I have just endured one of the most uncomfortable interviews of my life. Sir Rufus Glyde made a point of calling on me after he had set you down. He felt it his distasteful duty to relay the most shocking news. He wished to warn me of a thoroughly unsuitable friendship you have contracted.'

She caught her breath. So this was Glyde's new plan. He intended to use her own grandmother to intimidate her and enforce his threats.

'I had to sit there,' Brielle continued bitterly, 'while he was kind enough to inform me that my granddaughter is acquainted with a man who is a proven thief, an out and out villain, a man who has been shunned by his own family and is not accepted in decent society. This is a man apparently that you know well. But let us not be mealy-mouthed, a man you have stayed with alone in a solitary country inn. Sir Rufus was nothing but courteous, but can you imagine my feelings when he told me this? He expressed concern for your safety. He knows this man well and said he would be most anxious if it were his own sister involved. His feelings do him credit, which is more than I can say for yours, Amelie. You have let me down badly – in fact, your scandalous behaviour has let the whole family down.'

Her grandmother's harsh words struck a deep chill in her heart. There was no defence she could make without revealing her feelings for Gareth. And that could do nothing but make the situation a hundred times worse, if that were possible.

'I acquit you of any deliberate wrongdoing,' her grandmother was saying, 'but your naivety and lack of prudence are likely to make you the talk of this town and beyond. If that happens, you will be lucky ever to live it down.'

Questions nagged in Amelie's mind and forced her to speak, though she knew it would infuriate her grandmother further. 'How could Rufus Glyde know I spent time at the inn with this man? And what right has he to accuse him of such wrongdoing?'

'He *is* a wrongdoer. Sir Rufus would not voice such a serious charge if it were not true. And as for him knowing of your indecent stay with this man, he has been most discreet, never hinted that he imagines there is any more than a casual acquaintance between you. He did not have to say more – I worked that out for myself. The patient you looked after so devotedly? An older man whom no one else could care for? How could you have deceived me so? Have I not deserved better?'

Amelie turned a stormy countenance towards her grandmother.

'You are unfair, ma'am. You must know I would never hurt you. Please believe that I have done nothing wrong. I was at the inn by accident, that is the truth, and I only withheld the full story because I did not want you to worry unnecessarily, not because I wanted to deceive.'

'It is certainly necessary for me to worry now. How are we to avoid this becoming common knowledge?'

'I left the inn as soon as I could and no one knows I was there, except you.'

'And Sir Rufus, if only by supposition. However, he

appears to be an honourable man and I am sure will not spread rumours. In the circumstances he is hardly likely to. We must trust that the scandal will not leak out.'

Her grandmother looked at her sharply. 'You are extremely fortunate that, after this dreadful misdemeanour, a man like Sir Rufus is still willing to marry you.'

She turned sheet-white as her grandmother's words sank in. Of course Glyde was willing to marry her. He would get his desire and she would no longer be able to say a word against it. She had lost any moral advantage. Brielle was right. Her family would consider it very fortunate that anyone wished now to marry her, least of all a notable member of the *ton*.

Brielle looked at her granddaughter's woebegone face and her heart softened. Amelie was so like her mother. She remembered seeing too often that same expression on Louise's face when things between her and Miles Milverton had begun to go awry. She took her granddaughter's hands in hers.

'You have made a bad mistake, but you can recover. I have every faith in your good sense. Whatever may have happened in the past, you must immediately cut any links you have to this unsuitable man.'

Amelie said nothing and her grandmother tried to rouse her with a brisk smile. 'Put this behind you, my dear. You are still very young and you have your whole future in front of you. You should give thought to what that future is to be. Sir Rufus is not the only man who admires you. It is possible...' she pursed her lips thoughtfully '...that an early wedding will prove the best way out of this predicament.'

She felt too distressed to ask her grandmother what she meant and excused herself as soon as she could. Crushed by the weight of her troubles, she could barely drag herself up the stairs. Fanny was waiting for her, bearing a cup of camomile tea and a handkerchief soaked in lavender water. Within minutes she had whisked Amelie's clothes from her and slipped a nightgown over her mistress's shoulders.

'I shall never sleep this early,' Amelie protested.

Fanny said nothing but spread the covers wide. It was too tempting. She climbed into bed and closed her eyes. Then fell into an exhausted sleep.

# Chapter Nineteen

It was daybreak before she stirred. As she swam out of slumber, a tide of wretchedness swept through her and drowned her in its misery. She longed to bury herself deep beneath the sheets never to emerge, but she knew she must rise and dress and pretend all was well. At breakfast her grandmother looked approvingly as she sat opposite, pale-faced but composed. Whatever ailed the girl, Brielle thought, she had spirit and would recover.

'I thought we might make a short visit to the Pump Room this morning.' Her grandmother buttered a second slice of toast.

'If it's possible, I would prefer to spend the day quietly,' Amelie returned. The thought of a crowded room and noisy chatter filled her with something near despair.

'Very well—' Brielle smiled agreement '—but we cannot have you withdraw from society for too long. That way rumours start.'

She knew her grandmother spoke the truth. She would have to appear in public again very soon and could only hope that when she did, she would be able to wear an indifferent face. After a meagre breakfast she picked up one of the marble-backed novels recently arrived from the Circulating Library, thinking to divert herself, but it turned out that she had no interest in fantasy worlds. All the time her mind was tussling with yesterday's dreadful news and she could give thought to nothing else. Whatever occupation she chose, it was no different. She started to write a letter but never finished it, picked up her embroidery but set only a few listless stitches and at the piano practising a new piece, her attempt was half hearted at best. Hour followed hour and each felt more wearisome until at last the long day finally dragged to its close.

Two equally long days later Brielle rose unusually early and made her preparations. By the time Amelie came down to breakfast, she found her day already arranged and to her grandmother's liking.

'Perry Latham is calling this morning. We have not seen him since the picnic and I thought it a friendly gesture to discover how he goes on.'

Amelie smiled absently and took a sip of tea. Whether he called or not was unimportant. Her grandmother, though, continued to pursue the subject.

'I know he has business at Duffields and I thought you might wish to accompany him and choose some new reading for yourself.'

She didn't bother to disagree. Brielle was obviously eager that she took a walk with Sir Peregrine this morning and, since she felt guilty at upsetting her grandmother so badly, she was more than willing to go. She was even persuaded to wear the bronze-and-green walking dress that became her so well and to allow Miss Repton to dress her hair. She was determined to make it up to her grandmother in whatever way she could, short of consorting with Rufus Glyde.

When she came down to the drawing room, Sir Peregrine was already there discussing with her grandmother the weather prospects for the next few days. 'Lady Blandford holds her open-air ridotto the day after tomorrow, but the omens are not good. It is said that the Blandfords have spent huge sums on the party. No doubt an attempt to launch the youngest daughter in some style. A nice enough girl, but rather too plain to take, I fear.'

'It will need more than a ridotto to launch Georgiana Blandford successfully,' her grandmother was saying caustically as Amelie entered the room.

'Miss Milverton—' Perry Latham leapt to his feet '—allow me.' And with an amiable smile, he drew out a chair for her. 'Lady St Clair tells me that you have been a little unwell. I hope you are now fully recovered.'

'I am, Sir Peregrine, but thank you for your concern.'

'You have been missed, let me tell you. You have been constantly looked for. Your army of admirers will be delighted to see you return.'

'You were talking of a ridotto, I believe,' she said to deflect the conversation away from herself. 'That sounds exotic.'

'Not so exotic if we do indeed suffer the thunderstorms that are threatened. But I don't wish to put you off – I hope you will come.'

Her grandmother looked meaningfully at her. 'We have certainly received our invitations.'

'Of course we shall come,' Amelie said quickly, 'but perhaps take our umbrellas.'

Brielle relaxed and Sir Peregrine smiled with pleasure. 'We should not need them this morning in any event. I hope you feel able to accompany me to Duffields Library, Miss Milverton?'

'That would be most enjoyable – it's time I explored the shop,' she lied glibly. 'I understand that you have already selected your volumes.'

'It is most exciting. I have ordered them especially from London. They are serious histories of this part of the country and one in particular is lavishly illustrated. If you are interested, I would be most happy to loan the books.'

'That is kind of you.'

'Perhaps you had better start for the library or they will be closed for luncheon,' Brielle reminded him. He looked concerned and rose quickly from his chair before he remembered his manners.

'Only when it is convenient with Miss Milverton.'

'I am ready to leave now. I'll fetch my bonnet and gloves.'

Walking through the Sydney Gardens reignited uncomfortable memories for her. Had it only been a few days ago that she had met Gareth here and he'd said those fateful words? That he needed her to trust him, that he wanted to tell her something that might change her feelings towards him? In the event, he had never told – someone else had and it had rocked her world.

Sir Peregrine continued to make gallant conversation as they threaded their way through the park. She felt sorry for him, trying so hard to entertain a companion whose thoughts were far away. When she looked up, she saw that he had led them to the small summerhouse in which she and Fanny had taken shelter, the place she'd had her last meeting with Gareth.

Her instinct was to flee from the spot, but instead she asked with only a slight tremor, 'Sir Peregrine, why are we here? I thought we were making haste to Duffields.

'You must forgive my little deception. We will, of course, go to the library but I was hoping to have a few words with you in private and I thought this would be a perfect setting. I know how much you like it.'

She wondered fleetingly how he could have got things so wrong, but it was his desire for a private interview that gave her greatest pause. Before she had time to question, he had begun on what was plainly a well rehearsed speech.

'Miss Milverton... Amelie, I would like you to know how much I honour and respect you. These last few weeks your company has given me enormous pleasure. It is not too much to say that you have transformed my life. Meeting you has given me a second chance of happiness.'

Alarmed at this passionate declaration, she held up her hand as if to stop him, but he was now well and truly embarked on his address and he was going to finish come what may.

'I said I respected you, but my feelings run far deeper than this. I truly love you, Amelie, and I ask you to do me the honour of becoming my wife.'

She was stunned into silence, but he continued to speak. 'In case you might think your grandmother would not approve, I have confided my feelings to her, and she has given me permission to address you.'

So this was the reason for Brielle's cryptic comment that an early marriage would be the most satisfactory outcome. Her grandmother had decided that it was time for Perry to declare himself. At this moment he was looking at her beseechingly. She felt sorry for him and angry with Brielle for her interference.

'Sir Peregrine, Perry,' she managed. 'I esteem your good opinion very highly and am greatly honoured that you wish to marry me. You are a true friend, but I fear that is all. I regret I cannot accept your kind offer.'

He looked crestfallen. 'Perhaps I have been too precipitate,' he suggested. 'You may wish for time to think it over and I am more than happy to wait.'

'No, Perry, it is only fair to tell you that I am quite sure of my decision. I need no further time. I am not in search of a husband.'

'I see. I was led to believe that you would not be averse to marriage.'

'Then I regret that you have been misled.' She saw his face fall further. 'I hope that we can still continue friends. I would not wish this uncomfortable situation to make that impossible.'

She held out her gloved hand to him and he took it in a limp hold. 'Naturally I shall always be your friend,' he murmured chivalrously, looking abjectly into the distance.

'Shall we continue to Duffields? Or would you prefer to abandon our visit?'

'No, not at all. We must continue.'

'I am sure you are eagerly awaited. The shop will be looking forward to showing you the volumes they've obtained.'

For the first time his face relaxed a little. 'By Jove, yes,' he exclaimed. 'I had almost forgotten them.'

She took his arm and they once more moved off, this time towards the delicately wrought iron gates which led them out of the gardens. His step had a slight spring in it now and by dint of talking to him about the publications he had ordered and getting him to describe them in every particular, they managed to arrive at the library with Sir Peregrine in unusually good spirits for a man whose marriage proposal had just been rejected. In her desire to console him, she had for the moment forgotten her own plight.

Once in the shop he made haste to the counter and was soon lost in his new treasure. She left him to his reading and began to wander around the shelves, picking up and putting down books at random without any real intention of borrowing them. She drifted towards the back of the library where the shelves were even higher and the tomes even more dusty. A large volume bound in dark brown calf took her eye. The gold lettering seemed to leap out of the battered cover as though the title were intent on seeking her attention. She lifted the book from the shelf better to decipher the words on its spine and found herself looking through the empty space at a face she knew well. In a second, Gareth Heywood had walked quickly around the end of the bookcase and was at her side.

'I have visited every shop in Bath these last few days, trying to find you,' he began abruptly. 'Where have you been hiding?'

'I don't hide, Mr Heywood. I have been indisposed.' Her words hid a well of pain.

'And are you fully recovered?'

It was unlikely she thought that she would ever recover, but she must answer him as best she could. 'Thank you, I am well.'

'I wanted to find you,' he repeated. 'I have things I need to say.'

'There really is no need.'

'I think there is. Let me speak. I will be brief.'

'There is no need, I tell you.' There was real anguish in her voice. 'I already know what you are about to say.'

'How can that be?'

'Others have told me.'

'Others? What others?'

That was something she would not answer. His brow furrowed. 'Glyde? Was it Glyde?'

She said nothing but misery was writ large across her face. The furrow deepened. 'How did he know I was in Bath?'

'He saw you as we were driving back into town a few days ago and was kind enough to apprise me of your history.'

'What exactly did he say?'

'Do you really want to hear?'

'Yes. I imagine his account differs markedly from mine.'

'He said you were a card thief – a card sharp, I think he called it – who preyed on naïve people and made your living by taking their money. He said that usually you worked on the Continent, but had not been successful lately and returned to England to try your luck here.' Her voice was dead and her eyes opaque. She could hardly bear to hear what she was saying.

He reached out and took her hands. They were ice cold through her light gloves. 'Let me tell you the truth,' he urged.

'Truth? You once told me that my relationship with the truth was slippery. Yours, I think, does not exist. Spare me any more lies.'

With a sharp jerk she snatched back her hands just as Perry Latham came into view. He had been lost in the dream of his new acquisitions, but had suddenly remembered he was escorting a lady and one he had just asked to marry. He came bustling up to them, raising his hat to Gareth whom he vaguely remembered.

'Your servant, sir. Amelie, I am so sorry I abandoned you. Call it the excitement of an enthusiast. I cannot wait to show you the books that have arrived. They are truly magnificent. I know you will be as entranced as I am.' He fairly danced with pleasure.

'Books!' Gareth's voice was a growl.

'On the history of this area. Priceless volumes. Could it be that you are an amateur historian, too, Mr Heywood?'

Gareth's expression was a mixture of astonishment and rage. He wheeled around to face Amelie. 'I cannot talk to you here. Come with me.'

And without a further word he grabbed her arm and pulled her through the shop, leaving Sir Peregrine to gape helplessly after them. Once outside, he hailed a passing hansom and bundled them both inside. It was all too reminiscent for Amelie of a previous journey she had taken with him.

'How dare you kidnap me in this way!' she protested.

'I need to be alone with you.' With that he pulled down the blinds on the cab windows and commanded the jarvey to drive on.

## Chapter Twenty

'Where to, mister?'

'Anywhere, drive in circles if you wish, just leave us to be private,' he said abruptly.

'I geddit.' The jarvey gave a low whistle.

Incensed, Amelie made to open the cab door, but before she could jump to freedom, they had jolted forward and were bowling along the cobbles at speed. He steadied her with one hand and turned to face her.

'You must listen to me, Amelie. Whatever Glyde has told you is a distorted version of what happened. Give me the chance to tell my story.'

'It would seem I have no option.' Her voice was cold and she stared rigidly ahead.

For days she had spent fruitless hours trying to hate this man, remembering every slight she had suffered, every insult, every mockery. She had told herself again and again that for all his charm he was as untrustworthy as any man and worse, guilty of a low crime for which he had been justly punished. Pure chance had brought him into her life and now the dice had rolled once more and chance was setting her free. But try as she might, she could not forget him, let alone hate him. He was always there, always with her wherever she went, catching at her heart at each and every unexpected moment.

Undaunted by her silence, he began to relate the events of that long ago evening. She listened, at first smarting and angry at being kept against her will, but then with growing concern as a very different account emerged from the shadows. Imperceptibly, her heart began to lighten; she wanted so badly to believe him.

'Why would Glyde have marked the cards?' she asked guardedly. 'What was in it for him?'

He shook his head. 'I have no idea. He must have known that I had little money and Lucas not much more. Petersham is a very wealthy man, of course, and as for the General, I imagine he's reasonably well-breeched. But to risk a thing like that makes no sense.'

'And to accuse you? That makes no sense either.' Maybe, she mused, it didn't have to. Glyde was simply a vicious man.

As if to echo her thoughts, Gareth said, 'Lucas insists he did it out of malice. That he resented me for having what he didn't – a loving family and a promising future.'

'And do you agree?'

He shook his head again. 'I can't think a man like Glyde would care a jot about family and as for a golden future, his own was secure enough. It was an excessive thing to do out of spite. He hardly knew me.'

'If it was spite, he was successful.' She reached out for his hand and gripped it very hard.

Gareth's expression was bleak. 'My grandfather disowned

me on the spot and we remained unreconciled. Whatever Glyde's motives, he ensured that I lost everything.'

'And you have never tried to clear your name?' She so wanted things to be right.

'A small matter of how,' he said grimly. 'I was without money, friends or influence. Glyde, on the other hand, was rich and well respected, if not greatly liked. I had not a shred of evidence against him.'

'And is that still the case?

'Evidence? No, none.'

'But you have friends – Lord Avery for instance. And you appear now to be in better circumstances.'

He looked at her sharply, but then relaxed. She could have no inkling of his changed position. 'Let's say that I've come to a point in my life where it's immaterial to me whether society believes my story or not.'

'So why tell me?' she asked gently.

'I need *you* to believe, to trust me sufficiently that you will heed my warning. Glyde will not easily give up his pursuit. He is a ruthless man and so steeped in vanity that he'll go to any lengths to achieve his goal.'

She snuggled closer, a happy curve to her lips. Somewhere her heart began to sing. Gareth had faced scorn, faced shame, in order to warn her and keep her safe. Perhaps his feelings did go deep. Perhaps he loved her after all.

'I will be doubly on my guard,' she said at last, 'but I have always known that beneath his mask Sir Rufus was a vile creature.'

'It seems that others do not – unfortunately the ones who should protect and care for you.'

'I'm lucky, then, that they don't include you. If indeed you do care for me.' She blushed at her boldness.

His answer was slow in coming and when he spoke it was to say obliquely, 'You could wreak havoc on my life, Amelie, and I on yours. But I'll not let that happen.'

His reply left her hot with embarrassment at having once more exposed herself so baldly. How stupid she was! He did not care for her, at least not enough. She was more to him perhaps than the women who had previously skimmed the surface of his life, but she was not the anchor that would bring him home for ever. Well, she had her pride. She would take his warning and expect nothing else. He need not fear she would hang on his shoulder.

Silence crowded in on them. He sat unseeing, a lock of hair shadowing his set expression. She sensed he was waiting for her to speak, but she felt too mortified to utter a word and the silence gradually built in intensity. So intense it could shatter the carriage walls. But then he was turning to her, slowly, almost unwillingly. 'You *do* believe me?'

The urgency in his voice made her look up and she found her eyes caught and held by his gaze. The unexpected longing that she saw there shocked her.

She was stunned by the emotion that she had glimpsed and tried for a light reply. 'Would you prefer I believe Rufus Glyde?'

But lightness was not his touchstone. He pulled her roughly towards him. 'Don't ever say that name again in my hearing.'

Held tightly against his chest, she felt the heat of his body weave its spell, stifling her doubts, submerging her hurts. Shyly she lifted her face to his, aching for his touch. It was not long coming. In a moment more she was in his arms and he was smothering her with kisses, his breath warm on her skin, his mouth hard and demanding.

Even as she opened her lips to him, he knew that he should stop. He had told her what he needed to say and she had believed him. That was all that mattered. There could never be anything more. He did not belong in her world, nor she in his – they were destined always to journey apart. But her mouth was so soft and inviting that he could not bring himself to break away. Instead his lips sought hers more urgently. He needed to taste her, all of her. He slid down the loose sleeves of her dress, exposing her shoulders to his kiss, his mouth working its way towards the soft swell of her breasts. His lips lit a fire in her. She was breathing quickly and he had an unbearable yearning to make her his if only for this time. He must fight it, he knew, but she was matching him kiss for kiss. She was stroking his body until it was burning out of his control. He laid her down on the seat and she moaned with pleasure. He would allow himself this one moment; he would take the memory with him and cherish it.

Suddenly the carriage came to a juddering halt and their entwined bodies were forcibly parted. There was loud shouting coming from close by. Dazed, they scrambled to their feet and Gareth carefully inched the blind upwards. A scene of carnage greeted him.

'There's been some kind of accident,' he said. He was still breathing hard. 'There's a large crowd milling about and people shouting at each other.'

She rapidly put her dress to rights and joined him at the small pane of glass. They were at a crossroads and an overturned cart blocked the road opposite. Scattered sacks of potatoes bore witness to a collision and loud accusations of blame rent the air. She was alarmed at the number of people standing so close to the cab. At any moment someone might notice them at the window or might even choose to open the door. She could not afford to be recognised.

'I must go,' she gasped. 'If someone sees me and tells my grandmother...'

'Your grandmother knows of me?'

'Glyde has told her. She has warned me that I must never see you again. If I disobey, she is certain to send me back to my father.'

'Then you must go. We should say our goodbyes now, Amelie.'

She had been drifting on a hazy cloud of love, but this splinter of ice shook her from her dream. 'But why, why must we say goodbye?'

'I will be gone from Bath very soon and we are unlikely to meet again,' he replied tautly.

'But—'

'Don't make it more difficult. This has to be. You know my story now – convince your grandmother of its truth and she will send Glyde packing. Then you may look forward to a peaceful future. But it's one in which I have no part.'

His face wore a blank expression and she felt like hitting him very hard. How could he be so obtuse? Whatever he was, whatever life he led, she was now a part of it. Glyde's shocking intelligence had forced her to confront her deepest and truest emotions. Even when she had thought Gareth a cheat and a liar, she had loved him and longed for him.

An idea flashed into her head. It was daring and dangerous, but it was what she wanted most in the world. 'Come to me tomorrow.' Her voice rang out clear and joyful. 'Meet me behind the Abbey after the lunchtime service. I'll be on my own – Grandmama attends the Catholic Church early in the morning.'

He shook his head. 'We cannot continue to meet, Amelie.'

'Come to me,' she pleaded urgently.

'I should not. We should not.' He felt a wild confusion of tenderness and desire wash over him.

'Come!' she beseeched.

At last he said, 'I will be there,' and his voice was thick with emotion.

He held her fingers to his lips for an instant and then she was slipping out of the carriage.

They had stopped near Pulteney Bridge, a walk of only a few minutes to Laura Place, and she hurriedly made for home. Before Perry had a chance to speak to her grandmother, she needed to concoct an explanation for her sudden disappearance from Duffields. But pausing for a moment, she glanced back at the crossroads where an angry crowd of people still spilled across the road. She could just spy the top of Gareth's carriage.

'Such a shame you had your ride curtailed.' A cold, reedy voice sounded behind her.

She wheeled around. Rufus Glyde blocked the pavement, a sneer on his face. But where had he come from? He must have taken to tracking her through the town. She shivered inwardly at the thought of this base creature dogging her footsteps.

'I cannot think why you should choose to travel in such a disreputable conveyance,' he continued, gesturing in disgust at the distant hansom. 'And with the blinds closed.'

'I don't understand you, Sir Rufus.' She felt her stomach clench.

'Do you not? I believe I spoke in English. You alighted just now from a hansom cab, eccentric behaviour in itself, but with the blinds down? My dear!'

She flushed involuntarily, but her gaze did not waver even as he taunted, 'You are surely not bored already with the delights of Bath? Or was the view inside particularly enthralling?'

'Your remarks are offensive, sir. Allow me to pass, if you please.'

'Not so fast. I have, after all, a vested interest in your conduct.'

'On the contrary, my conduct has nothing whatsoever to do with you.'

'There we must disagree, yet again.' He sighed softly, but his face was alight with malice. 'I consider myself your affianced husband, barring the formal announcement, and as such I have every right to concern myself with your activities.'

'You will never, ever be my husband,' she rejoined wearily. 'Accept my decision and let me alone.'

'You are very wrong, my dear. I shall be your husband and soon.'

She shook her head with impatience and he said sourly, 'Let us have no more of this nonsense. You will do as I require. If you think to make a fool of me, you had better think again.'

'Only you can make a fool of yourself, sir. Now let me pass.'

'You *will* show me respect whether you like it or not. I have only to tell your grandmother that you are still consorting with a known criminal, and she will shower me with blessings if I still agree to marry you.'

'You may tell her what you wish. I have no fear of you or your threats.'

'I think you will find you will be very afraid. I shall do more than tell your grandmother. I will make sure that I publish your loose conduct far and wide. Your disgrace will circulate way beyond Bath – it will make you the talk of London society.'

'I have little interest in what society says of me. Publish all you wish.'

'You may find that your interest quickens however, my dear Miss Milverton, when your grandmother ejects you from her house and the rest of your family shuns you in disgust. Where will you go? Who will shelter you? Not a pretty future, is it?'

'I think I can endure it,' she said lightly and slipped past his outstretched hand.

Glyde looked after her, his face distorted. He could not understand why she despised his threats. What could be lending her the strength to flout him? But that could not continue. If he was unable to intimidate her by menace or blackmail, he would do so by force.

Unaware of the cauldron of anger she had stoked, Amelie walked away with a smile on her face. Glyde was a repugnant creature and it had cost her dear to maintain her equanimity in the face of his threats. But throughout she had held tight to the magnificent idea that had come to her as she left Gareth. A ride in a hansom cab had changed everything. She had begun it believing she had given her heart to a man incapable of deep feeling, but ended knowing differently. The flash of emotion she had surprised in him had been a revelation. She had known then that she was loved. And that was sufficient.

She believed Gareth innocent of any wrongdoing and willed the world to believe it, too. It was clear, though, that he no longer cared for society's judgement. His mind was made up and she would not seek to persuade him differently. If he were determined to leave England, she was equally determined to leave with him. She would be ruined in the eyes of the world, but no more so than if Glyde made good his threats.

From childhood she had set her face against marrying, her mother's fate hovering always before her. But she had known that in reality she would be forced to conform; the best she could hope was to be tied to a dull, well-meaning suitor such as Sir Peregrine. Yet her whole being cried out to live life large, to live for passion. How splendid then to follow her destiny with the man she desired and to do so on equal terms. She would go with Gareth to the Continent and share the rigours of his life, travel where he travelled, sleep where he slept. She had no illusions. His way of life was transient and insecure and their future together might prove the same. Poverty imposed its own tunes and desire could become blunted. But whatever dangers she faced, she would be fully alive at last. Tomorrow when they met, she would tell him her plans.

## Chapter Twenty-One

She woke on Sunday morning deliriously happy. In just one day her life had been transformed. Her head had acknowledged the likely truth of Glyde's accusations, but her heart had always told a different tale. Now head and heart were one. Tomorrow she and Gareth would be together, friends, companions, lovers, for as long as he wanted her. She had discovered the freedom she had been seeking ever since her escape from Grosvenor Square.

Brielle did not appear at the breakfast table. She was still suffering from a chill contracted a few days previously and sent a message to say that she would keep to her bed this morning, but would take a light nuncheon with Amelie when her granddaughter returned from church. Amelie was relieved. There was no possibility now of an accidental meeting with her grandmother while she was hurrying to the tryst she had arranged.

Fanny was to accompany her to the Abbey and would have to be told of the appointment with Gareth, but she was sure that she could persuade her loyal maid to keep silent. It would be unfair to involve her any further than that. Whatever plans she and Gareth made this morning must be known only to the two of them. 'The two of them' – the phrase had a magnificent ring to it. He would be bound to oppose her wish to go with him to France and would paint in vivid colours the evils of exclusion from Polite Society. But in the end he would capitulate. She would persuade him that a life lived with him was all she desired – and she knew just how to persuade him. He would not hold out for long.

Her stomach was churning, her chest tight with excitement. Faced with the lavish breakfast laid out by Horrocks, she could eat little, and as soon as the clock struck twelve she slipped out of the front door with Fanny in tow. Together they began a brisk walk to the Abbey. She would wait until after the service before she revealed to the girl the meeting she had planned. It was pointless to worry her before it was necessary. The weather had changed dramatically and today the sun hid itself behind dark scudding clouds, but she was in no way downcast by the lowering skies. Deep inside she bubbled with joy.

As they approached the pathway leading to the Abbey's impressive front entrance, she paused for a moment at the lych gate. A few paces away a carriage had been drawn up at the side of the road. It had a strange, solitary air about it. No one was in sight and horses and carriage appeared abandoned. It struck her as odd. Normally residents walked to the Abbey for Sunday services or, if they were driven, their carriage was ordered to return for them at the appointed hour. She remarked on the waiting coach to her companion.

'It must belong to old Mrs Warrinder,' Fanny suggested.

'She hates to be kept waiting and never allows her carriage to return home.'

Amelie nodded and promptly lost interest, walking quickly along the paved way and in through the Abbey's main door. The church was full, as it was on most Sundays. Visitors and residents alike enjoyed the sensation of attending a service in such ancient precincts. The opportunity to show off one's finery and the chance to glimpse new arrivals in town was an added pleasure. At the entrance she glanced briefly around the congregation and at first recognised no one. But when she looked again, she saw Perry Latham sitting in a seat to the right of the pulpit. Hoping he hadn't seen her, she made her way to a pew at the back of the church. He had not visited Laura Place since she had left him at Duffields and she had still to offer an explanation for her abrupt departure. But this morning she could not afford to be delayed by conversation with anyone. Once the service had finished, she must make good her escape.

The well-remembered hymns and prayers proceeded at a leisurely pace. She heard hardly a word, making the responses automatically, her mind elsewhere. Surreptitiously, she looked at her pocket watch. In just over half an hour she would be seeing the man she loved, and for the first time they would be meeting as equals, all deception past. Then the rector was giving the final blessing and the congregation kneeling for a last prayer. As soon as she felt she could, she got to her feet and made for the door. Fanny had hastily to scramble upright and move at a trot to keep up with her mistress. They both shook hands briefly with the rector, who was waiting at the door to greet his parishioners, but they did not dally. A quick smile and a nod and they were through the church porch.

'Why such a rush, Miss Amelie? You mustn't worry about milady, you know. I'm sure she will be better soon.'

'I'm sure she will, too. Forgive me for hurrying you so, Fanny. It's not my grandmother I'm thinking of. I have an appointment to get to and I don't want to be late.'

'An appointment? Where? Who with, miss?'

'An appointment with Mr Heywood.'

Fanny drew a long breath and said with decision, 'I don't think you should go. That man is trouble if ever I saw it.'

'Nonsense. This is a business arrangement only. I shan't keep you long. I need to see Mr Heywood for just a few minutes and then we will be on our way. You may walk around the churchyard while we talk.'

'Would your grandmother like you to be meeting him?' Fanny asked feebly. She had a lively apprehension of what Brielle's reaction would be and who would most likely be held responsible for Amelie's rashness.

'My grandmother need never know. If you don't wish to be involved, I will understand. But I am going to meet Mr Heywood – you can come with me or not, as you please.'

'Miss Amelie, you know I would follow you anywhere, it's just...'

Her words died in the air. Two burly men had leapt from the coach they had noticed earlier, and blocked their path. The women looked startled, but before either could make a move, the men had scooped Amelie up and thrown her through the open door of the carriage. Fanny dashed after her, trying to hold on to her arm, but one of the men turned back and cuffed the maid soundly around the head. She fell to the ground, momentarily senseless. In a second, the horses had been whipped up and the coach was disappearing along the street.

'Fanny? It is Fanny isn't it?' A kind voice sounded in the maid's ear. 'Are you all right? You look terrible.'

It was Sir Peregrine Latham. He bent solicitously over the girl and tried unsuccessfully to drag her to her feet.

'My mistress,' Fanny whispered, 'Miss Amelie...'

'What about Miss Amelie?' Perry demanded. 'Where is she? I was trying to catch her up to have a word, but you both left the Abbey so quickly that I lost sight of you.'

The maid sat up groggily. She was shaking now, hardly able to speak. 'My mistress,' she moaned, 'my mistress.'

'Yes?'

'The men – they kidnapped her.'

'What men? There are no men, Fanny. You must be suffering from concussion. You will have hurt your head when you fell.'

She looked blankly up at Perry, who was still bending anxiously over her. 'They hit me around the head and then I fell.'

'Hit you around the head? In Bath, in broad daylight? And on a Sunday? Surely not!'

She nodded in a bewildered fashion while Sir Peregrine struggled to understand what had happened. 'Who are these men? Who could be guilty of such barbarism?'

At this, a jumble of disjointed words gushed forth from the tearful Fanny. 'I don't know, I don't know. They were waiting... My mistress and I were passing a carriage and they sprung out and grabbed her and I tried to hold on to her but the one with the crooked teeth turned round and hit me round the head and I wasn't able to hang on any more and now they've taken her.'

She collapsed back onto the pavement, sobbing violently. Sir Peregrine began to feel extremely agitated. He was not sure whether the poor maidservant was deluded or telling him some monstrous truth. And he had no idea how to cope with a woman deluged in tears. He was very worried that at any moment she would succumb to hysterics. It was obviously time to be decisive.

'We must return to Laura Place and tell Lady St Clair what has happened.'

'But my mistress…' Fanny moaned.

'Yes, yes,' Perry said soothingly. 'Her ladyship will know what to do, I am sure.' His voice carried a certainty that he was far from feeling.

It was a matter of minutes before they arrived back at Brielle's house. With encouragement from Sir Peregrine, Fanny haltingly told her tale. Brielle looked first astonished and then infuriated.

'What nonsense is this that you are telling me, girl?'

The maid looked crestfallen and ready to burst into tears again. Perry Latham thought it prudent to intervene.

'My lady, the girl is speaking the truth when she says she was attacked. I found her lying on the pavement, clearly having been injured in the head.'

'And why should that mean she has been attacked? She could have tripped. This girl has a history of not telling the truth. I have never found her to be wholly dependable.'

She bent a basilisk stare on the unfortunate maidservant.

'But, Lady St Clair, your granddaughter is missing,' Perry pleaded. 'She has vanished into thin air.'

The stare became more pronounced. 'And precisely where is my granddaughter, Fanny?'

'I don't know, milady,' she sniffled. 'Miss Amelie was took. I couldn't stop them.'

'Are you expecting me to believe that my granddaughter has been abducted in broad daylight?'

'Yes, ma'am,' Fanny asserted, her voice trembling.

'As she came out of church?'

'Yes, ma'am.'

'Ridiculous,' Brielle pronounced. 'And who do you suggest is responsible for this outrage?' Her dawning fear was making her more imperious than ever.

'I think I recognised one of the men,' Fanny managed. 'He had crooked teeth.'

'Yes...' Brielle prompted crossly.

'He was at the picnic Miss Amelie went to.'

'What picnic?'

'The one at Severn Abbey. The one organised by Sir Rufus Glyde, milady. He was one of Sir Rufus's men, I'm sure.'

'Are you suggesting, you stupid girl, that Sir Rufus Glyde, a respected peer of the realm, has abducted my granddaughter? How dare you! If it were not so laughable, it would be a shocking accusation.'

Fanny hung her head. 'Miss Amelie was plenty afraid of him,' she muttered defiantly. 'She was scared he would force her to marry him.'

Sir Peregrine had listened to this interchange in growing bewilderment. The idea that Amelie might be forced to marry a man she feared, and that this man had been responsible for her disappearance, seemed to him something out of one of the local legends he so eagerly devoured rather than anything approaching real life.

'Sir Peregrine, will you put a stop to this nonsense once and for all? Please call at Sir Rufus Glyde's lodgings and ascertain his whereabouts. I am sure we will find that he is as ignorant as we are of Amelie's plight. In the meantime I will send Horrocks and the footman to make enquiries. I am sure there must be a rational explanation for my granddaughter's disappearance and—' she favoured the maid with a contemptuous glare '—for this girl's sudden malady.' Inwardly, though, she had begun to feel very uneasy.

Sir Peregrine was not long in returning. His face was grave as he entered the room.

'I regret to tell you, Lady St Clair, that Sir Rufus has not been seen at his lodgings for some hours. Apparently, he quitted his rooms quite suddenly. The landlord was given no notice of his departure and...' Perry coughed delicately '...I understand there is a considerable amount of rent owing.'

'I cannot believe that of a gentleman such as Sir Rufus.' Brielle looked ashen. 'I am sure if we can discover where he has gone, he will be able to tell us something of Amelie or at least reassure us that he has had no part in her disappearance.'

'As to finding Sir Rufus, the landlord has no idea where

he might be.'

'And you?' Brielle looked painfully at her young friend.

'I regret, my lady, that my acquaintance with him is of the slightest.'

There was a soft tap at the door. The butler had returned from his mission and came quickly to the point. Neither he nor Thomas had been able to find any trace of the young mistress. The rector remembered a girl who matched her description leaving the Abbey at the end of the service, but after that the trail had gone cold.

When Horrocks had bowed himself out, Brielle rose with unaccustomed difficulty from her chair and began slowly to pace the room.

'Who on earth can we turn to in this predicament? Who is likely to know where Sir Rufus would go? Who can we trust?'

There was no answer from her small audience. Suddenly she turned on Fanny.

'Sir Peregrine said that you were lying on the pavement *beyond* the Abbey. You must therefore have been walking away from the church. Why was your mistress heading in the opposite direction to her home?'

The maid swallowed hard, but did not reply.

'Come, girl, the truth, if you care anything for her.'

Fanny's voice was barely a whisper. 'She said that she had a business meeting.'

'What do you mean, a business meeting? What has business to do with Amelie? Who was this person she was meeting and why?'

Fanny saw no escape from the question. 'I don't know

why she was meeting him, milady,' she stuttered. 'Miss Amelie didn't tell me, but it was a man called Gareth Heywood.'

The name galvanised Brielle and she rushed over to the girl, and shook her violently. 'You allowed your mistress to meet that man? A man she was expressly forbidden to see?'

Sir Peregrine intervened in his quiet voice. 'I don't think we can blame Fanny, my lady. She would only have gone with her mistress to protect her.'

Fanny nodded gratefully and Sir Peregrine continued, 'I am sure she knows as little as we about this man. I have met him on a few occasions. A somewhat fierce person, I thought, but decidedly a gentleman.'

He turned to the maid. 'Where was this meeting to take place, Fanny?' he asked her gently.

'Behind the Abbey, Sir Peregrine. I was to walk around the churchyard. Miss Amelie said she would only be a few minutes.'

'Then we must go there and find this man immediately. He may know more.' Brielle was reinvigorated now that she could take some action. 'Sir Peregrine, would you be so good as to assist in this?'

With an inner sigh, Perry Latham agreed and once more hurried from the house. The day was proving unusually energetic.

# Chapter Twenty-Two

Gareth knew he should not have agreed to the stolen encounter. He had needed to tell Amelie the truth of his past, needed to be sure that she understood the full wickedness that was Glyde. But once she had heard his story, he had vowed that he would bid her a final goodbye. Why had he been unable to keep that vow?

Ever since he'd met her, he had been acting irrationally. How could a slip of a girl do that to him? He had never felt love for a woman, but that had been no hardship. Exiled from home and country, he had been swift to put on an armour of indifference. And an unsettled existence roaming Europe demanded nothing emotionally. But then Amelie had erupted into his life. The minute he had seen her pirouetting uncertainly above him on that ridiculous rope, he had felt drawn to her. He had been drunk, but not so drunk that he hadn't realized the pearl he had stumbled on.

Since then he had fought a constant battle with himself. Over and over again he had argued the stupidity of a serious involvement with any woman, least of all with this green girl, and by dint of concentrating on her deceptions, her lies, he had thought he had managed to keep her from invading his heart. But it seemed that the heart wasn't interested in this tired ploy; it had its own ways to follow.

Sitting close in that musty cab, watching her beautiful face alight with happiness, and feeling those soft curls against his cheek, he had been overwhelmed not only with desire, but something deeper. He had been unable to resist the urge to hold her, to caress and be caressed, to give himself to her body and soul. To take with him that one moment of love – yes, love. He had been crazy; it should not have happened.

Yet here he was, arrived early at their meeting place, and foolishly longing for the moment when he would see her again. This time, though, there must be no repeat of yesterday's lovemaking. He could never offer her the marriage she deserved. Even as the rightful earl, the taint of scandal would follow him wherever he walked and he could not bear to expose her to the venom of a spiteful society. She would say she cared nothing for her peers' judgement, but in time she would come to. They were destined always to walk different paths. His bags lay half-packed at Lucas's house: that was his future. Hers was the sensible marriage and no doubt Sir Peregrine Latham was being groomed at this moment for the role of husband. As for Rufus Glyde, he would cease to be a threat once Amelie's engagement to another was announced.

He made himself as inconspicuous as possible while he waited for the end of the service. The patch of grass where he loitered was shaded by overhanging trees from the churchyard and he was able to watch people coming and going without himself being seen. For some time there was little activity, but then the Abbey bells rang out and churchgoers began to saunter past in twos and threes. He felt a rising impatience. He tried to remind himself that they had only a few hours left to them, but all he could think of was forbidden delights: to touch her, smell her, taste her again.

Time moved on and still Amelie did not come. He began to wonder if she were unwell or perhaps had been forcibly stopped from keeping the appointment. Perhaps her grandmother had discovered their intended meeting and kept her at home. The minutes ticked by. Surely, though, she would have sent an emissary to tell him if she had been prevented from coming. That maid of hers, Fanny, was a devoted servant. She would have found a way of slipping out of the house and letting him know what had happened.

He stopped his pacing for a moment. She might have decided not to come. She might have thought better of it. In the fervour of their encounter yesterday she had appeared to believe his account of that night at Watier's. But when he recalled their conversation word for word, he realised that she had never actually committed herself. When he had asked her if she believed him, she had pushed the question to one side. What if she'd had second thoughts in the quiet of her own room? Perhaps she was unsure that this was finally the truth. After all, he had consistently lied to her or at least avoided being honest. She might imagine that this story was yet another deception. She might think that the heat of the moment had misled her and, now in the coldness of a new day, she would doubt. And doubting, she would not come.

Or perhaps this had always been her plan. The monstrous thought struck him off balance, apprehension turning to anger. She had never any intention of meeting him today. She had meant him to wait fruitlessly. She had enjoyed the physical pleasure he offered but she didn't trust him. She didn't love him. He was the deceiver and always would be. This was her final riposte: she would be the one to practice the last deception.

That was the explanation, he was sure now. Why had he ever imagined otherwise? Amelie Milverton was no different from any other woman he had ever met. They had shared a fleeting passion and that was all. He turned to go, disgusted with himself that even for a short time he had thought he could know love. As he walked towards the corner of the street, a familiar figure came into view. Peregrine Latham, her chosen go-between, he thought bitterly.

Perry Latham raised his hat and looked uncertainly at the glowering man in front of him. 'Mr Heywood, do excuse me for accosting you in this fashion,' he began with a worried look on his face, 'but would you be so good as to accompany me to the house of Lady St Clair.'

'Why on earth should I?' Gareth asked belligerently.

'Her ladyship is most anxious to speak to you.' Perry employed his most placating manner.

'But I am not anxious to speak to her ladyship. I have nothing to say to her.' Not only was he to be made a fool of by his false love, but he was to receive a raking-down from her grandmother.

Perry tried again. 'Lady St Clair is most worried about her granddaughter and feels that you may be able to help. I hope you will reconsider your decision.'

'Worried – why is she worried?' Gareth was seized with sudden foreboding.

Sir Peregrine answered repressively. 'That is something I cannot discuss in the street. If you will be so good as to accompany me, we can speak of the matter in private.'

'Has something happened to Amelie?'

'If you would come with me, Mr Heywood?'

'What's happened to Amelie?' Gareth rasped out, grabbing the other man by the coat lapels and nearly lifting him off his feet.

'I beg you, sir,' Perry gasped, 'let me go. All will be explained.'

Gareth reluctantly released his hold. All thoughts of Amelie's supposed treachery fled from his mind. She was in trouble and he must get to her.

Brielle looked long at the man who was ushered into her drawing room. He was lean and tanned and his dark hair fell carelessly over eyes that were as blue as a summer sky. At the moment they were blazing with a mixture of anger and alarm. As a woman Brielle could appreciate why her granddaughter had proved so wayward, but as a grandmother she recognised danger when she saw it. This man had no time for social niceties, she could tell – he was a soldier of fortune, a vagabond.

She wore her most haughty expression, but Gareth

met her with an equal disdain. Neither might care for the other, but both were united in their desperate concern for Amelie.

'What do you know of Rufus Glyde?' she began.

'He is a villain,' Gareth replied shortly.

'You are entitled to your opinion,' Brielle conceded, even now finding it difficult to accept that she had been so badly mistaken in the man. 'But I meant – what do you know of his habits? Where might he go if he left Bath suddenly?'

'What is this about? I am here because something has happened to Amelie, not to discuss a blackguard such as Glyde. If she is in trouble, I need to know.'

It was Perry Latham who once again intervened at a difficult moment. 'We very much fear that Miss Milverton has been abducted, and possibly by this man Glyde.'

'What!' Gareth's voice exploded in their ears. 'And you are sitting here doing nothing!'

Sir Peregrine glanced anxiously at Brielle, but she remained sitting bolt upright, her lips firmly compressed. 'Her ladyship hoped that you might know where this man could have taken her,' Perry explained tentatively.

Gareth regained something of his calm. Now was not the time for outrage. He needed to be in control of himself, to think rationally and to think fast.

'Glyde has a country estate some thirty miles from Bath,' he said curtly. 'That would seem a likely destination. Do you know what he was driving?'

'Fanny described a coach and pair.'

'Hardly designed for a lengthy journey, so I doubt he

has decided to leave the county.'

For the first time Brielle looked directly at Gareth. Her voice shook very slightly. 'Do you have any idea of why he should do such a dreadful thing?'

'His threats against Amelie have failed. Your granddaughter is a spirited woman – intolerable to a man like Glyde. My guess would be that his abduction is a way of punishing her and making sure he wins any contest of wills.'

Brielle suddenly looked a very old lady and Gareth felt a stirring of compassion. 'I will find her,' he promised, and his voice held absolute conviction. 'I'll travel on horseback – that way I can ride cross-country and get there quicker. Time will be of the essence.'

Brielle nodded, her face a study of wretchedness, understanding his meaning only too well. She came forwards and shook his hand. 'Mr Heywood, if you can rescue this dear child I will be for ever in your debt.'

'I have no need of gratitude, my lady. I do this as much for me as for you.'

He walked swiftly to the door and was gone. Sir Peregrine, who had been hovering by the window, felt it an opportune moment to escape. He preferred his dramas to be safely confined within the covers of a book.

Left alone, Brielle sank into her chair, exhausted and sick with fear. She had believed Gareth Heywood when he'd pledged himself to find Amelie. Despite what she knew of his reputation, she had trusted him. But he did not know the local country well and he was just one man. It was clear that Glyde had hired a team of thugs to do his bidding.

What if Gareth never found Amelie or, having found her, was overpowered, which seemed more than likely? She could not bear to contemplate what might happen to her beloved girl. And she, Brielle, would be responsible. She had promoted the pretensions of a man who had turned out to be a scoundrel. How could she have fallen into such gross error? She had always felt pride in her judgement, but now she would never trust herself again. And Amelie, all the time in this very house, fearful and alone, not daring to tell her grandmother of the threats against her. The tears began to trickle down Brielle's cheeks and she put her head in her hands and sobbed.

She was not allowed to indulge her grief for long. A diplomatic tap on the door by Horrocks heralded another visitor, and one who could not have been less welcome.

'Lord Miles Milverton, milady,' the butler announced.

'How good to see you, Brielle.' Lord Milverton's hearty voice sundered what little peace was left. He seemed to fill her dainty drawing room with his presence and she was forced to her feet, offering him a feeble smile as he came towards her.

'Miles, what a surprise! Whatever brings you to Bath?' she asked somewhat inanely.

He looked nonplussed for a moment. 'Amelie, of course. My daughter? I need to see her. She is here, I take it?'

Brielle made a brave attempt to mask her discomfort. 'I hope to see her soon,' she extemporised.

'When exactly?' She thought he sounded agitated and wondered why. 'I have urgent business with her. I have been travelling since dawn to get here.'

Brielle looked closely at her son-in-law and saw that he was looking tired and travel stained.

'I'm so sorry, Miles. You must be dreadfully fatigued. Where are my brains wandering?' She rang the bell. 'Horrocks will bring refreshments and I will have a room made up immediately.'

'Yes, yes,' he said testily, 'but Amelie. When will she be back?'

'Why is it so urgent to see her?' Brielle parried.

It was his turn now to look uncomfortable. He shifted uneasily on his feet and fixed his gaze on the far wall. 'You might as well know, Brielle, I have been a damned fool. The man I was intent on her marrying has turned out to be a complete blackguard.'

'Sir Rufus Glyde?'

'Yes, Rufus Glyde. The man is a very devil. He has deliberately set out to ruin this family!'

Sir Miles began pacing jerkily up and down the room, evidently labouring under a great upswell of emotion. Hoping to calm the situation, Brielle gestured to him to sit down beside her.

'He started with Robert, you know,' he blurted out. Then tried to compose his voice. 'It was gradual, drawing him into gambling well beyond his means. Truth to tell, the boy needed little encouragement, but until he met Glyde the sums he wagered were within reason. Since then he has become more and more reckless. I have had to sell just about every piece of property we have ever owned to cover the boy's debts. The last straw was the mortgage on Grosvenor Square.'

Brielle said nothing, but took his hand. His face was one of utter defeat. 'I believed in Glyde,' he continued. 'I thought that if he married Amelie, the family would be saved. And she would have a secure future.'

'And now?'

'Robert came to me late last night. For once he wasn't drunk and he hadn't been gambling. He told me a dreadful tale. A young friend of his had blown his brains out. Just twenty-two. Such a tragic waste. He owed money to Glyde and Glyde was threatening to foreclose on his parents' property.'

Brielle could not speak. This was the monster who had taken Amelie. She hoped desperately that the story was false or at least exaggerated.

'Could there have been any mistake?'

'No mistake, I'm afraid. Robert said that as soon as the suicide became known, half a dozen other young men came forward with similar stories. They had gambled with Glyde, lost heavily and been encouraged to pledge more and more until they were ruined. Glyde would make sure they paid up – his threats were taken seriously.'

'And nobody realised what was happening?'

'Not until now. The young men – boys really – were reluctant to publish their troubles.'

'How dreadful,' Brielle said faintly.

'Dreadful indeed. It was the shock of losing his friend that gave Robert the courage to tell me just how badly things have gone with him. And it is worse than I knew. There is nothing I can do about the money or the estate – the Milvertons are ruined. But I can prevent another of my children becoming Glyde's victim.'

Miles opened his arms as if to plead for absolution. 'I have been so stupid. I knew that Glyde had followed Amelie to Bath and I hoped she would get to know him better here and be more willing to contemplate marriage to him. That's why I left her with you.'

'It didn't make her any more willing. She hated Glyde and has continued to hate him despite every effort he has made to attract her.'

'Thank God for that.'

'Don't be too thankful.' Brielle was finding it almost impossible to speak. 'I fear that Sir Rufus Glyde has lived up to his reputation.'

'What do you mean?'

'I hardly know how to tell you. Glyde has abducted Amelie.'

'Abducted!' Miles Milverton's voice reverberated around the room, making the crystal decanters on the sideboard tremble.

'If you please, Miles, we must be as calm as we can.'

'Calm! How can I stay calm when you tell me my own daughter has been abducted and by this out and out villain? When did this dreadful thing happen?'

'This morning. Amelie attended the lunchtime service at the Abbey and Glyde's men swooped on her as she walked away from the church.'

'And what has been done to get her back? Has Bow Street been alerted?' His face had turned a bright red and he once more began furiously to pace the carpet.

'You really must seek to compose yourself, Miles, or you

will become ill. I am trying to find Glyde privately. Calling in the Runners would lead to a scandal that neither of us would want.'

'But how are you trying to find her?' Miles pulled his usually sleek silver hair into something resembling a haystack. 'Can you trust the servants you have sent?'

'I haven't sent servants. A man called Gareth Heywood has gone. He knows where Glyde's country estate is situated. He is a friend of Amelie's.' She passed over this quickly, hoping he would not enquire too deeply.

'I have never heard of him. What do you know of this man?'

'Little except that Amelie trusts him and he is intent on finding Glyde and bringing her safely home.'

'And meanwhile we are to sit here and wait like clunches.'

'What else do you suggest we do?' his mother-in-law asked, an irascible edge to her voice. Her nerves were overwrought and the constant effort of appearing self-possessed was beginning to take its toll.

Miles pulled himself together. 'You are right. It would not be sensible to career around the countryside looking for this wretch. We can only pray that this Heywood fellow runs him to ground. If he rescues my girl, he will have deserved the highest reward – though God knows I have nothing left to give him.'

Brielle thought otherwise, but decided to keep her counsel.

## Chapter Twenty-Three

It seemed as though she were emerging from a pitch-black tunnel. The echo of far-off sounds filled her ears, but she could see nothing. A suffocating darkness enclosed her and her breath came in short, sharp gasps.

Now the tunnel was expanding and the darkness was not so opaque. There seemed to be a slight chink of light in the distance. She opened her eyes a fraction and pain arrowed through her head. In response, her eyelids quickly shut and she drifted back into a black haze.

When she tried to look again, she was sure that she could see sunlight. Her head was heavy and throbbing and seemed detached from the rest of her limbs. Minutes ticked by and gradually her body began to come back to life. She stretched out her hands and realised that she was lying on a bed. A shaft of light lay brightly across the faded counterpane. Cautiously she turned her head and saw the sun streaming through dusty, mullioned windows. She turned her head in the other direction and this time the shape of a door swam into her vision. She felt wretchedly sick.

There was a bitter taste filling her mouth, which she couldn't understand. Her throat felt raw. She puzzled over this for some time and gradually her mind began to recall incidents, voices, actions. She tried desperately to focus her wandering thoughts, to piece together fragments of memory. She had been in a coach she remembered and her arm was hurting badly. She had been in a coach, against her will – yes, that was it. Someone had thrown her into the coach and she had hurt her arm. A large rough hand was covering her mouth. She had struggled, she had bitten that hand and freed herself. But not for long. Her head was being jerked back. What then? A hot evil-tasting liquid was forced between her lips – she had been drugged! Two men there had been, nasty and brutish. She had recognised one of them from somewhere. And Fanny had cried out. Fanny, where was Fanny?

And where was she? Gingerly she tried to raise herself into a sitting position, but instantly fell back onto the bed. The walls were moving in disturbing circles. After a while she tried again and saw that she was in a large room, wainscoted with dark oak panelling. Heavy Jacobean furniture filled the chamber, sombre and intricately carved. The bed she lay on was massive, the bedstead as black as jet. Leaded windows filled the entire side of a wall, diamond-shaped panes giving on to tall trees which swayed in the wind. Their branches scratched against the glass. She was in an old house and in the countryside, but whose house and where remained a mystery.

She lay back on the pillow and tried to concentrate, but it wasn't easy. Waves of nausea constantly engulfed her. She had been with Fanny, she remembered. They had been walking along the pavement, just past the Abbey. They had been to Sunday service and were going to... meet Gareth, she finished in a rush. She had been going to meet Gareth when two men had jumped down from the coach she'd seen earlier, scooped her up and thrown her into the carriage and driven off at high speed. She had struggled, but it was hopeless. She had been forced to swallow the drugged liquid and she'd known no more. Until now.

She sat up groggily, then very slowly swung her feet to the ground. So far, so good. She tried to stand, holding on to the bed for support, but was forced to sit down again as the floor spiralled up to meet her. Allowing herself a short rest, she once again tried to stand. She had to get out of this house, wherever it was. She had to get back to Bath and find Gareth.

He would think she had failed their appointment, that she was no truer than any other woman he had met. He would decide very soon that he was wasting his time. His eyes spoke a depth of feeling that took her breath away, but she knew that if he thought himself rejected, he would cut his losses there and then and start on his journey. She had to get to him before he left Bath.

Dragging herself up to a standing position, she shuffled very slowly to the door. She tugged at the handle, a huge plaited-iron circle, but the door did not budge. Even more slowly she inched her way in the other direction towards the windows. Looking through their dusty panes, she saw that she had been right: she was in the countryside. Rolling hills were the backdrop for what appeared to be a neglected park. The grass almost reached the window sill and ragged bushes ranged far into the distance. The room had an air of neglect and the gardens were no better.

If she could just open one of the windows, she might be able to climb over the sill. She fumbled with the latch, but it was stiff with rust and appeared to be jammed. As she struggled with it, the door of the room opened. She turned quickly, too quickly. Head spinning, she clung to the window seat to prevent herself from falling. She looked at the man framed in the doorway. She had always known who it would be. Rufus Glyde. It could be no other.

'I am delighted to see you on your feet, my dear. You have a strong constitution, which is most gratifying.' In the gloom of the doorway, his thin mouth was like a knife slash across the white face.

She tried to speak with authority, but her mouth was dry and her voice came out in a hoarse whisper. 'You are a villian, sir, to serve me thus.'

'A villain? Quite possibly, although I have been called worse.'

'You have drugged me, kidnapped me and now I am imprisoned.'

'Yes all those things. But it will get better, I promise.' His thin face broke into a mirthless smile.

'Let me go immediately.' Her voice was stronger and it gave her courage.

'I don't think so. At least not immediately. What would be the point of all the hard work in bringing you here? There is some business outstanding between us and we must first attend to that.'

'What possible purpose can you have in locking me up here?'

'I warned you, did I not, that you would bend to my will?' The ice in his voice cut through any small hope she had. 'My purpose is to ensure that you do just that. Really it's quite simple.'

'And what is your will?'

'I think you know very well, Miss Milverton. By the way, do tell me when you think I may call you Amelie. Miss Milverton is a trifle formal, I feel, for what lies ahead of us.'

'If you are referring to marriage, you must surely know that I will never agree.'

'Indeed I do.' He sighed with tedium. 'However, I regret that I must disappoint you. I find I am no longer desirous of marrying – at least not just yet.'

'Then why am I here?'

'So that we can become more closely acquainted. What else? And what better place to get to know each other intimately? No one lives within ten miles of this house and there is no staff to speak of. Only your two gallant companions of the coach and they, of course, do my bidding like the faithful dogs they are. We shall be completely alone. Won't that be pleasant? Just the two of us, getting to know each other.'

As he spoke, her face had grown even paler. He seemed to notice. 'You must not despair, Miss Milverton. Not entirely. I may still discuss marriage at a later date. We shall have to see how you please me.'

When she said nothing, his voice became harsh and peremptory. 'And you *will* please me, you know. You are completely at my disposal.'

She sank back on to the window seat. Her body was

weak, but her mind was racing. Let him but go and she would try the window once more. Ten miles was a long way, but if she could once reach the road, she might garner help from a passing traveller.

He seemed to know exactly what she was thinking. 'I do hope you will not try to escape. It would be so tiresome. As you have already discovered, the windows are bolted and the door securely fastened. You will remain locked in this room and whenever you leave it, for whatever purpose, you will be accompanied. I shall leave you now. You will find hot water by the dressing table and fresh apparel in the wardrobe. I wish you to wear the dress I have selected for you.'

Despite her weakness, Amelie felt her temper rising. 'My own clothes are sufficient, I thank you.'

'Evidently I did not make myself clear. You will do as I command. Your own clothes are no longer fit to be seen.' And he gestured with distaste at her dusty skirt and torn bodice.

'And who is responsible for that?' she demanded angrily. 'The men you employ are thugs.'

'Regrettably so, but very efficient, would you not say? I am sure you will find the clothes I have provided more than ample recompense. You will put them on and wait to be fetched for dinner.'

Her heart lurched. Might this provide her with an opportunity for escape? The relentless voice told her otherwise.

'So far you have been treated with restraint, but if you should attempt to escape or resist in any way, you will be bound closely. Do I make myself understood?' He strode out of the room, banging the door behind him, the iron key grating noisily in the lock.

For a long time she sat looking into nothingness. She would not weep. That was wasted energy. And she would not think of the threats Glyde had made. More wasted energy. Instead, she must concentrate her mind on flight. Somehow she must find a way to escape this evil man. But looking at the locked door and bolted windows, her spirits faltered. The sun that had been shining earlier had now disappeared over the horizon. Cold shadows had stolen into the room and their gloom found a cheerless echo in her heart.

Once he had left Brielle's house, Gareth moved rapidly. He went first to the livery stables and ordered them to saddle their fastest mare as quickly as possible. His tone sent the usually sleepy ostlers scurrying to do his behest. From the livery stables he hurriedly retraced his steps along the main thoroughfare towards the Averys' house. The family was visiting friends and he was relieved to find only the servants at home. No time would be lost trying to explain the situation. He dashed off a brief note to his friend and left it with the footman to give to Lucas immediately he returned. Then up to the bedroom two stairs at a time and a rapid change into riding breeches and top-boots, headlong down the staircase once more and quickly back to the stables.

The head lad was fastening the last buckles on the harness as Gareth walked through the gate. Minerva stood waiting, her legs twitching with anticipation and her head jerking up and down as if to shake off the bridle and be gone. He was in the saddle and away within minutes.

The location of Guestling Manor, Glyde's country estate, was already known to him. Just last night, Lucas had related the latest *on-dit* from town, now going the rounds of Bath. It was said that Sir Rufus Glyde's affairs were not flourishing and he would very soon be putting his country estate up for sale. It was generally held that he would be lucky to find a purchaser. The mansion was old and dilapidated and its surrounding park untamed. It would require a mountain of money to make any improvement and was, in any case, not large enough for the needs of a gentleman and his family. It was large enough to conceal a prisoner though, Gareth thought grimly.

He was soon out of Bath and making for the country roads beyond. Almost immediately Minerva fell into an easy stride, devouring the miles seemingly without effort. But Gareth did not relax for they had far to travel and the time was short. The image of Amelie, bewildered and frightened and in Glyde's power, tormented him and he was tempted to spur the horse forward in a headlong gallop. But he knew he had to save her strength for the cross-country riding, which would soon be upon them. He felt the mare trembling with excitement, eager to speed like the wind, but reined her in and forced her to maintain a slower pace. The hedgerows were ablaze with pale gold honeysuckle and the scarlet of poppies newly opened, but he saw none of it.

Amelie was the picture that filled his mind. He knew she would fight with every breath in her body, but how successfully could she defend herself, a vulnerable girl held prisoner in a hostile place? He could only guess what Glyde intended towards her and none of it was good. Brielle's mention of that scoundrel's name had sent his mind blazing, hot enough to set her drawing room on fire. He had been overwhelmed with the need to choke the life out of a man who sowed wickedness wherever he went. Such bloodthirsty ferocity was new to him. As a youth, wandering Europe friendless and penniless, he would have given his soul to wreak revenge on the man he suspected had authored his downfall. But he had lacked the power to do so; all his energy and ingenuity had been employed in simply keeping alive.

His situation today was very different and he might have avenged his injuries any time since he returned to England. Yet he had not done so. He had not wanted to soil his sword on such a contemptible creature, but in truth he no longer cared enough. He was sure it was Glyde who had sent him into exile, but it was exile from a society he despised. Sure that Glyde was responsible for severing the ties to his family, but his grandfather had proved cold and unforgiving. Was avenging such wrongs worth more scandal and possible death? He had considered not. But now it was no longer just about him. It was about a girl who had lodged herself deep within his heart. His face hardened as he considered the revenge he would exact.

And he would exact revenge. He had insisted to Lucas that he knew nothing of love, unwilling to acknowledge the powerful emotions Amelie had stirred in him from the very beginning. It had been easier to concentrate on her shortcomings. He had pretended to himself that all they shared was a physical passion that would burn itself out as quickly as it had ignited. But if he'd ever doubted that he knew the true meaning of love, it had been put to flight the instant he'd realised she was in such desperate peril.

He would rescue her or die in the attempt. He would bring her safely back to Bath and to those who should have the greatest care of her. She would, she must, find happiness in a match deemed suitable by her family and for all his title and wealth, that could never be him. It was ironic that after all the years of uncaring liaisons with women of the *demi-monde*, he should have fallen in love with a virtuous daughter of *ton* society. He'd had a taste of that society as he'd stood in the doorway of Watier's salon. He would not be ignored – his inheritance would make sure of that – but he would attract the worst kind of attention. For himself, it mattered not a fig, but for Amelie... Confronted by the whispers, the nudges, the nuanced glances, she would die a thousand deaths. She would trust him to defend her and he would be unable. He loved her too much to submit her to that. No, she was destined to be another man's bride and when he found her it would be to say a last farewell.

His mind thus occupied, he rode onwards, hardly conscious of time passing. The going was easy at this stage, the country lane soft underfoot. For the first hour, he made excellent time but just outside the village of Marksbury he received a check. Precious minutes were wasted at the toll where the keeper had absented himself. Gareth was forced to bribe a small boy to go and find him. After what seemed a lifetime, the guardian of the tollgate returned very much the worse for drink and was only persuaded to allow Gareth through by another hefty bribe. It was fortunate that only that morning he had withdrawn a large sum of money in anticipation of his journey to France.

The experience of Marksbury decided him to avoid the toll roads and begin to travel cross-country where possible. The young boy had described a short cut through Witham Woods, which lay ahead and to one side, its eastern border running parallel to the toll road. The morning's dark clouds had gradually cleared and the day become hot, but the woods were blissfully cool. Strong branches reached skywards, interlocking overhead to form a shadowy vault, hardly pierced by the sun. The mare showed her appreciation of this welcome change of temperature by a willingness to pick up speed once more, but Gareth again reined her in. The forest floor was uneven; dead branches were strewn here and there and tree roots erupted haphazardly through the soil. The path, pleasant though it was, meant potential danger. Whatever happened he had to keep the horse in good shape.

From Witham Woods he took the path which skirted the southern end of a lake. Once past this large expanse of water, the countryside opened up and he could at last allow the horse an unrestrained gallop. Pounding over the soft turf, he made up the minutes that he had forfeited earlier. And even when open country was left behind, he continued to make good time, speeding through leafy lanes and along rough tracks. Candlelight began to appear in the few lonely cottages he passed, but still he travelled on, never slackening his pace.

The sun's last rays had created shaded folds in the patchwork of surrounding hills. It was a beautiful sight and a beautiful evening, breezy but warm, and the pink tinged clouds that streaked a wide sky promised another fine day on the morrow. But he was too anxious to care much for nature. A dilapidated signpost had warned him that the manor house was still some five miles distant. He had to get there before nightfall. A moon, now gently climbing the sky, offered little help, its light diffused and pallid behind the scudding clouds. The thought of Amelie in Glyde's power as night closed in was unbearable. Once more he spurred Minerva onwards, whispering in her ear to make one last effort. She whinnied softly in response, and though her breath was beginning to come short and fast, she redoubled her pace. They were back now in open countryside and leaning low over her neck, he urged her to a last gallop. The miles once again flashed by. The mare was almost spent when the rusting iron gates of Guestling Manor at last came into view. They were locked and barred, but an overgrown screen of dark ilex surrounded the property. Gareth sidled the horse along the hedge and very soon found a small gap. He pushed the mare through and prayed he was not too late.

## Chapter Twenty-Four

Reluctantly, Amelie took the gown from the wardrobe. It was an elaborately embroidered silk gauze and the diaphanous folds billowed over her arms. A very expensive dress, she thought, its amber sheen lustrous and its beadwork intricate. But when she slipped it over her head and viewed herself in the tarnished mirror, she hated what she saw. The sheer material and the low cut neckline made her feel horribly exposed and she looked in vain for a handkerchief to cover her naked skin above the plunging bodice. Eventually she tugged a faded cloth from the small table which stood nearby, and fastened it around her shoulders. It made her feel considerably braver. The shoes she was forced to wear were as flimsy as the dress, and would surely make any chance of escape impossible. She saw with satisfaction that her face was chalk-white and made even paler by the deep gold of the gown. Her hair was left tumbled and unkempt. She aimed to be the least attractive of dinner companions.

She had only just finished dressing when the ancient lock once more ground into action and one of her erstwhile captors stood on the threshold.

'Come with me,' he ordered abruptly, seizing her by the arm.

She found herself dragged out of the room and along a maze of flagged passages. Small, cell-like doors dotted the stone walls, but appeared to lead nowhere. There was no other sign of human life. They seemed to walk for ever, the man striding ahead and pulling her roughly behind him. It took all her strength to remain on her feet. She had completely lost her bearings by the time they arrived at a door that was more imposing and less dilapidated than the rest. The man's knock was discreet, a surprise given his general brutishness. But she imagined that Glyde was an unpleasant master and his hired hand would want to stay as inconspicuous as possible.

'Come!' The thin tone rose clear in the air and she shivered. She could never hear Glyde's voice without feeling an upsurge of disgust.

She was pushed unceremoniously into the room and the door locked behind her. The furnishings here were slightly more comfortable, but the room still bore all the signs of prolonged neglect. The brocade curtains, once a deep sapphire, now hung greyly at spotted windows, their fraying material incubating layers of dust. The *chaise longue* below the window had lost most of its gold embellishment and the two wing chairs which guarded either side of the fireplace had sunken seats and stained coverlets. Someone had attempted to polish the large rectangular table that dominated the middle of the room. Its surface reflected the light of a wrought-iron chandelier hanging above, also newly cleaned, it seemed. The table was set for two.

Glyde was lolling at his ease in one of the massive carved chairs drawn up to the table, but as she stood wavering in the doorway, he rose in a leisurely fashion and moved towards her. With a twitch of his hand he tore the material from around her shoulders and cast it on the floor.

'Allow me to see what my very considerable efforts have purchased.' The familiar sneer made her clench her fists. If only she were strong enough to use them.

For what seemed minutes on end, he stared at her, his sulphurous eyes undressing her inch by inch. She could do nothing but stand and endure his gaze. Then reluctantly he stepped back, waving a negligent hand at her to take a seat.

'Come to the table. You must be hungry after the exertions of the day.'

She had never felt less like eating, but she feared that he would return to her side if she did not obey. She could not bear him anywhere near. She moved slowly towards the end of the table and sat down. Glyde had evidently been drinking while he waited. His face was already slightly mottled and drops of red wine stained the frilled white shirt he wore beneath a suit of rich ruby velvet. He saw the direction of her glance.

'Don't worry, my dear. I have merely been filling in time until you got here. No more wine this evening – at least not for me. *I* need no Dutch courage.' He smirked unpleasantly. 'But allow me to pour *you* some. You will undoubtedly find it beneficial. Such an excellent relaxant.'

'I thank you, no.'

'You will drink some wine. It is my wish.'

He said it with a finality that suffered no dissent. Before

she had time to realise what was happening, he was at her shoulder and filling her glass to the brim.

'Now drink,' he ordered.

She did as she was told, but tried to sip as small an amount as possible. Satisfied that he was being obeyed, he resumed his chair and reached for the tattered bell pull. Its noisy clang echoed through the passageways beyond. Almost immediately, the man who had brought her to the room appeared in the doorway. He carried large bowls of soup and was followed by his companion bearing the remaining entrées. He was the man identified so accurately by Fanny, the man with the crooked teeth.

'This is most enjoyable,' Glyde murmured expansively, supping from the bowl in front of him. 'The moment has been so very long in coming. But triumph is even sweeter when it is hard won.'

She made no answer, but played with her spoon, pretending to consume the soup while in reality watchful and alert, hoping for a chance to escape. She had noted that this time the door behind her had not been locked. It was possible that Glyde's two henchmen were lurking just beyond, but she reasoned they would have to return to the distant kitchen after each course to collect the next serving. For a few minutes at least the door would be unguarded. If only she had not been forced to wear these stupid shoes! Perhaps she could slip them off under the table without being noticed. She hoped Glyde might forget his vow and begin drinking again. She needed him torpid and lacking in vigilance.

When the next course arrived, though, it was brought

by just one man. Where was his companion? She could not be sure and if she made a dash for the door and he was on the other side, she would have lost any chance of escape. Her fate would almost certainly be another drugging, only this time when she awoke she would find herself securely bound.

Serving followed serving and there was never more than one man in the room at any time. She felt bitterly disappointed.

Glyde read her mind with uncanny ease. 'Escape is impossible. Resign yourself to the inevitable, my dear, and enjoy the evening. For my part I can assure you that many hours of pleasure lie ahead.' He leaned hungrily across the table, but almost immediately recovered himself and continued smoothly, 'The food, for instance, is in a class of its own. Not cooked, of course, by the clods who have served it, but produced by the finest chef that money can buy.'

She wondered, but only for a moment, whether the chef was still on the premises and, if so, whether she could appeal to him for help. 'Naturally he is no longer with us.' Glyde had read her mind once more. 'There is just Amer and Figgis - they do have names, you see - and myself. A cosy little foursome, do you not think? Though naturally Amer and Figgis will be absenting themselves very shortly.'

She tried to eat slowly and delay each round of food as it came to the table. He saw through the ploy immediately. 'I have all the time in the world, Miss Milverton. Do please savour your food. I like that in a woman. It suggests appetite.'

She continued to eat at the same pace, trying to maintain an air of indifference. All the time he watched her intently, the thin gash of his mouth fixed in a mocking smile. 'The longer the meal, the greater the anticipation and the more satisfying the finale. Do you not agree?'

All too soon the fruit was removed and coffee served. She was allowed to decline the liqueur, which Glyde tossed off in a single gulp. He nodded sharply at his two henchmen, who were clearing the last vestiges of the meal, and they disappeared promptly. The occasional noises emanating from the passage gradually ceased.

Glyde strolled to the door and turned the heavy rusting key. He returned to his chair and leaned back, the same mocking smile on his face. She cast around for ways of deflecting him, anything which would win her freedom.

'Sir Rufus,' she ventured, 'my grandmother is a wealthy woman. She would come to an accommodation with you – you have only to say the word.'

His expression was one of incredulity. 'You foolish chit, I do not desire money. Money is mine whenever I wish,' he boasted. 'What I require is a far rarer prize, as you well know. Spare me the playacting. After all, you are hardly an innocent.'

'You have been misinformed. I am a virtuous woman.'

He scanned her cynically. 'As you wish, my dear. Your recent conduct would suggest otherwise. The man in question is fortunate to be many miles away, else I would have ordered his disposal. Chastity is not a requirement of mine – virginal pleasures in my experience are much overrated – but when I make a woman mine, that is how she will stay.'

He gestured to her. 'Come here to me, Amelie.'

She made no move.

'Now,' he barked, 'unless you wish me to come and drag you here.'

She got up and walked with as much dignity as she could summon to stand in front of him. He pulled her down on to his lap, his eyes devouring her greedily.

'You are very beautiful and you are mine – mine as and when I desire. You will stay with me here until I have finished with you. If you entertain me well, I may consider renewing my proposal of marriage.'

One hand fitted itself around her waist while the other stroked her hair. She was overcome with nausea and fervently hoped that she might be sick over him.

'However, if you do not please me, you will be sent back to your family,' he continued impassively. 'They may do as they wish with you though their options will be severely limited. Damaged goods are so difficult to sell. And the family home will be no more. I will be forced to foreclose on the mortgage. Dear, dear, let us hope that it will not come to that.'

She was dazed by his depravity. Her body was rigid, withdrawn into itself in a desperate attempt to avoid contamination, while he held her tightly against his chest. He began stroking the inside of her arm and crooning to himself. It was too much. She leapt to her feet and ran across the room to the window.

'Of course, I must not forget how young you are.' His jeering voice followed her. 'Naturally you wish for more excitement. I am only too willing to oblige.'

And he was there beside her, grabbing her around the

waist again, only this time managing to encircle her whole body with his arms and pulling her tight against him. His shirt smelt of wine and his breath on her bare skin was noxious. She tried to escape his grasp, but this only caused him to tighten it still further.

His right arm imprisoned her, holding her so that her face was buried in his chest and she could hardly breathe. With the other hand he began caressing the soft cream of her shoulders. She cried out in disgust, but this seemed only to excite him further. He pulled at her dress trying to untie the ribbons single-handed. Taking advantage of his preoccupation, she managed to tear herself away. But not for long. He came after her immediately.

This time she had fled to the corner of the room nearest the door in a vain attempt to effect an escape. But there was no help from that quarter – the door was impenetrable. She was fighting for breath and knew she would not be able to hold off her abductor for much longer. A vision of Gareth, sparkling eyes and warm smile, sprang improbably to her mind. She clung to it as though it would somehow save her. But how could that be? It was a figment, a phantom only. By now he would be well on his way to France, unknowing and perhaps uncaring of her fate.

Glyde was advancing on her once more, incensed now by her recalcitrance, and tore at her dress, exposing her breasts to view. For a moment he stood back, examining her with a salacious intensity as she cowered partly naked against the wall. Then he threw himself at her, hoisting her skirt upwards while he fumbled with his breeches. She knew that he would have no compunction. He would rape her, here in this dreadful room. She closed her eyes, trying to abstract her mind from the frightful deed that was to be perpetrated on her.

A loud crash sounded from across the room. Suddenly all was changed. There was a whirl of movement, a muttered curse from Glyde, and she was left alone, her hands trembling and scrabbling to cover her nakedness. An intruder had smashed his way through one of the leaded windows and stood brandishing two swords. One he retained in his right hand while the other he threw to Glyde, who caught it awkwardly. The man waited for his adversary to regain his balance. Glyde, deliberately ignoring the courtesy of touching swords, lunged without warning at the stranger, attempting to catch him off guard while the man's eyes were still adjusting to the lighted room. In response the intruder cut the chandelier cord and brought it tumbling down on to the table, the small crystals tinkling eerily as they shattered. The only light was that of the moon, now floating free of its cloudy cover, and streaming through the open casement. The two men faced each other.

# Chapter Twenty-Five

Moonlight glittered through the window pane, lighting the centre of the room as though it were a stage complete with its actors. The two figures circled each other cautiously for some minutes, their swords disengaged. Then Glyde, impatient to free himself of this unwanted visitor, delivered a lightning strike. In return he was deftly parried. He lunged again and was once more countered. Over and over again he pressed forwards, often seeming to be on the point of breaking through the other man's guard, but miraculously his opponent always regained his position, meeting Glyde's blade with steel.

In one of the pools of darkness that filled the corners of the room Amelie stood, hardly daring to breathe. Her lips were parted and her eyes wide. She had recognized Gareth instantly, a phantom miraculously made flesh. He had found her! How he had done so, she had no inkling. It was enough that he was here and fighting for her life. And for his. A darting force, lithe and nimble, biding his time, waiting to make a kill. She saw his eyes glow with the primitive joy of revenge.

The fight went on, their blades clashing harshly in the

silence of the room. Glyde continued to attack fiercely, but his opponent was able to parry the blows with ease. Gradually the younger man began to gain ground, his thrusting sword pushing Glyde back farther and farther. It seemed he would pin his adversary to the wall. Then, in a sudden violent movement, Glyde gathered all his strength into the riposte and with his whole body weight lunged straight at his opponent's chest. Gareth stepped back as quickly as he could, but the blade caught him on the arm and ripped the sleeve of his shirt. A trickle of blood seeped through the white cambric and began to drip on to the floor.

Amelie's eyes closed in horror, but when she looked again she saw that Gareth had managed to steady himself. Tight-lipped and with a deep furrow scarring his brow, he had recovered his ground. He began to fight more defensively, waiting for an opportunity to occur that would enable him to snake below his enemy's guard. Sensing his advantage, Glyde continued to assail his opponent savagely, strike after strike. At any moment Amelie expected to hear the dull thud of her lover's body falling to the floor. A dozen times he might have been run through, but always he managed to block the attack, disengage his blade and return to the fray. He was tiring, though. The loss of blood was taking its toll and he was no longer as nimble on his feet nor was his swordplay as sharp as it had been. Every fresh charge from Glyde tired him further. His face had turned ashen and his breathing was laboured.

Glyde's face wore a devilish expression. Once more he drove forwards, intent on making an end of it. But with an almost superhuman effort, Gareth blocked the blow and with a supple flick of his wrist twisted his sword in a rapid half-circle and slid smoothly under his opponent's guard. Glyde's sword hand wavered and he staggered back. With a mighty slash, Gareth struck the weapon from his hand and directed the point of his own blade to the other man's throat.

'Villain, I have you.' He was breathing raggedly, but his voice shook with triumph.

In a moment he had staunched his bleeding with a tightly bound strip from his shirt sleeve. The fallen man, his face whiter than ever, snarled defiance. With the point of his sword Gareth pricked the skin of his enemy's neck and brought a pinhead of blood to the surface.

'If you wish to live, you will do as you are told.' He looked down on the prostrate figure.

'And what might that be?' Glyde spat.

'You will grovel to Miss Milverton for the pain you have inflicted and then tell her exactly what happened on the night you say I cheated at cards.'

Glyde, his head awkwardly angled away from the sword point, looked contemptuous. 'I will not grovel. Naturally as a *gentleman*, I apologise to Miss Milverton for any misunderstanding.'

Gareth's expression remained one of iron control, but his sword hand gripped the weapon ever more tightly. 'You are a cur and I would whip you if *I* were not a gentleman!'

'A somewhat besmirched gentleman, however. You will never free yourself of that particular stain, I fancy.'

The sword quivered and the gash on Glyde's neck grew redder. 'You mistake – you are about to free me from the lies I have lived with for too long.'

'How very dramatic. But hardly likely.' Glyde's smirk became more pronounced even as the wound in his neck began to bleed freely.

Gareth ignored him and continued in a voice that was icily indifferent. 'You will recount the circumstances of that evening and you will do it truly. If not, I can assure you that you will feel more than the tip of my sword.'

His implacability seemed to affect his enemy more than any show of anger. The man glared at him, his face sullen and set. 'I must first ask you to remove your weapon from my throat. It is hardly conducive to talking.'

Gareth reluctantly withdrew the point of his sword a little, but still held its position fast.

'You have it. Now talk.'

'What am I to say? It was an evening like any other. I was engaged to dine with Petersham and we wandered into the Great-Go to make up a table with the General and whoever else was in the mind for a little light gambling.'

'Hardly light, as I recall.'

'Not for a Johnny Raw, that's true. It was unfortunate for me that you and your friend Avery, such an innocent, should happen to arrive at that moment. I would have preferred a plumper bird for the plucking.'

'That was your purpose for the evening?'

'I had some debts that were becoming a little pressing.'

'And you decided to pay them by cheating those you played with.'

'Not entirely, but the cards fell badly for me that night. I really had no choice.'

'So you marked the cards?'

'A very little, just sufficiently for me to recognise the ones I needed.'

'And when it was discovered?'

'I was amazed. That old duffer Tilney spotted it. His eyesight must be a good deal sharper than his brain. Nobody else at the table had a clue. Petersham is so indolent that he hardly looks at the cards. And so disgustingly rich, that the result of a game matters nothing to him.'

'When General Tilney alerted the table to the cheating, you didn't own up.'

'Are you mad?' Glyde's voice was waspish with irritation. 'Of course I did not "own up". One would think I was some cadet on probation.'

'But you had no compunction in implicating me.' Gareth's hand quivered on his sword, but he controlled his fury and kept its point just short of Glyde's throat. He was finding that after all such gross treachery roused an incendiary rage.

'None whatsoever. Striplings who think they are old enough to play with the grown-ups get all they deserve.'

'You must have known that I had little money of my own.'

'That's what made it so perfect. I saw in a moment that you were the one who would shoulder the blame. The General was out of the question, Petersham is too rich and as for Lucas Avery, everyone knew that his trustees were liberal to the point of insanity and would pay his debts instantly. But it was also common knowledge that your esteemed grandfather kept you on a tight allowance. So who more likely to cheat than you?'

'And that was your sole reason to tarnish the name of a man you hardly knew?'

'There was an additional pleasure, I must admit. I had a score to settle with your grandfather. You settled it nicely.'

'And now? Are you still settling debts in the same way?'

'One must live and, contrary to society's opinion, I am not a wealthy man. Fortunately, there is an inexhaustible supply of callow youth. The money I have won off that fool Robert Milverton has kept me afloat for many a month.'

Amelie's eyes had grown wide with dismay, but now she looked stricken. It was bad enough that her brother had gambled so stupidly, but to know that his downfall had been deliberately plotted by this depraved man was horrifying. She could not stop herself crying out, 'You are the worst of men.'

'Indeed, and it is a great pleasure to know that I exceed in this.' His voice was gloating.

'And Miss Milverton, was she to be part of the debt?' Gareth asked savagely, thrusting the sword once more against Glyde's throat.

'We are all fools for something, are we not? She has been my one failure. I should have known she would be more trouble than she was worth. But as soon as I saw her, I meant to have her. The mortgage on Grosvenor Square was a master stroke. I had thought to make her my wife and then sell the house to provide much-needed funds. But damaged goods...'

Gareth's weapon cut into Glyde's flesh. 'You will pay for every moment of suffering you have caused her.'

'How touching,' the injured man croaked, his voice faint with pain.

Gareth ignored him and for the first time looked directly at the frightened girl standing transfixed in the corner of the room. He gave her an encouraging smile.

'Unlock the door, Amelie, and ring the bell for those ruffians to come.'

She emerged uncertainly from the shadows. 'Are you sure we should? They may overpower us.'

'Have no fear. They are as cowardly as their paymaster. I need a light and paper and ink. This black-hearted monster is about to make a full written confession, a little keepsake from our encounter this evening.'

The prostrate man recovered sufficient strength to utter a snarl. 'I will not be signing anything. My men will finish you in a second.'

But when Amer and Figgis appeared over the threshold and saw Glyde's situation, they seemed in no hurry to come to his aid. Gareth snapped out his orders, warning them to follow his commands or he would execute summary justice on both them and their master.

They scurried from the room and he looked down at his antagonist.

'Somehow I can't see them staying too long. I would guess they'll be gone from the house as soon as they can make their escape.'

In a few minutes the men returned, bringing with them the items Gareth had demanded. He moved towards the door to take the lighted candlestick and momentarily released his sword grip. In that moment Glyde staggered to his feet, his hand crept into his pocket and he withdrew a small duelling pistol. Standing behind him, Amelie saw in an instant what he meant to do and shouted a warning.

Gareth spun round as his adversary lifted the gun to eye level and made ready to fire. He waited for what seemed an eternity, knowing there was no way he could escape, but then Glyde's body was crumpling to the floor, the gun harmlessly firing into the ceiling. Amelie, her breath coming fast, stood clutching a branch of the broken chandelier.

Gareth wore a wry smile. 'You certainly know how to fell a man,' he murmured.

'Have I killed him?'

He felt for a pulse. 'Fortunately not. We don't want him dead just yet.'

Amer and Figgis turned tail at this new course of events and made off towards the nether regions of the building. Gareth, meanwhile, had bound Glyde's legs with curtain ties and was busy throwing a jug of water from the table over his face. He came round, groaning and looking decidedly green. Gareth dragged him roughly across the floor and into a chair, propping him up against the solid oak table. He dipped the quill in the ink and placed it in Glyde's hand.

'Now write to my dictation.'

For long minutes, the pen scratched across the paper, the writer looking ever more sickly. Inwardly, Amelie fretted that he would faint or worse before he could finish, but she remained silent while Gareth's inexorable voice spelt out the long confession. When the last word had been written, and Glyde's signature appended, he carefully rolled the document and stored it safely in his shirt front.

'That is the price for my not killing you.' He reached down to bind his adversary's hands behind him. 'The price of my silence, however, is a little more exacting. You will leave England within the next five days. And leave for good. You will never show your face in society again.'

Glyde started angrily, but his legs were still bound and he was unable to move.

'You would do well to heed my words,' Gareth warned. He patted his chest. 'I have here the means to expose you to your peers for what you are.'

'And if I choose exposure?'

'Somehow I don't think you will. A life wandering the world is not the most fulfilling, as I can testify, but better far than being blacklisted by your fellows. Think, too, of all those opportunities to exercise your talents. Johnny Raws are everywhere!'

He opened the door and ushered Amelie through. Glyde was already struggling with the ties that bound him as Gareth turned to speak.

'Remember,' he warned, 'five days and you will have left these shores.'

His voice was implacable and with a last hard look at his enemy, he followed Amelie into the passageway and walked her slowly through the hall and out of the front door.

# Chapter Twenty-Six

Once outside she turned to him and said wonderingly, 'You came.'

'How could you doubt that I would?'

She gave a small smile in response and held her hands out to him. He took them only briefly. She wondered at his reticence, but a more important matter needed an answer.

'Why did you let him go?' She was perplexed. Gareth had had this evil man at his mercy, yet he'd allowed Glyde his freedom and the opportunity to spawn wickedness wherever he went.

'What else could I do? If I called in the Runners, your abduction and my pursuit would be the talk of the town for months. There has already been too much scandal and I don't want any more to taint your life. This way, Glyde has his liberty, but only to spend it miserably – and you are free of him for good.'

'But if he disappears, you may not properly clear your name. People may continue to think ill of you.'

'I have his signed confession, but, in any case, I have no interest in what people think. You know the truth and that's sufficient.'

He smiled down at her and she looked once more for the warm embrace she had been expecting ever since they left Glyde to his fate. Instead he tossed her up into the saddle of the waiting Minerva, laughing as he did. 'I'm afraid that this time you *will* have to share a horse with me.'

The mare, still tired from her earlier ride, ambled along the same lanes that she had flown down a few hours previously. Although night had fallen and the surrounding countryside was in inky darkness, a shaft of moonlight revealed clearly the thread of packed earth that was the pathway leading back to the main Bath road. Amelie nestled in her rescuer's arms, weary but overwhelmingly happy. Above, the clear night sky was silvered with a cascade of stars and only a breath of wind sighed through the trees as they passed on their way.

It was she who spoke first. 'How *did* you know where to find me?'

'I didn't. I knew it was Glyde who had abducted you, thanks to Fanny, but I had no means of knowing for certain which direction he had taken. It was a hunch. I'd been told that his country estate lay nearby and I guessed that he would instinctively go to ground there once he had his prey.'

She shuddered. 'You talk of him as though he were a wild animal.'

'What else is he, beneath the paint and the polish?'

'But how clever of Fanny to recognise Glyde's men.'

'She got precious little thanks for it.' Gareth smiled reminiscently. 'Your grandmother has the devil of a temper. Do you know that?'

When Amelie didn't reply, he said, 'Like grandmother, like granddaughter, I guess.'

'Why do you say that? Is that what you thought when I didn't meet you at the Abbey? That I was angry and wanted to punish you?'

'I thought you might have regretted making the appointment.'

'But we made a promise to meet.' There was a short silence before she burst out, 'You didn't trust me to come, did you?'

'Of course I did,' he blustered.

'No, you didn't. You didn't trust me!' She paused. 'But then I haven't trusted you either.'

There was a longer silence between them until she said quietly, 'Neither of us is blameless, Gareth. We've both been guilty of deceit.'

He bent his head and his lips brushed lightly against her soft curls. 'We have done a lot of silly things,' he murmured, 'but they are in the past. Now we can both face our futures honestly.'

She hardly noticed the odd expression and once more laid back against his strong frame while Minerva slowly and surely carried them towards Bath. They had been riding almost in the dark along a stretch of road where the trees overhung, pressing tightly together and barricading the moon from view. Then quite abruptly the trees fell away on either side and they found themselves in clear country, with the lake before them, a shaft of moonlight shimmering across its surface like a lustrous ribbon. The mare began to pick her way carefully around the shoreline. The warm night air wrapped them in velvet. All was tranquil.

But dozing in Gareth's encircling arms, Amelie suddenly became aware of a warmth dripping onto her hand. She raised her fingers slowly and gasped when she saw them blood-red.

'Gareth, your arm!'

In the semi-conscious state into which he had sunk, he hardly heard her.

'Gareth, wake up. You are bleeding and badly. We must stop. We must bind up your arm immediately.'

She tugged urgently on the reins and the horse came to a halt. Slipping from the saddle, she pulled him down, trying to support his weight as he slid to the ground. His face in the moonlight was ghostly, but he was alert now and tried to reassure her.

'I am pretty sure it's just a surface wound.'

'Surface wound or not, you seem to be doing a good job of bleeding to death.'

'One of your faults, Amelie, is that you are prone to exaggeration.'

'One of your faults, Gareth, is that you are prone to stubbornness.'

And with that she pulled down her silk petticoat and ripped off a large strip of soft white material. She led the way down to the lakeside and gently took off his shirt. The wound looked livid. She only hoped it was not already infected and bathed the angry weal with care, binding it up again, this time more tightly and thoroughly than Gareth had managed in the heat of conflict. With some difficulty he shrugged on the remains of his shirt.

The horse had followed them down to the lake and was now drinking its waters. After a few moments they took hold of her bridle and led her back to the trees where she began placidly to crop the grass.

'She should have a rest,' Amelie said, 'and so should you. Here...' and she quickly pushed a mound of leaves together to form a bed '...lie down for a while and try to sleep.'

He protested, but only feebly. He knew that if he were to return her safely to her family, he needed to be in stronger case. In less than a minute he was asleep while she watched over him. At length when he showed no sign of waking, she curled up beside him and slept herself, her head on his chest, the glinting curls fanned out across his body.

∼

It was one of those curls tickling his chin that finally woke him. He ran his fingers through the ruffled tresses and kissed her awake. Her eyes opened and for a moment she was filled with fear, remembering the locked and darkened room of her imprisonment. But the rustle of leaves and the breeze on her cheeks brought her to full consciousness and steadied a racing pulse.

Gareth was looking down at her, his expression tender. 'I have no idea how long we have been sleeping, dear child, but your grandmother must be going out of her mind with worry. It's time we were gone.'

He looked over at Minerva. 'The mare is well and truly rested. She should carry us swiftly back to town.'

Amelie stretched lazily. Her ordeal was over and the

man she loved was by her side. 'I have never thanked you properly for rescuing me.'

'Thanked me? What nonsense is this?'

'You risked your life.'

'But think of the prize,' he said lightly.

'You came for me because I'm yours and always will be.' Her voice grew husky and her eyes glistened with unshed tears.

'You will always be the one girl I have truly loved, Amelie.'

He said it carefully and she felt a shiver of apprehension. 'Why does that sound like a farewell?'

'Because it is. As soon as we reach Bath and you are reunited with your grandmother, I must be on my way. Lucas will be wondering what on earth has happened. I have my valise half-packed and ready to go.'

She sat bolt upright. 'You cannot still mean to leave England.'

'I must, Amelie.'

'I don't understand you,' she cried passionately. 'Why must you go? You have a confession from Glyde. Everything is changed.'

'Not everything, my love. I am still the same man with the same history – and it's not an edifying one. I am not a proper suitor for you.'

'But you have proved Glyde a villain. You can clear your name.'

'No matter how much I may wave his confession at people, scandal is like to follow me wherever I go. You deserve better.'

'This is nonsense.'

The alarm in her voice hurt, but he knew he must keep his vow for her sake. 'It's the way the world wags,' he said as calmly as he could. 'And your grandmother will know that better than anyone. She will advise you.'

'You mean in the same way she advised me about Glyde.' Her tone was acid.

'She has learned a painful lesson, I think you'll find. She will be anxious to discover a man who is good and kind and not at all like Glyde. And not like me either. Someone whose skeletons from a misspent life will not always be threatening to reappear.'

'I don't care how many skeletons are hidden deep in your past, Gareth,' she said in a taut voice. 'They may all make an appearance if they will. I want no other man, and I intend to have no other.'

'Fighting talk,' he said. It was a sad attempt at a joke.

'And why not? You have just fought for my life, but now you seem intent on denying it to me. So, yes, it is fighting talk.'

In the silver light that flooded the landscape, her face was ardent and her eyes sparkled with indignation. 'Why am I not to be allowed to choose my own destiny? Why should everyone feel they have the right to make my decisions for me? First my father, then my grandmother and now, unbelievably, you!'

In her vexation she had moved a little away and sat facing him, her back ramrod straight and the tendrils of her hair blowing in the breeze. The torn dress had been hastily patched together, but now slipped from her shoulders revealing an expanse of luminous skin, gleaming pearl-like in the moonlight. Gareth had to force himself from feasting on this vision, for both his heart and his body were urging him to forget his resolve to walk away and never return.

He cast around in his mind for an argument that would convince her, but she was in no mood to listen.

'I have made my own decision,' she said proudly, 'and I will allow no one to gainsay it, not even you. When I asked you to meet me at the Abbey, it was to tell you that I wanted to go away with you, that I wanted to live with you for as long as you desired me.'

Astonishment ranged across his face. Did she love him so much that she was willing to relinquish her family, her friends, the world she knew?

'And I still want to,' she announced defiantly.

'But—' A vagrant part of him leapt hungrily to life. His resistance was crumbling, the power of her love destroying his last defence.

'No buts. I am sick of buts. Sick of other people trying to arrange my life. You followed me to Glyde's prison and from now on I intend to follow you – wherever you go.'

'What a spitfire!' He was gathering his scattered wits. 'I see you do have your grandmother's temper.'

'I may pull caps with you from time to time,' she admitted, 'but only when you deserve it. Will you still be able to love me?'

In response he pulled her roughly into his arms, the misconceived vow consigned at a stroke to oblivion. 'Now it's your turn to hear *my* decision, my fiery one,' he whispered into her ear. 'You *will* go with me wherever I go, but with a wedding ring on your finger.' A shadow passed across his face. 'If we stay in England, it will not be easy. There will be gossip, innuendo, even direct snubs. You will have to learn to bear it all with an indifferent face. Do you think you can?'

'I can and I will, but I'll need kisses. Endless kisses.' She sighed slyly. 'You have been particularly mean with them of late.'

He pulled her down onto their bed of leaves and searched her face. His eyes were the deepest blue, dark and mysterious, and her heart gave a small lurch.

'You are sure of this?'

'I couldn't be more sure.'

She closed her eyes, drinking in his musky scent, her body melting like warm honey. His arms wrapped her tight.

'I see your wound is a good deal better.'

'Don't be pert, miss, or...'

'Or?'

'Or this,' and with one deft movement he rolled her beneath himself, fitting his form to hers. A long, lingering kiss and the heat of his mouth made her hungry for him. Her fingers buried themselves in his dark hair and pulled him closer as his kisses covered her face, her arms, her neck, with a fierceness that left her breathless. Her body was ablaze, every fibre singing with hot pleasure. The world around her vanished into nothingness – the soft grass, the hushed lake, the clear night sky. Her world was contained only in this moment and she was ready to give herself up to it.

But very gently he pulled away. 'We must get you back to Laura Place,' he said. Then seeing her dazed expression, he whispered, 'There will be a right time, Amelie, I promise.'

## Chapter Twenty-Seven

Neither Brielle nor Miles Milverton could bring themselves to eat. They sat at either end of the mahogany table, maintaining the pretence of dining while their faces, mirrored in the sheen of the wood, reflected back an overwhelming anxiety. Horrocks carefully served the modest meal: soup and entrées followed by salmon, then a braised ham and a haunch of venison, and finally an assortment of pastries, jellies and creams. They sat in silence as the butler expertly brought and removed courses. But every dish was returned to the kitchen barely touched.

Once the dismal meal was at an end, they removed to the drawing room and settled themselves by the fireside. It was early June, but Horrocks had thought it wise to kindle a small blaze and provide a little cheer. Both had given up trying to make polite conversation and instead gazed intently into the flames, sunk in their own thoughts. Forbidding images danced in front of them, pictures of Amelie terrified and alone, at the mercy of a villain they had both championed. Older heads had not been wiser and it was their lovely girl who was paying the price.

At around ten o'clock Horrocks brought in the tea tray. They sat still silent, cradling their two cups, as though needing to hold on to something, anything. Neither could keep their eyes from the grandmother clock, its hands slowly ticking away the minutes. It was an hour later that the door bell pealed. Miles, slumped in the brown leather chesterfield, jumped from his seat in one movement. Brielle held up her hand for silence and strained her ears. Two voices sounded from below, but she was certain one of them was Horrocks. Could it be that Gareth Heywood had returned empty-handed? She sat perched on the edge of her chair while Miles paced up and down, unable to rest.

Horrocks opened the drawing room door and in a voice muted by disappointment announced, 'Lord Lucas Avery.' The servants, too, were keeping their own vigil below stairs.

Brielle pulled herself together sufficiently to make the necessary introductions. Their visitor looked uncomfortable, but also extremely worried.

'Please accept my apologies for this intrusion at so late an hour, Lady St Clair. Only very real anxiety for my friend's welfare could prompt me to impose on you in this way.'

'Your friend?' She knew Lord Avery only very slightly and his friends not at all.

Lucas was overwrought and the words poured out unchecked. 'I had a note from Gareth... he is staying with me... I couldn't make head or tale of it. Something about his having to leave Bath at short notice, but that he would be back to collect his baggage. He was due to leave for France tomorrow.'

He paused for breath and then continued more slowly though with some awkwardness. 'He mentioned in the note that Miss Milverton was in danger. Naturally, I have no wish to intrude on a private family matter, but Gareth has not returned, and it's now many hours since he left.'

'There is no need to apologise, Lord Avery. As you see, we are in similar case, waiting helplessly for news.' Brielle sank back down in her chair. She looked very tired and very old. 'You are most welcome to sit and wait with us.'

'But where has he gone, ma'am?'

'To find Rufus Glyde. It appears that the man we trusted—' and she included Lord Milverton in her gesture '—is an out-and-out villain.'

'That I have always suspicioned, but your granddaughter?'

'Abducted,' she said abruptly, but could not keep the quaver from her voice. The young man looked horrified.

'This is the most shocking news. What can I say? But do not despair, Lady St Clair. Gareth is a resourceful man and a tough one. He has had many years shifting for himself in difficult circumstances. If anyone can help your granddaughter, it will be him. Depend on it, he will bring her safely home.'

'So I hoped when I agreed to his going, but that was many hours ago. Will he even find Glyde?

'I am sure he will. Glyde will not travel far with an unwilling girl in tow. His country estate is close by and Gareth knows its general direction.'

Brielle refused to be comforted. 'Glyde is not alone. Amelie's maid has told us that two ruffians in his employ swooped on her mistress. Your friend is just one man. How will he fare against the brutality of such low creatures?'

'And Sir Rufus is a notable swordsman,' put in Lord Milverton, still pacing the room and in despair for his daughter's safety.

'Gareth is a first-class fencer. He will be more than a match for Glyde.' Lucas said this staunchly, but his heart felt leaden. He had a very good idea of the odds his friend would face. If only he had waited. But Gareth would have refused his help, he knew. Lucas had a wife and children and the mission was dangerous, if not suicidal.

Frustrated, he suggested riding out towards Glyde's estate. 'I could try to discover news of them. At least I would be doing something useful.'

Brielle shook her head. 'I appreciate your offer, but I doubt that you would learn much. You might, however, give rise to speculation. The reason I was persuaded to let your friend go alone was the need to keep this whole shocking business from becoming an open scandal.'

Lord Milverton gave a sombre shake of his head. 'We shall know soon enough what has happened to them, I fear.'

His words effectively silenced the trio and they sat mutely, each encased in private thought. Horrocks appeared regularly to make up the fire and offer unwanted refreshments. The minutes ticked by, the hours wore on, and Gareth's mission looked increasingly hopeless. By the time the small hours arrived, what little spirit had been present had vanished entirely.

The breaking dawn, chill and grey, found the three of them dozing fitfully by the embers, unwilling to give up their watch but knowing in their hearts that whatever news came now, it could only be bad. Then a bell pealed below. A sudden noise, a flurry of voices, footsteps springing up the marble staircase, and the door flew open.

Gareth and Amelie stood framed in the doorway, tired and travel weary but with hands held fast and faces lit with happiness. Brielle started forward and flung her arms around her granddaughter, tears streaming down her face.

'It's all right, Grandmama. I'm all right,' Amelie calmed her.

She smoothed Brielle's hair and kissed her on both cheeks and then, putting her grandmother gently aside, moved towards her father where he stood alone and forlorn. His emotions choked him and for a moment he could only cling to his daughter, silently hugging her to his chest.

'Papa, why are you here?'

'My darling, thank God you are safe. Thank God.' His voice choked again. 'Will you ever forgive me?'

'There is nothing to forgive.'

'Indeed there is. I was the one intent on forcing you into marriage with that villain. You must believe me, I had no idea what manner of man he was. I have only just discovered the evil he has practised against our family and I came immediately to warn you. But by then he had done his worst.'

'Not quite his worst, Papa.' And she turned with a radiant face to her lover. 'I have my rescuer to thank for that. Grandmama, I believe you already know Gareth, but, Papa, let me introduce you. This is Gareth Heywood.'

The name made Lucas Avery's brows twitch, but Gareth signed to him to hold his peace.

'I don't think we have met before,' Miles was saying, 'but you have my most grateful thanks for what you have done this night. How can I ever repay you?'

'I wish to marry your daughter, Lord Milverton. To have your consent will be ample repayment.'

Miles Milverton looked taken aback. 'That will need some discussion, young man,' he began to bluster, but Brielle interrupted, giving him one of her basilisk stares.

'Her father means that he will be only too pleased to give her to a man of courage and principle.'

'Is that what you wish, Amelie?' Miles spoke more mildly.

'More than anything, Papa.'

'But I had such hopes for you, my dear. Mr Heywood is obviously an honourable man who deserves the highest consideration. I would not wish you to think that I am unappreciative of what I owe him. However, marriage is another matter and I am sure he would himself agree that you could look a lot higher for a husband.'

Once more Brielle interrupted her son-in-law. 'Miles, we have already made the most dreadful mess of Amelie's life between us. Do you not think that she knows her own mind best?'

'I do,' Amelie said firmly. 'I am going to marry Gareth and I hope you will be happy for me. But I shall marry him even if you are not. He is the only man I will ever want and I intend to share the rest of my life with him.'

She looked mischievously around at the gathering. 'I

shall make an excellent vagabond, I'm sure!'

'There will be no need for that,' her father rejoined hastily. 'Mr Heywood may not be the husband I had in mind, but he is a man of integrity and if he is your choice, I am happy to give my blessing. But not,' he added, 'to a life of vagabondage. I am sure that between us—' and he glanced across at Brielle '—we can start this young man in a respectable profession and provide a home for you both.'

Brielle nodded her head vigorously. 'It will be quite unnecessary, Mr Heywood, for you to resume your former life.' Gareth smiled at the thought of the inward shudder she must be suppressing.

The presence of Lucas Avery had all but been forgotten, but now he was staring at them open-mouthed as though he could hardly believe what he was hearing. Then he began to laugh. Amusement bubbled up in him, mixed with relief at his friend's safe return, and exploded in a riot of noise which rang around the room. The company turned to him in surprise. Gradually his mirth subsided and he whisked out a handkerchief to dab the tears from his eyes.

'I am so sorry. Forgive my merriment. But to hear you talk about setting Gareth up in a profession...!'

He had all their attention, their eyes fixed on him in enquiry. He was in danger of bursting into laughter again, but managed to splutter, 'I think you will find Gareth already has a profession. Meet the new Earl of Denville.'

Lord Milverton and Brielle looked at first astounded, then their faces flooded with relief.

'But why are you travelling in this fashion?' Miles asked him in amazement.

The whole sorry story of Glyde's villainy had to be told and the signed confession passed around. Lord Milverton read it and reread it, shaking his head and muttering inaudibly from time to time. Then he looked up from the sheaf of papers and spoke with determination.

'Glyde is already widely discredited and I will make sure that everyone of my acquaintance, and their acquaintance, too, is aware of this confession. *You* may have promised him silence, but I have not. If I have any influence, the tale of his infamy will soon be known to every member of the *ton*.'

He reached out to his future son-on-law and clutched Gareth's hand. 'It is clear that you have suffered even greater harm from this devil. No one could be more worthy of my beautiful daughter.'

'Your beautiful daughter has something to say for herself.' Amelie had kept silent, her lips firmly sealed, but now she turned a furious face on Gareth.

'Were you by chance ever going to tell me who you really were?'

Brielle heard the biting tone and saw the indignation flooding her granddaughter's lovely face and made a decision. 'It is more than time that we all had some rest,' she said briskly and moved towards the doorway with surprising speed. In an instant she had shepherded her companions out of the room.

The door had barely closed behind them before Amelie repeated her question, her tone even more imperious. 'Well, were you ever going to tell me who you were? Or perhaps it just slipped your mind that you had inherited a title?'

'Strangely enough, it did. Or at least has done these past few weeks.'

His eyes held an errant sweetness and she longed to reach out and feel him close again, but steeled herself against his charm.

'How could it slip your mind? It isn't possible. You vowed there would be no more secrets between us, yet the very biggest you have kept hidden. How can I ever truly believe you?'

'You must, Amelie. You must believe me when I say that for weeks the Earl of Denville has been pushed from my mind. You met me as Gareth Heywood and I have loved you as he. The earl is as foreign to me as to you. We must both get to know him.'

For a long minute she did not speak, her eyes scanning his face intently, searching and searching again, and she knew that he spoke the truth. Her anger drained away. This *was* the final deception and the first brick, too, in the bridge of trust they would build together.

He was by her side and looking directly into her eyes. She felt a wild, dancing joy surge through her. His arms were back where they belonged, his lips close.

'I love you, Amelie Milverton,' he whispered.

'I love you, too, Gareth Heywood,' she replied.

# About The Author

Merryn Allingham was born into an army family and spent her childhood moving around the UK and abroad. Unsurprisingly it gave her itchy feet, and in her twenties she escaped an unloved secretarial career to work as cabin crew and see the world.

The arrival of marriage, children and cats meant a more settled life in the south of England, where she's lived ever since. It also gave her the opportunity to go back to 'school' and eventually teach at university. Merryn loves the nineteenth century and grew up reading Georgette Heyer, so when she began writing herself the novels had to be Regency romances.

For more information on Merryn and her books visit **http://www.merrynallingham.com/**

You'll find regular news and updates on Merryn's Facebook page
**https://www.facebook.com/MerrynWrites/**
and you can keep in touch with her on Twitter
**@MerrynWrites**

If you enjoyed reading *Dance of Deception*, do please leave a review on your favourite site. Authors rely on good reviews - even just a few words - and readers depend on them to find interesting books to read.

www.ingramcontent.com/pod-product-compliance
Ingram Content Group UK Ltd.
Pitfield, Milton Keynes, MK11 3LW, UK
UKHW021258120325
4964UKWH00040B/301